The Bloody Bord

The Bloody Border

**Book 7 in the Border Knight Series
By
Griff Hosker**

The Bloody Border

Published by Sword Books Ltd 2019

Copyright © Griff Hosker First Edition

The author has asserted their moral right under the Copyright, Designs and Patents Act, 1988, to be identified as the author of this work.

All Rights reserved. No part of this publication may be reproduced, copied, stored in a retrieval system, or transmitted, in any form or by any means, without the prior written consent of the copyright holder, nor be otherwise circulated in any form of binding or cover other than that in which it is published and without a similar condition being imposed on the subsequent purchaser.

A CIP catalogue record for this title is available from the British Library.

Contents

The Bloody Border i
Prologue 1
Chapter 1 3
Chapter 2 16
Chapter 3 30
Chapter 4 43
Chapter 5 59
Chapter 6 72
Chapter 7 83
Chapter 8 94
Chapter 9 104
Chapter 10 118
Chapter 11 130
Chapter 12 143
Chapter 13 154
Chapter 14 168
Chapter 15 182
Chapter 16 197
Chapter 17 205
Chapter 18 217
Chapter 19 230
Epilogue 241
Glossary 247
Historical Notes 248
Other books by Griff Hosker 250

Prologue

Stockton 1231

It was good to be back in Stockton. After the rigours of a campaign, I would enjoy time in my manor and my valley. My daughter, Isabelle, was with child and due to give birth. My lands were at peace and I had time to enjoy my grandchildren, my children and my wife. It had been many years since I had been left alone at the Battle of Arsuf. I had fought in the Holy Land, Sweden, Poitou, Wales and Scotland. I had lost many warriors and I was tired of war. For once I agreed with my wife. I would enjoy being a lord of the manor. Sir Edward, who had been one of my squires and then knighted, had lost the use of his left arm in the battles to retake Poitou. He was now an increasingly fat and comfortable old warrior. If he could enjoy the life of lord of the manor then why should not I?

The King had shed himself of advisers. He ruled England if not well then at least with an iron fist. Like me, he had been betrayed by those he had trusted and was warier of the motives of others. I had hoped he would be a better king but he had time for he was young. He had seen just twenty-two summers yet he had been king for thirteen years. I had helped to guide him but I was not the Warlord. I knew I would never be the man who had been the knight who had saved England. When the Earl Marshal had moulded King Henry II, he had dedicated his life to make him a great king. I had the Warlord's blood but I was not him. I was a sword for hire who had managed to claw back his manor and his valley. I was not destined for greatness. That did not worry me for I knew what it had cost Earl Alfraed of Stockton. The small church in my castle was a testament to his losses. I would make Stockton as vibrant as it had been when he had ruled the valley. That would be my achievement.

Part One
Thomas, Earl of Cleveland

Chapter 1

"The baby is coming, Sir Robert!"

My son-in-law and I were in the Great Hall in Stockton. I had always planned to give Sir Robert a manor but I was selfish enough to keep my daughter and her family as close as I could for as long as possible. I took Sir Robert to walk my walls. Birthing was woman's work and neither my wife nor my daughter, Isabelle, would thank me if I allowed the father-to-be to stalk the corridor outside the bedchamber. Even the castle doctor, Erasmus of Ghent, kept away. My son and squire, William, walked with us as did Richard, Sir Robert's squire and brother. The two squires were good friends and they walked behind us.

"When the child is born, Sir Robert, you will be ready for a manor, eh?"

He smiled and we paused to look over the river, "My wife is more than happy to be here. She worries about you, Sir Thomas. The wounds you received in Poitou caused her great concern."

"Aye, well, she has no need to worry now for there are no wars. The King is busy consolidating his power in London and Wales is now settled. He may well wish to go abroad but I will not go. This is my land now." He nodded. "So, a manor?"

"Elsdon was a small manor, lord, I do not expect a large one. My ambitions died with my first wife and my folk."

"Redmarshal is without a lord. When I go to Durham to speak with the Bishop about the dubbing of my son, I will ask his permission to give you that domain."

The Bloody Border

Behind me, I heard Richard speak to my son, "You are lucky William! A knight eh?"

William was older than Alfred had been when he had been knighted. He deserved the knighthood but he knew the responsibilities which came with such a title, "I will have to buy my own horse, armour and pay for a squire. It is not all pleasure, Richard. When my father began, he was so impoverished he had to hire out his sword."

I stopped and turned, "Fear not, my son, that will not be your fate. Thanks to the prowess of you and my other men we are well off. Stockton is prosperous. When you are knighted then there will be money coming your way. Your Aunt Ruth left a large sum and she wished it to be used by her family."

Aunt Ruth had had no family save mine and she had made me promise, before she died, to use her money for my children. I did not need it. I was not profligate. I did not buy objects simply because I could. I bought what I needed and not what I wanted. There was a difference. Just at that moment, I heard a shout from below and then, a moment or two later, Eleanor, one of my wife's ladies, came rushing out of the west tower, "My lords, you have a son and you a grandson! The bairn is healthy and with a fine set of lungs!"

I clasped Sir Robert's arm, "And so it begins for you. Go, see your son. Now is your time. We will join you in a little while." When he had left us, I said to my son, "And now that my daughter has given birth, we can give our attention to the small matter of your knighthood. We will ride on the morrow to Durham. It is courtesy to tell the Bishop and I can ask about the manor of Redmarshal."

Richard asked, "Will the Bishop not have his own man in mind, lord?"

"He might, Richard, but Bishop Poore owes me so many favours that I think he will accede to my request." He nodded, "I have to ask you, William, you are prepared for the vigil and the challenges which you will have to face?" Thanks to King Richard knighting me on the battlefield I had never had to endure the rituals of knighthood. My son would.

He nodded confidently. When he had been my page his brother had gone through the ceremony and William had

The Bloody Border

watched it all. Since Alfred's death, he had known this day would come. I looked to Richard, Sir Robert's brother, "And you will be ready soon eh, Richard?"

He shook his head, "We are a poor family. You are happy that there is peace, for my part, I would that we had a war so that I could take a knight for ransom."

I laughed, "I like that you are confident that you could do so."

"It is not arrogance, lord. I have learned much from both you and your son. I have held my brother's banner and seen how you fight. Thanks to Ridley the Giant and Henry Youngblood I am more skilled with a sword than I was. I always knew how to fight but now I know how to win."

That skill had come from me. I had chosen sergeants at arms who had the same philosophy. I had been a sword for hire. I had not learned to be a knight at tournaments and jousts. I had learned my skill when fighting enemies who sought to kill me and not take me prisoner. My swordplay was functional rather than beautiful. I had seen knights who could use a variety of sword blows yet they had died because their opponent wanted to win more.

We headed down the stairs to the Great Hall. William said, "I need to speak with Alan Horse Master about a horse."

I nodded and as he was leaving I added, "See Henry about the men we will take. We will need just four men at arms with us. Choose single men." I had many more men at arms and archers who were married now. They trained each day but I was loath to take them from their families for a day or two. I knew how precious time was with wives and families.

Richard and I went to the jug of wine on the table. I poured us both a goblet, "To my grandson and your nephew!"

"My nephew!"

Eleanor came back into the hall. In her hands, she held bloody cloths, "My lord, Master Richard, her ladyship says you can greet the baby."

We went to the birthing chamber. My daughter was cuddling the baby and my wife looked pleased enough to burst. Sir Robert stroked his wife's hair. Isabelle turned the red-faced babe so that I could see his countenance, "Here, Thomas, is your namesake.

Here is your grandfather and the greatest knight in England, Sir Thomas of Stockton."

I shook my head, "Do not give the poor bairn such high expectations of an old man!"

Margaret went over and took the baby from Isabelle, "I have had my cuddle. He had better make the most of the times he gets to see you, eh husband?"

I held the tiny babe carefully. He looked so helpless. I shook my head, "I told you, wife, my days of wandering are over. I shall stay here in the valley." Thomas opened his eyes. I knew that he could not really see me but I smiled and spoke anyway. "I promise, if God spares me, Thomas, that I will protect you until you become a man. I will show you how to be a knight and I will do all in my power to see you grown, knighted and married."

My wife laughed, "You are getting soft and sentimental in your old age." The baby began to cry. "And the child has had enough of your sentiment already!"

Isabelle shook her head. "He wants a feed, that is all. Give him here, father."

As I leaned over to place him in her arms, I kissed her on the forehead, "And right glad I am that you are well too."

It was a good time to be lord of Cleveland. With new members of the family and all of us safe we enjoyed a peaceful time. It was a wrench to leave Stockton but William and I had duties. He was now on the threshold of knighthood and he had to learn about fealty. William and I left for Durham. It was the time of year for taxes to be paid to the Bishop. There would be many knights in the city. I had paid mine already. I paid promptly. It was my way. Others liked to wait until the last moment or to go in person to the Bishop to appeal against what they saw as exorbitant taxes. I knew it was not so. When King John had been king then there had been abuses but King Henry had learned. He was still fearful of the barons but he now used a parliament to allow his peers to have their say. It guaranteed him his coin. He did not like it but he understood the necessity. Richard had asked to accompany us. His brother was somewhat preoccupied. I did not mind.

We visited with Sir Edward when we passed his manor. We told him of the birth of my latest grandchild. He had children of his own now and, with Sir Gilles to run the manor for him, was a man of leisure. I was pleased for him. Few warriors enjoyed a happy retirement. That would be me soon enough.

As we left to head up the Durham Road, Richard asked, "How does he remain content with life with just one arm which works?"

"He lives, Richard, and that is what is important. My father died when he was younger than I am now. Think of all that he missed which I now enjoy. You are young and see war as something which is glorious and a chance for you to show your prowess. I do not criticise you for that but it is not my philosophy and, I think, it is not that of my son."

William nodded, "I have changed my opinion since the death of my brother."

Richard was silent for the rest of the journey to Durham. Thanks to our visit with Edward we did not arrive until late in the afternoon. We were admitted to the castle immediately. The Bishop was dealing with visitors from the Archbishop of York but we were taken to chambers. There was a time when I would not have received such a warm welcome. Thankfully that was another life and I was no longer considered an outlaw and a murderer in Durham. Our efforts on behalf of the Palatinate had been rewarded with smiles and comfortable chambers.

"His Grace will see you at the evening meal. I fear it will not be a special one, my lord."

"That is not a problem. We are warriors."

I took Richard and William into the cathedral. I knelt and prayed. I knew that I was getting older. Would I live to see my grandchildren grow? I prayed to God and to St. Cuthbert that, if I should die, they would be safe and live to be adults. That was all that one could ask. When we were outside, on the green, I said, "And did you pray?" A man did not ask another what his prayers were for. My son and Richard, however, were keen to tell me anyway.

William spoke first, "I prayed that I would be as good a knight as my brother."

I nodded.

Richard said, "And I prayed that I would be a knight."

"Then I hope that you are both rewarded as you deserve."

The Bloody Border

Richard Poore was not the sort of priest who enjoyed a dull cuisine. We ate well that night. If this was not a feast then I would like to be there when he did enjoy one! He seated me at his left hand. My son and Richard had to serve. It was the way of the world. It was part of their training to become a knight. They learned how a knight should eat and conduct himself at a feast.

"The King has an iron fist now, Sir Thomas. For one so young he has exercised his power well."

"He had a tricky beginning. I am pleased with our monarch. He is not perfect but King John was imperfect in many ways."

"Aye, you have the right of it." He leaned into me. "My lord constable at Norham tells me that the Earl of Fife is less than enamoured of you."

I laughed so loudly that some of the priests who were close to us looked around, "The day I worry about upsetting a Scotsman is the day they will put the lid on my grave. The man tried to take English land and he lost."

"The trouble is the Scots believe that Cumbria, Westmoreland and Northumbria are Scottish, my lord."

"They might believe that but it is not true." I turned to him, "You are saying that they have not yet lost their ambition to take English territory?"

He nodded, "I am no fool, my lord. I have spies and I speak to the lords who command the border castles. They are quiet now and that is thanks to you."

I sipped the wine. It was a good one. "That is disturbing. The King thinks that the fact that Alexander is married to his sister will prevent another incursion."

"No, my lord, they will come again. My knights are on constant alert." I detected a plea in his voice.

I decided to change the subject slightly, "I came here, Your Grace, to ask for permission to give the manor of Redmarshal to Sir Robert of Elsdon."

"Of course. He did great service when you defeated the Earl of Fife. I give it to him gladly for you are a buffer against all sorts of enemies and a source of the best men we use when we have to fight. Although I had hoped to have Elsdon given to one of your knights."

I shook my head, "Sir Robert could not return as there would be too many bad memories and I would not wish my daughter to be so far from me. She has just been delivered of a son."

"Just so."

"And the other reason was to inform you that I shall be dubbing my son, William of Stockton."

He beamed. "Your son is a fine young man. This is good. I shall send him a present for he, too, has served the Palatinate." He toasted me with his goblet of wine, "And if you have a knight you think could hold Elsdon for me…"

"I will put my mind to the problem, be assured of that Bishop."

I learned much that night and ideas were planted in my head. We left after two days with the seeds growing in my mind. I spoke with William as we rode down the Durham Road, "I have decided to give you your spurs the same day we christen Thomas. It will be an appropriate time. Then we will put our minds to selecting two squires for us. I have been remiss. When I made you a squire, I should have had a page prepared to be ready for this moment."

My son shook his head, "You have been in the service of the King. Perhaps I may know of one."

"Who might that be?"

He smiled, "Matthew and Mark are the sons of John the Tanner. They are twins and were named after disciples for their mother was a religious woman who hoped they would be priests or perhaps go on crusade. She died two years ago. They are both strong."

"And how do you know they would be suitable?"

"Before I was your squire, I would go with Will son of Robin to help train the men of the manor at the butts. Those two were good archers but more when Padraig started to train them with the sword the two of them showed great skill." He shrugged, "Since we have returned, I have visited the butts with Will and Padraig. I have spoken with the two of them. They asked Padraig how they could become men at arms. They have two older brothers who work in the tannery."

"Then when we have visited with Father Harold to arrange the vigil and the christening you and I will see John the Tanner and his sons."

When we reached my castle, I could see that my wife was displeased that I had been away so long, "Husband this is not like you to tarry when there are tasks to be done. The child needs to be baptised!"

"He is healthy is he not?"

"He is but…"

"Our son will be dubbed when Thomas is baptised. That pleases you does it not?"

"I am pleased that our son will be knighted for he deserves it but not about the consequences of knighthood. I lost one son when he became a knight and William is my last."

"When a man straps on a sword he is at risk of losing his life. It matters not if he is a knight or a farmer. Our son will not suffer as Alfred did."

William and I first went to Father Harold who agreed to make the baptismal arrangements. "The ceremony of knighthood is not the work of the church, my lord, I leave that in your hands." He did not say it in a churlish manner but he was right. The dubbing of a knight involved a church but not a priest. Then we went to my town. I had visited on more than one occasion since my return but it was still not enough. My father had told me that a good lord of the manor understood his people as well as he understood his horse. It had taken time to build up the confidence of my people. In the dark years, when I had been away, they had suffered. The town was now prosperous and as we headed north towards the tannery, we had to stop to pass the time of day with folk who were keen to congratulate me on my new grandson.

The smithies were close to the tannery. It was the part of town my wife did not like for it had the smell, noise, smoke and fire from the anvils and forges which was mixed with the stench from curing hides. I knew that they were necessary. Old Henry was working at his forge. A young boy was working the bellows. They stopped as William and I approached. Henry had never left the town. He had lived there when taxes had almost destroyed it. He was proud of Stockton for his family had lived there when the Warlord had run the manor. Alf had been the first smith in the town and Henry was his great-grandson, "Congratulations on your new grandson."

"Thank you, Henry. He is healthy and has a fine set of lungs. And who is this young titan working your bellows?"

"That is my grandson, John."

"Good morning, John and would you be a smith like your grandfather?"

He shook his head, "I would be a warrior, my lord!"

I laughed as Henry shook his head, "His father despairs of him. He has given him to me to see if I can rid him of these ideas."

"How old are you, John?"

"I have seen more than seven summers I think, my lord." He grinned, "Perhaps almost eight?"

"Well, John, you have some years to go before you can think of that. Working the bellows will give you the strength you need. If you are still of a mind in three years' time then come to my castle and speak with me."

His face lit up and Henry nodded, "That may be the best, my lord. I have other sons and grandsons who are happy to hammer metal but if the love of iron is not in your heart then you cannot beat it in"

I nodded and was about to leave when William said, "John, how would you like to be a page?"

I saw the boy frown. He did not know what a page was. "A page, Master William?"

I shook my head for William should have asked me first. The carrot was out of the ground and so I spoke, "A page serves a knight. He helps a knight's squire to polish armour and to sharpen his weapons. He waits at table."

John was young enough for complete honesty, "That sounds duller than working a bellows, my lord."

Henry shook his head, "John!"

"The boy is right, Henry."

William said, "Aye but then a page trains to be a squire and then a knight. I was a page and now I am a squire. In a few days, I shall be a knight!"

John's face lit up, "Then I would be a warrior!"

I looked at Henry. "I have a place for a page. If you wish it, then come to me at the castle and we will talk further. This is hurried and," I glared at William, "this is not the place for such talk!"

"Aye lord, we are honoured."

As we left William, who knew I was annoyed, said, "What is the difference, father? We now go to a tannery to see if Matthew and Mark wish to be squires. What makes this circumstance different?"

"Because the two we seek have already made a request. They are older too. You need to learn to think before you speak! You still have much to learn."

The stink from the tannery made my nose wrinkle. My wife would take our cloaks and have them washed when we returned home and have us don fresh surcoats! John the Tanner was unused to visits from the lord of the manor. He came and bowed, "You wish some leather, lord?"

I shook my head, "No John, I would speak with you privately."

"Of course, my lord. Come, the wind is from the east we will go to the river. The air is more wholesome there."

He was right. There was a wooden quay. The small ships which took John's hides away could tie up there and it made the loading easier. I saw seals swimming in the river. "My son tells me that your sons Matthew and Mark wish to be warriors."

"Aye lord, my wife," he made the sign of the cross, "God rest her soul, thought that as they were twins, they were destined for a better life than that of a tanner. Perhaps she was right. She had dreams of them being important men; merchants or even priests."

"Your work is valuable, John. Do not think less of yourself. Then how do you feel about it?"

"I have two other sons who will inherit the business and they are happy to work here. If Matthew and Mark wish to be warriors then so be it."

"And how would you feel if they were to be squires?"

I saw amazement fill his face, "My lord! That would be an honour! But two squires?"

The Bloody Border

"William is to be knighted and will need one. When he is dubbed then I will require someone to replace him." He nodded. "You know that this means they would be taken from your home and live in the castle with us."

He beamed, "Aye, but in heaven, his mother will be thanking me for fulfilling her dream. She hoped they might be priests but this is even better!"

"Then fetch them hither and we will see if they agree."

Of course, they both did. As they gushed their thanks, I examined them. They were already well muscled. Working with hides and training with the bow had done that for them. I could not determine the difference between them. They were big lads. They would do.

"You know that you will have to learn to ride a horse?" They nodded. "The work of a squire will mean you will have to serve at table. It will not all be training with weapons." The disappointment flashed across their faces but they nodded. "Then get your gear and make your farewells. We will return to the castle. Present yourselves at the gate when you are prepared. A new life awaits!"

My wife was less than pleased at the extra work which was incurred by the two squires and, two days later when Henry the Smith arrived at my gates with John the page, she voiced her opinion "As if I do not have enough to do with baptism and a ceremony of the knight! I have clothes to have made for three boys!"

I kissed her, "You know you love it!"

In truth, the work was for others. She had ladies who made the surcoats and tunics for the three new members of our household. They also made the simple white shift which would be worn by William for his vigil. The three would share a chamber. It was in the east tower and that was the coldest quarters. It was the one my wife reserved for the times when the castle was full. For the squires and the page, it was considerably better than what they were used to.

As William was busy preparing to be a knight, I gave them over to Richard. He had time on his hands. His brother was still enjoying fatherhood and Richard could tell the three what their duties were just as easily as William.

The night before the ceremony Matthew and Mark, along with John and Richard, helped prepare my son. He bathed. This was symbolic. It was like the dousing with water that baby Thomas would experience. Then he was groomed and dressed in a simple white shift. Bishop Poore had sent him a fine sword. I vaguely recognised it as one which had been taken from the Scots. Then the six of us marched to the church. My men at arms and archers made an arch beneath which we walked. Some would be following my son when he had his own manor. Once inside the six of us knelt and prayed. The tombs around us were a reminder of the duty we owed. Matthew, Mark and John had never been in the church. It was so small that the children of the town had to listen outside when we held services on Sunday. I saw the awe and wonder on their faces. My son held the sword before him like a cross and we left.

My men at arms and archers had dispersed. Richard looked back as we closed the door to the church. There were just two candles which lit the interior. He asked, "Will he not be afraid to be alone, my lord?"

"It is a vigil all knights must perform but he will be safe. The spirits of the past will watch over him. One day, Richard, and one day soon, you will undergo the same ceremony."

I had never had to undergo a vigil. When I saw my son the next day, I saw that he had experienced something I had not and that it had had a profound effect on him. I went into the church to fetch him. It was strange but that one night seemed to have made him age. He simply said, "I am ready now!" As with prayers, one did not ask a knight about a vigil. It was between him and God.

I took him to his chamber where Matthew, Mark and John waited for us. He was stripped and then dressed again. We put on his gambeson and his mail. We strapped on his dagger and his sword. We had decided that Matthew would be his squire and so he carried his helmet. Mark carried mine. We were ready. We descended to the hall. This would be just my family. I had not invited Sir Fótr, Sir Edward and the others. They would come for the baptismal feast in the evening. William had asked for a small ceremony. He was the one to be knighted and it was his choice. Sir Geoffrey and Sir Robert were the only knights who were present. All of us were dressed in our mail. We three wore spurs. John carried William's spurs. He looked more nervous than any. There was no set ceremony. King Richard had simply had me kneel before him and he touched my shoulders with his sword. I used the ceremony which appealed to me.

First, his mother handed him the surcoat she had made for him. It was the same blue as mine but instead of a yellow gryphon which filled the front, he had a small red one over his heart. It looked effective. When he had donned it she kissed him on the forehead. He had to bow his head to enable her to do so. I saw a tear trickle down her cheek. She was remembering Alfred.

William stood before me and all were silent. I drew my sword. "Kneel, William of Stockton." He knelt and bowed his head, "By the power vested in me by King Henry of England, I dub you Sir William of Stockton." I lightly touched his shoulders with my sword and then I sheathed it. I turned and John, who had been waiting for this moment, handed me the spurs. I gave them to him and then Matthew gave the helmet to John, taking the spurs from the page as he did so. "Rise, Sir William and don your spurs." Matthew fitted them and then stood.

Silence filled the room until Sir Geoffrey and Sir Robert stepped forward to clasp his arm. My son was a knight!

He turned to me and clasped my arm, "Thank you, father. I am pleased this was a small ceremony. I will see my peers later but for now, this is family and family is everything. I feel the presence of the Warlord."

"Aye, you are right." I touched the plaster-covered stone walls. "His spirit is in the very walls."

Chapter 2

The baptism went well. I say went well for Thomas did not cry when his head was wet. His mother had. We came back into my castle and my wife hurried off to organise the feast. My knights began to arrive soon after noon. Sir Fótr, Sir Edward and Sir Gilles arrived first, closely followed by Sir William of Hartburn. His sons, Richard and Robert, were also due to be knighted. When they came, they joined my son and Sir Gilles. Along with Sir Robert's squire, they were all keen to know what William felt. When a man was knighted then his world changed irrevocably.

Sir William of Hartburn said, "They are desperate to be knighted and, if truth be told, they should be but…"

I nodded, "But they cannot afford the expense."

He shook his head, "We have been lucky in the wars but most of my coin was lost when we fled La Lude. They need a war or a chevauchée."

"There is peace here on the border. Be careful what you wish for. Does Hartburn not provide all that you need?"

"It is a good manor but it cannot support three knights." Sir Robert had joined us, "I fear that you will find that Redmarshal can only support one knight too, Sir Robert."

"Aye, and Richard is now itching for his spurs. I can understand it."

"Your wife has money, Sir Robert. She had it from my Aunt."

"That is my wife's. I am not the kind of knight to take from his wife. No, my brother will have to be patient."

The Bloody Border

This was a celebration. My knights and squires enjoyed each other's company. I sat in my chair and watched them. I was content. Alfred's widow, Matilda, approached with a shy-looking Henry Samuel at her side. "My lord, my son would speak with you."

"What, Sam, surely you are not shy?" Once I would have picked him up and sat him on my knee. Now he was too big. He was close in age to John, our new page. "What is it?"

He pointed at John who was standing close to Matthew and Mark. "He is a page and I am nearly as old as he is."

I nodded, "Yet he is much bigger than you."

"I am growing."

I looked at his mother to try to read her face. I saw conflict. She knew that if her son was a page then he was on the road to becoming a knight. She did not wish to lose him and yet she knew that he was his father's son. Perhaps William had chosen the right path when he had added John as a page. "You could be a page." His face brightened. "Just so long as you know what that means. You would have to be at my beck and call while I was awake. You would have to serve us meals. You would need to groom my horses and help Mark to prepare my weapons. You would need to practise each day for many hours."

He nodded, "I can do that!"

"Well, then I give you a week to think about it. Follow John and Mark. See what they do. Speak to them. Return at the end of seven days and give me your answer."

"I am ready now!"

"Seven days!" I stood and shook his hand. He had seen warriors do that and knew what it meant. "Now go and speak with the others." When he had gone, I said, "I can see that you are unhappy with his request."

"I would be losing my child and he is so young."

"He will still live in the castle and you shall see him each and every day."

She put her hand on mine, "There will be no war, lord, will there?"

"I cannot divine the future and, although I do not see a war on the horizon you must steel yourself. One day war will come and when that day comes your son will need to be prepared."

"Then I pray I am old and grey when that day arrives."

Alfred, Rebekah and Sir Geoffrey's son, also asked to be a page for his father. It was hard for him to say no. My grandsons had taken the first step along the road to becoming a knight.

The next day, when all the knights left to return to their homes, the castle felt empty. My daughter, Rebekah, and her family left us. I began, along with William, the work of moulding the rough clay that was Matthew, Mark and John into warriors. They each had strength but no skills. Matthew and Mark had shown some skill with a sword but even Henry Samuel had had more training. This would be hard work. I used my men at arms to help me. We had wooden practice swords made and they sparred with the men at arms. I saw my grandson, Henry Samuel, watching enviously. He had used a small practice sword already and William had taught him basic moves. Now my son and the men at arms helped the squires and John. On the second day, we introduced them to horses. This was where Sam had an advantage. He had been riding since he could walk. Even though Alan Horse Master had chosen placid horses for them the three spent more time on the ground than in the saddle that first day. We alternated swords and spears on one day with horses on the next. They were given no respite at night for Geoffrey, my steward, taught them how to serve. This was the most alien of their tasks. In their own, humble homes, they ate with a spoon and their platter was often a piece of rye bread. They just drank small beer from a hand-turned wood beaker. In my hall, they had to learn about knives, plates, of goblets. It was much to take in. Once again Sam would have an easier time of it if he chose to be a page.

At the end of seven days, when I rose, Henry Samuel was waiting for me outside my chamber. I smiled, "Yes?"

"A week has passed, lord, and I have my answer." I nodded. "I would be a page."

"And you have told your mother?"

"Aye lord, she was upset. It did not make me change my mind. I will follow in my father's footsteps."

I took his arm, "Then Henry, son of Alfred, you shall be my page. We will get you tunics and surcoats. Go and find Mark. You begin your duties now!"

The Bloody Border

In many ways, it was easier now. The two squires were well matched and they could spar together. John and Sam also sparred. Although he was bigger and stronger, John could not best my grandson. He had been playing with wooden swords since he could walk. However, the longer a bout went on the more he tired. When it came to hoops, Sam was superior to all of them, Mark and Matthew included. I had played hoops with him since he could just waddle about. The training was robust. Of course, his bruises and lumps upset his mother and grandmother but it would make him stronger.

The training progressed well. Then, after months of work and practice, a rider came from East Harlsey. Sir Richard sent me a message, that the King was making royal progress. He would be heading for Stockton. Of course, that ended all training for we had quarters to prepare. It was not just the King we would have to accommodate, there would be his entourage. There could be more than three hundred people. Most would have to camp on the green by St. John's well.

Seven days after the message arrived the long column of riders approached the castle. They reached the river in the late afternoon. It was strange to see the King without his advisers. He was now surrounded by barons he trusted. I had been one once and, I daresay, he still trusted me but I was not one of his inner circle. I saw him looking at the crenulated walls. When he dismounted, he pointed to them, "They could hold off an army, my lord."

"Aye, Highness, and protect your river, the north and the main road south. I am ever your servant."

It was the right thing to say and he nodded, "We stay just the night for we are heading to Norham. First, we visit with the Bishop in Durham. When I have refreshed myself, I would have a conference with you."

Henry Samuel, John and the twins were now given duties they had not expected. They helped the King's servants to serve him. It was an experience. The King emerged from his chamber an hour after he had arrived. "Come, we will take a turn about your walls. I can talk and it will help my appetite!"

My men at arms knew the King and they understood his need for privacy. The sentries on my wall moved out of the way as we

The Bloody Border

walked around my fighting platform. "When I leave tomorrow I would have you and your son accompany me to the north. My sister and her husband have been invited to Norham." He smiled, "I think your presence might unnerve King Alexander, eh, Earl?"

I had bloodied the Scots, "Probably, Highness."

"I like Alexander but many of his lords are devious and seek power. We need to remind him and his lords that they now owe fealty to me. When that is done, I will take a ship from the New Castle. I have business in Gascony." I felt my heart sink. Such a voyage normally meant a war. Was he going to order me and my archers to accompany him? His next words brought joy to my heart. "As much as I might need your men and your archers my intentions are peaceful. I seek alliances. However, I know that the Scots still regard Northumberland, Cumberland and Westmoreland as their own land. I go to let King Alexander know that they are English and will remain so. Your presence will reinforce the notion. I do not think he will risk your ire."

I nodded, "I will ever protect England and its people."

He stopped and turned, "I do not want war. I will need all of my barons and lords when we eventually retake Normandy! I need my northern barons to be as a wall of steel. I want the Scots to fear us rather than risk the petty thievery they engage in. Bishop Poore thinks highly of you as do I. You are the one I leave in command of the north. You protect this border. I give you the power of Earl Marshal of the Northern Marches. I do not want you to go to war but I would have you ensure that my people and lords there are safe."

"Are there not others, closer to the border, whom you could leave in command, Highness?"

He stopped and looked at me, "You are the one man I can trust. The Earl Marshal's son showed me that I have to be careful about the men who are given power. I would not have it abused. You are sometimes too honest and plain-spoken." He smiled, "This is just such an occasion. There are many northern barons I trust but there are others of whom I am suspicious. You are the right man and the fact that you live so far from the border is an inconvenience. You, alone out of most of the northern barons, know the value of horses and your mounted archers are a legend. You will be the Earl Marshal of the North!"

The Bloody Border

I had refused the title of Earl Marshal before. The King's voice left me in no doubt. I could not refuse this command, "It would be my honour!"

His smile was genuine, "Good. I know that you will make a good job of this and you would rather be here than traipsing around Gascony with me, wouldn't you, Sir Thomas?"

I nodded, "Yes, your Highness!"

"See, honest and forthright! You cannot help yourself! Others would have flattered me and given me a comfortable lie. I have an appetite now. Let us eat!"

The journey north was a real test for our new squires and John. Thus far their rides had been in the bailey or on the green. Riding north they were under the scrutiny of lords and their King. I was proud of my grandson for he helped them all he could. I heard him offering advice as he rode behind us. I was just three riders behind the King. This was the first time he had been so far north and I saw him observing all that he could. I had no doubt that he took in the fact that it was barley and oats growing in the fields and not wheat. He saw sheep and cattle grazing together in fields. What he did not see were castles. After mine, the next one he would see was the mighty fortress of Durham. It would show him how frail was our grasp on this land.

The Bishop had been warned of the King's arrival and we were warmly greeted. The days of conflict between the King and the Bishop of Durham looked to be over. The cavalcade which had followed us from Stockton had to camp on the green before the cathedral. The King was a pious man and he entered the church with the Bishop where they prayed alone. I took the opportunity to speak to the knights he had chosen to bring with him. They seemed eager to speak to an old warhorse like me and they appeared to be good men. Battle would be the real test. They were largely young knights. I wondered at that. Did that mean he did not trust the older ones or had they chosen not to come with him?

Matthew, Mark and our pages found stabling for the horses. What our squires lacked in breeding they made up for with common sense. I saw other squires who just lounged around, waiting for the orders to stable their mounts. Ours had the best stalls for they reached them first. William came over to me, "I had expected dukes and earls to be with the King."

"As did I. Perhaps he is making his own court. We will just do as he orders." I smiled. "We are being used as a threat to frighten his brother-in-law. It would be best if we said little. Silence might intimidate the Scots more."

He shook his head, "It has taken us all day to reach a place we normally ride in less than a morning. Norham might as well be in Normandy! This will be a long journey."

I shrugged, "It is how kings travel. He will have his crown jewels with him as well as all of his armour. He does not mean to fight but he will need it When he goes to Gascony, he will have to be prepared for anything. A month or so and we will be back home again. The King will still be abroad. It is the way of kings."

That evening, as we ate, I found myself, along with my son, on a lesser table than the one with the King, the Bishop and the Sherriff of Northumberland. I saw the King and the Bishop with their heads together. The last time I had been at such a gathering of lords was just before we had headed north to punish the Scots. That was when I had first met Sir Robert of Elsdon. So much had happened since then. William had just been my squire and now he was a knight. I smiled as I watched our squires and John the Smith's son as they hurried to fetch more platters of food for us. I saw the youngest of them, Henry Samuel. He looked to be the one who was in control. This was his world.

When I saw the Bishop pointing to me, as he spoke, my heart sank. I was being singled out again. The problem with dining in the same hall as the King was that you could not leave before the King. It was at times like these that I wondered why I left my family. When I had first gone to war it had been out of necessity. I had to earn coin. Then, when my lands were taken, I had to fight to get a home. I had a home now but instead of enjoying time with my children and grandchildren, I was enduring a meal with men I did not know.

William was astute, "This will pass, father." He nodded towards the kitchen door. Henry Samuel was organizing Matthew and Mark. "See my nephew! You would not see this in Stockton. Geoffrey, your steward, would have taken the task from him. This is good for Sam. He is in no danger and yet he is growing and taking his first steps on the path to becoming a warrior."

"You are right and it may well be my age that makes me fret so."

When we left, the next day, the Bishop did not come with us. The King did not ask for me to ride next to him and I wondered what that meant. He sat in close conference with the Sherriff. Our next halt was Prudhoe and when we departed that castle the Sherriff left us. Hexham Priory was our last stop before Norham. There we were close to the lands which were claimed by the Scots. The houses of the barons we passed each had a tower. There were defensible ditches. I saw that the farmers worked in the fields but their bows were close to hand. This was the border. It was at Hexham that William and I were summoned to sit with the King and the Prior.

The King was never one for idle chatter. When he had something to say he came directly to the point. "When we were in Durham I spoke with the Bishop about the border. The Palatinate has many manors there. I asked why some were empty. Such an oversight allows those who wish to cause mischief, avenues which they can exploit to cause harm."

I nodded, "Aye, Highness, it caused the trouble the last time."

The King frowned. I had interrupted him and that was the wrong thing to do. He drank some wine and continued. "You, Sir William, are recently knighted. You are of your father's blood. The Earl Marshal was your grandsire. You need a manor. More, I need a baron who can protect my lands. Your father has other duties."

I knew what was coming and my spirits plummeted.

"Yes, Your Highness. I hope that my father may give me one in the fullness of time when I have earned it."

The King shook his head. He and my son were of an age and yet the King looked and sounded like a much older man, "England needs you now! I spoke with the Bishop in Durham and the Prior has confirmed what I had heard. The northern border is still lawless. Bandits and brigands raid from the debatable lands to the Tweed and Jed Water. You are to be the new lord of Elsdon. Many people have left the valley for the

Scottish bandits and border raiders still cause havoc. I command you to make the manor of Elsdon safe for our folk. You will ensure that Scottish forces do not use the road to attack the lands of England."

My son had no choice in the matter, he bowed his head, "I am honoured, Your Highness."

"You will need to provide twenty men. The manor will not support such a number yet for the manor has been raided too often. The Bishop will pay you forty pounds for two years to allow you to strengthen the manor. There will be no taxes for those two years."

Forty pounds would not even buy a destrier. Rouncys cost five pounds. His men would need to be mounted. The forty pounds sounded generous but it was not. As Sir Robert had discovered, Elsdon was a poisoned chalice. The difference would be that my son had no wife. He would not have to worry about a family.

My son was quick-witted, "And losses, Highness? I have fought these border bandits before. They hamstring horses. It will be expensive not only in terms of weapons such as arrows, spears and shields but also horses."

The King frowned. He did not like spending his own money. The Bishop of Durham was funding the manor. "Make an account and send it to the Bishop. Prior, I would have you write to the Bishop and ask him to make good any losses incurred by Sir William." The Prior nodded. The King then smiled, "Do this, William of Stockton, and there will be greater rewards in the future."

I bit my tongue. This was no reward. The pampered knights he had brought north with him would never have consented to such a duty. He was using my family. We never refused to serve England. The kings of England since the first Henry had done so.

"Thank you and what are the other manors which are close by?"

The King had the information readily to hand. "There are two. Sir Eustace at Rothbury and Sir James at Otterburn. Yours, as I am sure you know, guards the crossroads which leads to Morpeth and the East as well as Hexham and the south. Yours is the one which must be held."

The Bloody Border

I knew Sir James. He was an older knight. He had held his tower when the Scots had last invaded south. Sir Eustace was a new lord of the manor. His predecessor had died at the battle to recapture the captives. He was an unknown quantity. Sir Ranulf of Morpeth was an established lord. I wondered why he had not been asked to manage the border.

"You will come with us to Norham, Sir William. I have no doubt that your father will wish to visit the castle at Elsdon with you." He smiled, "He has a rare eye for attack and defence. His experience will stand you in good stead." He stood, "And tomorrow we leave before dawn. I have had enough of this snail's pace. We ride for Alnwick and the castle of Sir William de Vesci."

He swept out of the room. It says much about my son and his sharp mind that he did not dwell on his new circumstances but asked the question which was in the back of my mind. "Why did the king detour to Hexham when we could have stayed on the north road and stayed the night in Morpeth which was not far from Alnwick?"

I turned to the Prior. I knew him and he appreciated what had been done by my men and me when we had come north. Some of the captives we had rescued had stayed to live close to the Priory. "Prior, the King must like your Priory to come so far west when our business in the north is so urgent."

I saw him shift uncomfortably, "My lord, do not be so disingenuous. That is not the question in your heart is it?" I shook my head. He sighed and leaned forward, "The King came here to remind me that this priory exists because he allows it to. We need to pay more taxes for the privilege."

That made sense. The Augustines were not an order which espoused poverty. There were relics which pilgrims came to see. That generated an income for the town and the Priory benefitted. He had brought us here so that the Prior could see that the King was spending money for the defence of this land. The King knew the value of coin. He used it carefully. He was more cavalier in his use of men.

We retired to our chamber. The Priory was not huge and we had a canon's cell for the six of us. Only William and I had a bed. The others made do with the floor. For Matthew, Mark and

The Bloody Border

John, this was no hardship but Henry Samuel was not used to such privations. William and I spoke as Sam tried to get comfortable.

"I will need men, father."

"Of course, and you shall have them. I have more than enough and I do not need them as much as you. I will have Ridley the Giant choose some. They will, perforce, need to be single." Any other knight would have struggled to make men leave the comfort of Stockton for the wilds of the north and the bloody border but I knew that my son was held in high regard by my men. They would come. "I have coin enough. When we get to the castle do not be afraid to ask me for money. It will need improvement. We still have money from Aunt Ruth."

I saw the weight of his task sink in. He shook his head, "Am I ready for this?"

"No one would be ready for this task. If Sir Fótr were given the task he would struggle. The King is not being fair, and neither is the Bishop. They have neglected this border. We have been given an almost impossible task. I fear this is because of my name and the reputation of our family. We keep our word and we do our duty. I am sorry."

He laughed, "Do not be. I may not be the Warlord but I have his blood and yours. God has set me a challenge. When I prayed during my vigil I asked for a sign. He has answered me. If I do not relish the task it is not God's fault. I did not specify an easy life!"

The four youngsters had managed to get to sleep. I looked at them before I blew out the candle, "John can be your page. I do not think that your mother would approve of having her son and grandson both in such a parlous predicament." I would train Henry Samuel myself. William's fate was a warning. My grandson could be used too.

"Amen to that!"

We reached Norham two hard days riding later. We had met with de Vesci and William and I had been relegated to a lower table again. We knew our place. We left before dawn. Many of the knights had struggled with the pace. It seemed that the King was keen to complete his task and then head for Gascony. Norham was a fine border castle but it was no palace. We

The Bloody Border

camped. The constable had had a pavilion erected so that the two kings could meet. Berwick was not far away and the Scottish King and Queen would be accommodated there.

Our squires had led sumpters with spare clothes. A knight did not meet a King and his Queen wearing a soiled surcoat. This was the sort of expense Robert of Elsdon worried about. Now, of course, he would be Robert of Redmarshal. My son was the new lord of the northern outpost he and his brother had left. We washed and changed into new surcoats. Our squires and pages were learning that serving a knight meant far more than practising with a sword. They had to wash the dirty surcoats and find some way of drying them.

That night the King dined with just twenty of us. He needed to impress upon us all the tone he would adopt. He wanted no one to disrupt his plans. He meant, of course, me, "Earl Thomas, I must insist that you curb any desire to seek vengeance upon the Earl of Fife. He may well be present at this meeting. I have told you already about my suspicions. Remember the words I spoke in Stockton! I wish peace on the border but peace on my terms. I cannot have petty squabbles disrupting it." I bit my tongue. Petty squabbles to the King, safe in London, but matters of life and death here in the north. "I intend to let King Alexander know that I will not condone border raids. The lands his lords seek are English. It seems our last embassy did not work." He smiled at me, "Not your fault, Earl, they thought me distracted by Poitou. I will show them differently. They think I am still a boy. I will show them a man! They shall not ignore my words this time."

The other knights applauded and banged the table.

The King turned to me, "I would have you and your son present serious faces. Your visages can appear belligerent but your voices will be silent."

King Alexander and Queen Joan arrived at noon. King Henry had been kept waiting since the early morning. I knew he was unhappy at the slight. I saw, in the entourage, Malcolm, Earl of Fife. There were other nobles against whom I had fought. I studied the faces. Would I be fighting them soon? I saw my son doing the same. He was being introduced to his enemies!

King Henry was clever and he greeted his sister warmly. It was a snub to King Alexander but one which could not be contested, "Sister! How does the clime here suit you?"

"It is not Gascony, that is certain, but it does have its charm. It is good to see you, brother." She saw me and gave me a smile. For some reason, she seemed to like me.

The King took her to the throne which had been placed for her. His throne was the largest and I saw King Alexander take in that fact. His face showed his displeasure and his voice was almost petulant when he spoke, "So, King Henry, we have come as we were requested. What is it that you wish?"

"When I sent the Earl of Cleveland to speak with you about the border raids, I thought that I had made clear that Northumberland, Cumberland and Westmoreland are all English. I have heard of more raids across the border and, worse, I have heard that some of your lords," he stared at Malcolm, the Earl of Fife, "have also expressed the opinion that those lands are still Scottish."

The King of Scotland cast an irritable glance at his earl who just stared belligerently at me. "Brother, I cannot control what my lords think and I cannot ensure that bandits, who are of both English and Scottish blood, will not commit crimes. All whom we catch are tried and sentenced." There was deceit in his words. The sentence should have been death but the Prior of Hexham had told us that most of the bandits caught by the Scots were fined. "Perhaps you should make your side of the rivers stronger."

King Henry nodded, "And we have done so. Sir William, the son of the Earl of Cleveland, is now the Lord of Elsdon. His family know how to manage wrongdoers."

Until that moment the Scots, and Malcolm of Fife, in particular, had looked calm. As soon as the news was delivered, I saw a change. If my son was here then they risked my intervention. My family was often called the bane of the Scots. The Warlord had almost captured Prince Henry after the Battle of the Standards and he had been responsible for the capture of King William. The Earl and those around him stiffened. King Henry had surprised them.

"The Treaty of Falaise is still in place." King Henry glared at Fife and the other lords, "I will make the financial punishments instituted at that conclave seem like nothing if there is further trouble along this border."

It was a powerful statement. It left a silence until The Earl of Fife spoke, "King Henry, King Alexander is quite right. It is Scottish barons who do this. It is young headstrong knights who see the Treaty of Falaise as something dishonourable. They are young warriors."

The King gave a thin smile, "Then unless you wish to either ransom or bury them, curb them. The Earl of Cleveland will ensure that this border is safe!" The Scots left soon after looking a little less confident than when they had arrived.

Chapter 3

William and I left for Elsdon before dawn the next day. We had no men at arms with us and the six of us just slipped away as the early morning fog filled the Tweed Valley. There was little chance of reaching Elsdon in one day and so we planned on staying at Rothbury. It would give me the chance to speak with Sir Eustace. We would travel quicker than with the entourage of the King. Once he had finished with the King and Queen of Scotland we were forgotten. He had told Sir William what to do and he would quit England as soon as he could. I wondered why the Warlord had devoted his life to the Empress Matilda and her son, Henry. Perhaps Henry had been more grateful than mine.

We would head to Wooler where Baron Geoffrey of Wooler had a small castle. As we rode, I counselled our squires and pages. "What we do today is not the same as when we rode north. We are travelling the borderlands and there are dangers here. Keep your hands on your daggers and short swords. If we are attacked, forget the sumpters. Defend yourselves."

Henry Samuel asked, "Grandfather, are we likely to be attacked? I thought we were in England."

"We are, Sam, but there are bandits here. If we had our archers and men at arms then I would fear nothing but the four of you have yet to learn how to be squires and pages."

We had no shields with us but William and I had our helmets hanging from our saddles. I had not brought Crow but a good courser, Hawk. William had done this before and he was alert. The road had been built by the Romans and was largely straight but the contours of the land inevitably led to bends. In addition, the trees which had once been cleared had been reclaimed by shrubs, bushes and trees. There were many places where we could be ambushed. Each time we passed a village or hamlet, Crookham, Milfield, and Akeld, we made a point of paying for food and water for the horses. We also spoke to the locals. I did not need to but we engaged in conversation and learned much.

In Akeld I spoke with the smith who was beating a ploughshare. He was a large man and I saw a sword hanging from his wall. It looked to be well used. "How goes life here, smith?"

He stopped work and looked up at me, "It is good that you have not far to go, lord, Wooler has a good castle. If you wish my advice, I would hurry for the next few miles."

I cocked my head to one side, "Trouble?"

He laughed, "Not for the Earl of Cleveland but you have some young lads here."

"You know me?"

He nodded, "Cedric of Elsdon is my cousin. I followed you when we trounced the Scots. As they say around here, lord, 'gan canny'."

I saw Sam look puzzled. I smiled as I explained, "It is the local dialect for '*go carefully*'. Thank you, smith." I flipped him a penny, "That is for your trouble."

He slipped the coin into his apron, "No trouble, lord. Folk around here respect you and your name."

As we mounted, I said, "William, ride at the fore with Matthew and Mark. The smith was warning us of danger. I will ride with John and Sam."

As we left the village, I saw that the road was straight for almost a mile but then it entered a wood. There lay the danger. I had Sam on one side of me and John on the other. John was still a poor rider. He was getting better but he had little confidence in his ability to stay in the saddle when his horse galloped. Sam was younger but was happy to turn in his saddle to watch the horses behind. John was concentrating so hard that a bandit could have crept to within ten paces and he would not have been seen. I said, quietly, "If we can traverse those woods then I believe we will be safe for Wooler is not far on the other side.

The Bloody Border

Remember, if there is danger, hold the sumpter's reins in your left hand and take out your dagger. If we are attacked then you two stay behind me."

"Aye, grandfather."

I drew my sword. It would do no harm and the smith's words had been a warning that I ignored at our peril. I left my helmet on my cantle. William would spot the ambush before I did. I was now convinced that the smith had been warning us. He would have known there were bandits. He could not afford to make enemies of them and so he had been obtuse in his warning.

We passed through scrubby trees into the woods proper. The Romans had built a ditch on both sides of the road when their legions had constructed it. Time and nature had filled it in and bushes had joined the weeds to encroach upon the road. Even as William raised his sword to shout a warning the first arrow flew from the trees. In all, four arrows came from the undergrowth which lined the side of the road. We were lucky that they were sent towards William and me. We had mail. The arrows were simple hunting arrows sent from hunting bows. Had they hit flesh they would have caused a wound. They did not. One hit my shield and another struck my surcoat and mail. Donning my helmet, I spurred Hawk and rode into the woods. The arrow which was sticking from my mail and surcoat told me that it had come from my right. I knew that I was abandoning my grandson but if I stayed with him then a lucky arrow might hit him and he wore no mail. William and I had to take on these bandits, no matter how many there were!

I saw an arrow come straight for me. I even saw the archer. He was a small red-haired man. I swashed my sword before and miraculously managed to deflect it. He turned to run. I twisted Hawk's reins and leaned forward. I swept my sword from the right and it bit deeply into his neck. The speed of Hawk's hooves took me beyond his falling body and my sword slipped out. To my left, I saw another bandit pulling back on a bow. These were poorly made bows. He was concentrating on sending an arrow towards the road. Even as he let out his breath to release the arrow Hawk's head hit his left hand as my sword hacked across his back. I heard the clash of steel and urged Hawk back to the road.

I saw Matthew lying on the ground and John, Sam and Mark with daggers drawn defending his body. Three bandits, one with a short sword and two with axes were advancing. Of William, there was no sign. I did not hesitate, I roared a challenge and spurred Hawk. It made the three of them turn. As they did so Mark lunged at one of them and his dagger ripped into the man's upper arm. The other two made the mistake of hesitating. As I reached them, I pulled back on the reins. Hawk's hooves clattered into the skull of one of them while I split open the head of the other. The man who had been wounded suddenly found three daggers aimed at him and an angry knight with a sword. He dropped his axe and fell to his knees.

I looked up as I heard movement through the trees. William had his sword in the back of another bandit. "The rest are fled or dead." He looked down and saw Matthew.

I dismounted and handed my reins to Sam. Matthew was breathing. I saw his chest moving up and down. He was still alive. I turned to his brother, "What happened, Mark?"

"His horse put her hoof in the ditch and he did not keep the saddle."

I smiled. A bloody coxcomb would soon heal. "Sit him up. John, find some cord and bind the hands of these two criminals."

William said, "There are two dead on this side."

"We will take these two back to Wooler. His lordship can deal with them and then rid the woods of the bodies and the ones who survived."

I turned as Matthew came to. "I am sorry, Sir William. How can I be a squire when I cannot sit on a horse?"

My son laughed, "Let us say it will be a challenge but the four of you showed today that you are no cowards." I glared at the prisoners, "Unlike these bandits."

It was almost dark by the time we reached Wooler Castle. The two bandits had slowed us down. Our attire gained us entry and the Lord of Wooler, Sir Geoffrey, waited in his lower bailey. He was older than I was. He was about Edward's age. He was overweight. He had not hunted bandits in his woods. He had enjoyed the venison it provided and had drunk mead and ale.

"I am the Earl of Cleveland and this is my son, William, the new Lord of Elsdon Manor. We were attacked by these two bandits and others in the woods north of here. We slew some but the others escaped."

I dismounted. Baron Geoffrey walked over to one of the men and lifted his chin, "I might have known. Brian Sheep Stealer. He turned to the other, "And this would be Andrew the Scot. Both are wanted for sheep stealing."

"I am guessing, lord, that they have a camp in the woods."

He gave me a guilty look and nodded. Shaking his head, he said, "Then I will stir myself and rid my land of these parasites. I apologize, Earl. I know your name and had you died in my manor then it would have been a stain on my honour."

I nodded. The baron was like many knights. They had a good income from a small manor. They kept few men at arms and did not rouse themselves when the levy was called. His small wooden castle would be too much for bandits or raiders but if the Scots ever chose to attack in force then he would perish.

"The travellers on this road need you to keep it safe, Sir Geoffrey."

"Aye lord, I know. I have been remiss."

He had a priest who looked at Matthew. It was as I had thought. A graze on the head. He would survive. The two bandits were kept in chains and, that evening, as we ate, the Baron told us that they would be hanged the next day. We did not stay for the hanging. I did not wish Sam to see it and we left as dawn broke. I wished to be in Rothbury as soon as possible. This time, when we rode, our squires and pages were more alert. They had learned a valuable lesson!

Baron Eustace of Rothbury appeared to be a real warrior. He wore good mail and had a fine sword hanging from his belt. He had men at arms on his walls and his castle had a stone base with wooden palisades. The gatehouse was made of stone. I knew him from the battles with the Scots. He had been a young knight then and had sought a manor. His action against the Scots had brought him a good castle and a rich manor. As we sat in his hall, I told him of the visit with the Scots and the attacks of the bandits. "Old Geoffrey likes his Malmsey a little too much! He is lucky. Norham guards the north and we guard the south. The whole of Northumberland would have to fall before he was threatened." He turned to William. "I can tell you, Sir William, that I am right

The Bloody Border

glad that there is a lord of the manor once more at Elsdon. It was a shame about Sir Robert and I am pleased that he has found happiness. I confess I think you are a little young for the task." He was a bluff plain-speaking man and he held his hand up. "No offence intended."

"When I was little younger than William, Sir Eustace, I was knighted. My squire and I fought in the Holy Land. I do not think it is the age which makes a knight. It is in a man's heart and in his sword arm. Sir William has the qualities it will take to keep the border safer than it is at present."

"I believe you. We have all heard of the hero of Arsuf."

"Arsuf was a lifetime ago. Until my men can be summoned my son, his squire and his page will be alone here. Is there a reeve? A bailiff? Farmers?"

"Old Alan still watches over the place. He was a lay brother at Durham and when Sir Robert left the Bishop sent him. He does his best. As for farmers? There used to be ten or more farms. They ran mostly cattle and sheep. The raiders took most of them. There are three hardy families left and they farm close to the castle. Old Alan acts as a priest for the priest was slain too. Most of the houses in the village are abandoned. One or two widows live there still." He saw William's face. "I fear, Sir William, that you have one of Hercules' twelve tasks ahead of you." He shook his head, "But I will do as your father asks. I will send half a dozen of my men with you tomorrow and supplies for a week but I can do no more. You will need to fend for yourself after that. I need all of my men to keep my manor safe."

The rest of the meal was spent ascertaining the potential for the land as well as the dangers. It soon became clear that the Scots were insinuating themselves into the land once more. They were stealing cattle and sheep. When they could they took slaves. I wondered why Sir Eustace had not done more. Then I dismissed the thought. Sir James of Otterburn was old. There was no lord in Elsdon and Sir Geoffrey of Wooler would not be of much help. Now I saw why I had been appointed.

When we were in our chamber, I spoke with my son, our squires and our pages. "I will visit with the Bishop on my way home. I will impress upon him the need for a priest, supplies and animals. Then I will travel to our home and give your mother the

The Bloody Border

news. She will not be happy. The King could have told us his plans when we were in Stockton! I do not like this way of doing things. It is as though he does not trust us!"

"No father, it is not like that. I understand him. He had the crown thrust upon his head. His mother left the country and he had bad advisers. Who would you trust in such a situation? He is doing what he must for his crown and his throne. I am honoured that he chose both you and me for this task. I will make the best of it but I will not impose this sentence on others." He turned to his squire and page, "Matthew, John, if you wish to return to Stockton with my father I will understand."

Matthew looked offended, "Just because my father is a tanner, lord, do not assume that I cannot keep my word. I would be a warrior. It seems to me that this will be the best place to learn such skills." He laughed, "I will, however, need a good helmet and a sword. Brother, when you see our father ask for them for me. Tell him I will pay him when I can." Mark nodded.

William looked at John. He smiled, "Lord, fighting Scotsmen seems preferable to working at my father's forge. I will stay too."

Henry Samuel said, "And I can stay too!"

"No, my grandson, for I need a page to help Mark. You were always going to be mine but this has determined it. I just hope that you are ready for I have seen, here in the north, that this border is not yet ready to be at peace."

Elsdon looked to be very similar to Rothbury except that it was much smaller. It was a motte and bailey castle. The keep was made of stone and it was a small one. In the lower bailey were wooden stables and a kitchen. A steep slope protected the upper bailey. We saw it as we approached the road from Rothbury. The village was little more than a huddle of farms. The bridge over the river was wooden. It was a well-sited castle but it needed work. I could see that the damage from the attacks had not been repaired. There were some stakes missing from the lower bailey. The mill which lay close to the castle also appeared to be disused or damaged.

Godfrey of Etal who was the captain of the six men who came with us shook his head, "You have been given a hard task, lord."

"Aye, well, the Lord above will have to help eh?" My son would have to be positive. If he showed doubts then he could not hope to inspire others.

"That is the spirit, Sir William."

As we headed towards the gate, I saw that the church was small and although half built of stone was inadequate. This was a poor manor. I could do better for my son. Yet I knew he would not thank me if I offered him one on the Tees. He was as stubborn as I was.

An older man came from the hall to greet us. I took him to be the lay brother. He wore a simple habit but I saw that he had a sword about his waist. He bowed and said, "I am Alan of Bellingham. I am the Reeve of this manor."

Now that we were close up, I saw that despite his sparse, white hair, he had an alert look about him. He had kept himself fit. I dismounted and gestured to my son, "I am the Earl of Cleveland and this is my son, Sir William. He is the new lord of the manor."

He dropped to his knees and kissed his cross, "Thank you God for answering my prayers." He stood and said, "I have done my best to maintain the keep but…"

My son smiled and held out his arm for his reeve to grasp it, "Fear not, Alan, I am here now and when my father brings back my men, we will make this a safe manor once more!"

I let the others go ahead. I was examining the castle through the eyes of an attacker. The ditch was a good one but had fallen into disrepair. It needed cleaning and its edges sharpening. The gate could be improved and the palisade needed work. The outbuildings, kitchen, granaries, storerooms and bread ovens had been allowed to become run down and semi-derelict. The palisade around the upper bailey was a little better but the gatehouse was inadequate. The second ditch was also poorly maintained. There was a stable. I was pleased to see that the squires had taken it upon themselves to take the horses there. The keep was a square one. It looked to be three stories high. I knew what I would find before I went in. The gate at the bottom was for horses and animals. A stone flight of steps led to the entrance to the accommodation. I dismounted and Mark came for my horse. I pointed to the door of the keep. "Use this stable. Baron Geoffrey's men can use the wooden one."

"Aye, lord."

I climbed the steps. We could make this easier to defend too. I saw that the main living area consisted of three rooms. There was one room with a fire and a larger one with a table. The table was a little worse for wear. On the west side was a small room. It looked to have had a small table and chairs in it at one time. I saw the marks on the floor. It was now empty. I heard Alan explaining to my son what had happened to the furniture. I went up the ladder which led to the upper floor. There I found two sleeping chambers. They were both large. It looked like Alan had been using one. Another ladder led to the trapdoor which led to the roof and the fighting platform. I stepped out and saw that whoever had built it when the Normans first came, had known his business. Archers could send their arrows into the lower bailey and decimate any attacker. William would need archers, good archers! I ran my hand around the crenulations. The stone was rough but it was a well-built tower. There was no damage. Had Sir Robert defended his tower then his wife might still be alive. As I descended the stairs, I realised that if that was the case then Isabelle would still be alone and unhappy.

William looked a little downhearted when I saw him. "There is much work to do, father."

"Aye and my men will happily join you in that work. When I came back to England, I was just pleased that I had a hall. There were no walls but I had a hall. It was a start. You have a beginning. I had your mother, William and Rebekah. You are a bachelor knight."

"And this is no place for a woman, father. I am content to face the dangers without a wife." Alan stood deferentially to one side. Our squires arrived. The room had an empty cheerless look. "John, take Sam and find kindling. You are the son of a smith, I am guessing you know how to make a good fire. Let us brighten this place."

"Aye lord."

"Matthew, Mark, we need food. Alan, where do you cook?"

"The kitchen in the lower bailey."

"Take the food we brought and we will test your skills at cooking eh?"

They cheerfully turned to go. Alan nodded, "I will accompany them, lord."

My son had taken charge and that was good. Now I needed information. I shook my head, "No Alan, stay with us for we need to speak." There were still three chairs which were whole. "Come, let us sit and speak as civilised men. I am old and my bones ache from riding these days." We sat. William was still wrestling with the problems of his manor and I saw that he was distracted. "So, Alan, what is your tale for I can see that there is more here than a lay brother put out to end his days quietly away from the mother church?"

He smiled and nodded, "I was a Hospitaller, lord. I was a brother-sergeant. I was wounded when Jerusalem fell. I left the order and came home. I was born in Bellingham and thought to come back and find peace here. I went first to Durham to ask the Bishop if I could be a lay brother for the priest at Bellingham. This was during the Scottish invasion. It was after that when the Bishop remembered me. He sent me here." Alan slapped his sword, "I am a priest but I can be a shepherd to these people and protect them against the privations of the Scots."

William looked up, "One man against the Scots?"

He smiled, "When our Good Lord began his ministry, he was alone and then he found twelve to help him. Besides a man must make a stand. The few people who live here are good folk. They need someone to watch over them. They are the kind of people around whom I grew up. I am content, lord, to give my life for them."

I nodded, "My son is young and he will learn." He smiled. I could see that this Hospitaller had inner peace and that was rare. He had expected to die in the Holy Land. Each day was now a new beginning. I spied hope. "Forgive my son's words. He is young and recently knighted. Tell me, have you had trouble since first you came?"

"Bandits. They steal cattle and sheep. The only farms and farmers who survive are those who live within sight of the castle. They come here when the bandits are abroad and they man the walls. Since we have adopted this defence, we have had no losses."

"And they come from the northwest?"

He nodded, "Otterburn guards the road but these bandits just slip through the forests and take the animals. They are not warriors. They are predators. They are organized and they are well-armed."

"You were a warrior, numbers?"

"The largest band we had was when thirty of them came. It would have gone ill for us had not Sir James of Otterburn arrived with four of his men at arms. They drove them hence."

The boys had returned with kindling and a fire began to blaze. Alan said, "If that is all, lord, I would go and help your squires. They seem like good boys. I have told you all that I know." He stood, "I am happy that we have a lord." He smiled at me, "The son of the hero of Arsuf brings hope to my heart."

"Sam, John, go and help them prepare food."

Sam nodded, "Aye, Grandfather, for I could eat a horse with the skin on!" I laughed. That was one of Ridley the Giant's favourite phrases.

William said, "It looks hopeless."

"Really? I thought the opposite."

"The opposite?"

"If a lay brother and half a dozen farmers can thwart the bandits what can you, men at arms and archers not achieve? Tomorrow I ride to Durham and then Stockton. I will not tarry long in our home. I will return with men who wish to serve you. Until the King sends the monies he promised you, I will provide your coin but this manor has potential. There are trees to help you repair your walls and to improve the gatehouses. There is stone aplenty. You can build a barbican around your gateway into this keep. The archers can hunt in the woods. You will have food and our men can find the rat runs these Scots use. You train your farmers to fight and you encourage others to come and work the fields. It is not hopeless. It is hopeful. This manor has plummeted as far as it can. Anything which you do will improve it." My words seemed to show him the enormity of the task he faced but I hoped they gave him a plan. I would have much to do in Stockton and the sooner I returned home the better.

Hot food made his mood improve. He and his squire and page would have to camp in the keep for there was not enough furniture. Alan of Bellingham had slept on a mattress filled with hay. Beds could wait. My son had horses and we decided that he would take the men at arms and Alan and ride his manor, the next day. It would show the people that law had returned and would warn the Scots that their days of banditry were numbered.

I confess that as I left him, the next morning, I was more than sad. I felt as though I was abandoning my child. I was leaving him at the edge of the world. I was deserting him on the bloody border. We rode hard. We had left all but one sumpter with my son and we made good progress. I spent just one night with the Bishop. I made it quite clear what I required. I ensured that we were alone when I spoke with him.

"Your Grace, the King plays a dangerous game here. The two of you could have appointed any lord to Elsdon, God knows it needs one. Yet you appointed a young knight and I have to ask myself why? Were the two of you thinking that my name would keep it safe?" His eyes flickered. I knew then that there was more to it. I shook my head, "No, the King is more devious and I am disappointed in you, Your Grace. You think that putting my son there means that I will bring my knights to his aid. The knights of the Tees Valley have a good reputation. You yourself sent for me when you last had trouble. You know that I would not desert my son. This is a way for the King and you to have warriors fight on the border without pay!"

He shook his head, "You do me a grave disservice, Sir Thomas. If you are needed then there will be a payment from the Palatinate but you are right, King Henry sees you as your grandsire. He sees, in you, another Warlord of the North."

I sat back in my chair, "And yet his father and uncle just used my family for their own purposes."

Richard Poore shrugged, "Sir Thomas, he is King. Kings are not like other men. If you expect them to behave like ordinary men then I think you are in for a disappointment. Fear not. Your son will have support. By the time you return with your son's men, I will have wagons with grain and other supplies for the winter. He shall not want. I will send a priest. Alan is a lay brother. I have families who seek land. They will come next year. King Henry might plan and plot but I am the Prince Bishop and I swear that I will keep the people of the Palatinate safe but to do so, lord, I need the aid of you and your son."

He was right. I could not expect a King to behave well. It was not in their nature. I had been forced into this corner and my life would never be the same.

Chapter 4

When I reached home without William I had first to beard my wife. She was not happy. "Why could I not say goodbye to him? I will come with you and see that his castle is well appointed!"

I held up my hand, "No, you will not. This is the borderlands. Our son has a dangerous task and the last thing he needs is to worry about his mother." I did not mention the attack in the woods although I was sure that Henry Samuel would blurt it out at some point. "When I deem it safe then I will take you. Until then you will write to him." I saw the tears well in her eyes. I put my arms around her. "I know how you feel. It broke my heart to leave him but he is a man. He has to make his own way in the world as we did."

"But he is alone!"

"He is not," I told her of Alan, Matthew and John.

She seemed appeased, "Then I will fetch the chests with his clothes! I will pack all that he needs." She glared at me, daring me to argue, "And I will send wine from your cellar and spices from our kitchens!"

I would not argue. I sent Mark to John's father. Our squires and pages needed arming. I provided the coin to pay, for armour did not come cheap. Then I sent for Henry, Ridley and David of Wales. "I need archers and men at arms to serve my son. I want single men for this is not the place for married men with bairns. I want volunteers. I need men who will serve my son as you serve me." Knowing what I wanted they left me. I was left with Sam.

"If I become a squire and then become knighted, I might have to leave here, grandfather."

"Aye, Sam. John will not see his mother and father again for a long time. He may never see them again. I am not getting any younger. William might not see me grow older. It is our life and we have to endure all that is put in our path."

He nodded, "I know. I am just thinking that I would make the most of my time with my mother. May I go and see her and my sister?"

"Of course. I will not need you again until we head north on the morrow. Mark's backside will be hardened to the saddle by the time we return here to Stockton!"

I headed to the stables. Alan Horse Master was my next port of call. I had left sumpters with my son but he would need palfreys. "Alan, I am sending men at arms and archers to Elsdon to be with my son."

"I know, lord, Henry Youngblood told me. I take it we will not see these horses again?"

"I doubt it."

"Then although we have enough the colts and fillies we have bred will not be ready as replacements. We will need to go to the horse fair at Appleby to buy more."

"See Geoffrey my steward and he will provide the funds. Do you have enough good animals? My son needs a courser."

"I had one for him already, lord. When you left for Norham I assumed he would be returning here. Eagle is a good horse. Not as good as Crow but Crow has destrier in him."

"Good. We leave in the morning."

"All will be ready."

I saw John returning through the gate. He carried with him a basket. He grinned when he saw me. "Mother wept when she heard of the attack. She has sent some of her preserves for us. Jams, relishes, chutneys and pickles." I nodded. That was the way of mothers all over. "And she has sent clean undershirts and hose. She does not want me to let the family down."

"And your father?"

"He is a weaponsmith. He had already begun work on swords, helmets and short mail byrnies for your squire and a helmet for me. Mine will not be ready today. He has said he will make them for Mark and Matthew. He hopes they will be ready for the morrow."

The Bloody Border

That set me to thinking about what else William might need. I left my castle and walked to Matthew's father's tannery. When I reached him, I told him that his son would be living in Elsdon and then asked him for hides. "Lord, do you need these as hides or as leather to be used by the men at arms and your grandson?"

"We will need hide jerkins and buskins for all of them. There is no tanner in the castle."

"The jerkin and the boots I have already. They just need finishing work. As for the belts and horse furniture, I have those ready to be shipped."

"Good. I will send Geoffrey with the coins to pay for them."

"There is no need, lord. It is for my sons and the smith's son. We are all of this manor."

"You are a craftsman and worthy of the hire. I will pay and it will help me to sleep easier. I will be in no man's debt."

By the time I reached my hall again, having spoken to all the tradesmen in my town, there were men at arms and archers waiting for me by the main gate. Henry Youngblood said, "We have the men who have chosen to come with you. There were others who wished to serve with Sir William but they were married. These are all the single men who now serve you, lord."

I looked along the line, "Your son, Young Henry, is here, Henry!"

He nodded, "Aye lord, it is hard to see a son leave home." He smiled, "As you have discovered too. He is of an age with Sir William and he has skill." He held out an arm as he introduced each of them, "Richard the Archer's Son."

"You did not wish to be an archer then?"

"I broke my left arm falling from a tree when I was ten years old, lord. The arm took a long time to heal. I can hold a shield and I can use a bow but I do not have the skill of an archer. I am content."

"Wilfred of Sheffield. None better with a pike." I clasped his arm.

"Roger Two Swords."

I saw that the man at arms had two swords in scabbards across his back. "They are short swords?"

"Aye lord, I can use a long sword and a shield but there are times when two swords can be more effective."

"Ralph of Raby."

Ralph was huge. He was almost as big as Ridley's son, Sir Peter. "Your size must draw weapons in a fight, Ralph."

"Aye lord but Ridley the Giant has given me tips."

"Harold Hart."

He was also a big man. Henry had chosen good men for my son. "I knew your father, William. He was a good warrior and served me well."

"As will I, lord."

"This last man at arms is a new sergeant at arms, lord. He has been with us for less than a month. Stephen Bodkin Blade."

"Do you find much use for a bodkin blade, Stephen?"

He grinned, "Aye lord. I fought in Poitou and some of the French knights there wore plate armour and full-face helmets. The bodkin blade finds holes in helmets. "

I knew the archers better. David of Wales had trained all of them, "Walther of Coxold, James, John the Archer, Idraf of Towyn, and Abel Millerson." Only Garth Red Arrow was unknown to me. He had arrived in the last few months but he seemed an affable young man.

"First, I thank you all for volunteering. Elsdon is neither a town nor does it have an alehouse. I know what you are giving up." I reached into my purse and, walking down the line, gave each of them five shillings. It was almost half a year's wages. They looked at me in amazement. They knuckled their foreheads and said, "Thank you, my lord."

Nodding I said, "Alan Horse Master has your horses. There are sumpters to pack. You will have arrows and spare tack to take with you. There is little up there and you will need to be resourceful." I would not sweeten the medicine.

After they had gone David of Wales said, "You had no need to be so generous, lord. They were happy to serve."

"I know but if it was your child at Elsdon would you not do all that was in your power to keep him safe?"

"Aye, lord."

"I will have six archers and six men at arms for my escort. We were attacked in the woods by Wooler. I would not risk my grandson's life again."

The Bloody Border

We ate together that night. Mark and Henry Samuel served us. I saw my wife and Matilda looking at Henry Samuel with new eyes. As I had expected he had not hidden the fact that he had almost been killed during the attack. When they left to fetch more food from the kitchen Matilda asked, "And will Elsdon be a dangerous place, lord?"

I would not lie to any of them, "Probably the most dangerous place in England at the moment."

My wife put down her knife and spoon. "And you care not that our son is there... alone! Sir Robert's wife died there! How could you allow this to happen?"

"That is easy, wife. The King commands. We obey! Would you go back to the life we had? Would you live abroad and be the wife of a sword for hire? I know not about you but I have grown to like this life we lead."

"But our son!"

"Our boy is stronger than you know. This is not forever. I will find a manor for him here in the valley but first, he must do as the King has asked. He will have support and you do not think that I will leave him alone do you?"

Mollified she nodded, "I suppose not."

"I will stay with him until he is secure and my men and I have had the opportunity to search for danger. He has the end of summer, the harvest and winter to come." I saw my wife begin to open her mouth. "And before you ask, I have no intention of allowing you to visit him. For one thing, it is too small a castle and for another, it is too dangerous. Resign yourself that you will not see your son for some time but I have impressed upon him the need to write to you."

We had found one of William's leather jerkins. I would give it to Henry Samuel. It had been Alfred's originally. Studded with metal it would slow down an arrow but if bodkins came his way then Sam was dead. I contemplated leaving him at home but knew that would only cause trouble. When we returned I would have armour made for him. We did not leave at dawn. My wife would not countenance such a thing. She wanted to say farewell and be presentable when she did so. Had I had time I would have ridden to Redmarshal to consult with Sir Robert. I did not. It was mainly a question of time but I knew that the discussion would

The Bloody Border

raise bad memories. I wanted him content for as long as possible. Isabelle deserved that.

We left as soon as the castle was roused and the tanner and the smith had brought the products of their labour. We had a long way to go. Ridley and David of Wales came with us. We would not be attacked, or if we were then our attackers would all perish. I did not go through Durham. I went closer to the coast for I was heading for the New Castle. I wished to have a conversation with the Sherriff. Brian son of Alan and Hugh de Magdeby jointly operated as Sherriff. When Brian son of Alan had been laid down by a winter pestilence the Bishop of Durham had suggested a second Sherriff.

Alan Horse Master provided good horses and we made excellent time. We made the thirty odd miles in one day although Mark and Sam were suffering by the time we reached the New Castle. We created a stir as we clattered across the bridge into the castle. My banner and surcoat told all who had arrived and my presence normally meant war.

That evening I dined with the two Sherriffs. I told them what we had done so far. They knew of the appointment of my son as the King had left from the port. Ship owners would profit greatly from the exodus.

"Your son is exposed at Elsdon, Earl. Rothbury, Wooler and Morpeth are all that stand in the way of an invader. If Scots come east then they risk Warkworth, Alnwick and this castle, not to mention Prudhoe but if they head due south then there is nothing until your castle. They could head west to Carlisle."

Sir Hugh nodded in agreement, "And Otterburn and Elsdon are little more than towers."

"Which is why I intend to help my son to strengthen it. My lords, I came here to plead with you. You are closer to this bloody border. If you hear rumour of danger then send to me. I know that you would help my son but I have the finest archers in the land. That is my secret weapon."

Sir Brian laughed, "Not so secret, lord, the Scots are terrified of your bows!"

"Perhaps but they have not seen the new arrows my archers have made. They can penetrate plate armour."

They both sat up. "Then that is a secret weapon."

The Bloody Border

Before I left, I had their sworn agreement to come to my son's aid if they were summoned and I was happier.

Although the road we took was not as good for at least half its distance, we made Elsdon in one day. We rode hard.

William, in the three days I had been away, had managed to repair the broken palisade but I was not surprised that he had not managed more. The men from Rothbury were reluctant workers and keen to get home. As we passed through the gate, I saw that they had also repaired the bread oven and the kitchens. "Mark, take the men at arms and archers to the stables. Sam, take my horse." He led Hawk away and I strode to the tower.

My son looked tired when he came to the door of the tower. "It is like the labours of Hercules, father. The closer I look the greater is the size of the task." He turned as Alan came down the stairs, "I am just glad that I have Alan of Bellingham. He is a good man."

"I brought some of my men at arms as well as your new men. There are eleven men who chose to come here. In truth more wished to come but they are married."

"Eleven is an adequate number. From what I have learned the bandits rarely operate in large numbers. However, should single men come to Stockton and should they wish a life of adventure, then send them to me."

"I will. We have ridden hard. We have brought food from home. Your mother has sent supplies for her son. While we eat, we will talk."

David and Ridley strode up, "It is good to see you, lord. This castle looks well made."

David nodded in agreement at Ridley's words. "Aye but we can make it even stronger. I saw a stand of ash by the river. I will have my lads collect branches to make arrows. We brought a number of arrowheads from John's father."

"Good. While we eat this night, we can discuss our plans."

Ridley shook his head, "We can eat together tomorrow, lord, but tonight we are tired and David and I need to talk to the men we will be leaving with you. Some have served at Stockton for less than a year." He smiled, "Besides you and your father, not to mention the squires and pages, have much to speak about."

The Bloody Border

Ridley was more like family than one of my men at arms. He had been with me longer than any. I had knighted his son. He was wise and I knew that I was lucky to have him.

One of the issues to emerge, as we sat and ate was the fact that the kitchens were in the lower bailey. The squires and pages complained about the distance and, more importantly, the temperature of the food. William was out of his depth. He had no solution to the problem. I drank some of the wine my wife had sent. It was one of my better wines! "It seems to me that there are two solutions. You either build a kitchen close to the keep or build accommodation close to the kitchens." He nodded but neither solution appealed. I could see his face and he was looking too closely at the problem. He needed to step back. "The keep is for defence. You will retreat here when you lose the lower bailey. Build a hall in which you can sleep. If you wish you can have four guards as guards for the keep but my suggestion would be to get dogs. They will alert you to any danger. You build a hall for you and your men in the lower bailey. I know not how long you will be here, but, until you have a wife, then you do not need more than a simple hall."

"That will take time!"

"Where will your men sleep? This night they are roughing it and sleeping in hovels but that cannot continue. Winter is around the corner and here it is harsh"

"But a hall! How can we build one quickly?"

"Tomorrow we hew timber and dig holes for the posts. I saw willow trees by the river. We cut them. There are farms close by and the farmers will be more than happy to give you their dung. You use daub. We can have a hall built in less than a week. It will be rough and ready but you will all be together. You will have hot food and you will get to know your farmers."

Matthew and Mark, not to mention, John, were my greatest allies. They were used to such work. When their fathers needed buildings then the families set to. William had been spoiled a little. He had witnessed bare earth turning almost magically into buildings.

He nodded, "And what of the bandits?"

"They are watching us now, William. They will be in the woods. They will have seen our arrival. There is no hurry for your presence will deter them, for a while. We have time. Hunting bandits is dangerous work. You need your men to be as familiar with this land as they are with the woods of Hartburn. I only know three of the archers well. You will need to get to know them all. You will have to choose a captain of archers and of sergeants. I know Walther of Coxold, as do you. If you wished my opinion, then I would choose him. He is the oldest. Since his wife died of the pestilence, he has shown little interest in women or a family. As for the men at arms? You will discover who the natural leader is."

Alan of Bellingham agreed with me when I mentioned the building of a hall. "I confess, lord, that when I came here first, I tried to live in the keep but found it unnecessary. The bandits do not attack castles. They know there is little within the walls for them. They want cattle, sheep and women. As for dogs, Rafe of Elsdon has a bitch which just whelped. There are too many for him. He will drown the surplus."

I smiled at the look of horror on Sam's face. John just accepted it as a matter of necessity. "Then, William, go and speak with this Rafe. Alan, you can show us where there are good trees for the hall."

Ridley and David worked well with each other. "You have the axes, Ridley. If you go with his lordship to hew the trees, we will dig the post holes and then cut the willow."

Ridley the Giant turned, "You heard the Captain of Archers. Take off your surcoats. This is dirty work! Today, you will earn your pay, for a change! Roger of Hauxley go and fetch the sumpters."

This was a wild country and we did not have to stir far to find trees. We headed to the north bank of the river. Alan pointed, "These are the best trees. They are about the right girth, lord, and it is not far from the castle. With your permission, I will return and light the bread oven. The flour you sent means we eat bread again! Real bread made from wheat!"

Sam was both too small and too young to be of much use but Ridley, who was a grandfather himself, saw a task he could do. He gave him a small hand axe. "See up there, Master Henry, there are ash trees. Use your axe to cut as many shafts for arrows

The Bloody Border

as you can. Nothing shorter than the length of your leg and nothing which is bent or curved."

"That is easy!"

Ridley laughed, "Tell me after we have hewed the trees and you still have less than a dozen shafts." Ridley was teaching my grandson a lesson. He respected archers and knew that arrows were difficult to make. There were few perfect pieces of wood. Inevitably the archers would have to work with the arrows to make them suit. It would keep him occupied. We had brought ale and food. We worked all day. We were not far from the hall and when I smelled bread then I knew that Alan had succeeded. The smell spurred us on. The sooner we finished the sooner we would enjoy fresh bread.

The men at arms worked well together. Ridley and the men who would be returning with me allowed William's men to work as a team. The side branches were trimmed. We would fetch them for kindling. The trunks were cut, using the saw we had brought, into similar lengths. By early afternoon I deemed that we had enough trunks cut. We used the horses to haul them back. It would take three journeys.

Sam had his arrow shafts but he had fewer than he had expected. "I am sorry, Ridley, I found less than twenty which were suitable."

Ridley laughed, "And that is ten more than I thought you would find. You have done well. When you stand in a battle line you will respect the skill of the archers for in a battle, they might loose a thousand of these! You have the shafts. Walther and the others will need to fit tips and then fletch them. In the short days of winter, they will toil in the hall we build for them."

My grandson was being given valuable lessons in how to be a warrior.

The holes were dug when we arrived back. Piles of willow were there too. They were trimmed and arranged in lengths. I stayed at the castle while the others returned for the rest of the wood. William was there too. He had four puppies. From the size of their paws, they were going to be big animals. That would be handy as there were still wolves in this desolate land.

"Rafe is a good man, father. He has three sons. They have a house which can be defended. It is almost as big as the hall we

The Bloody Border

are going to build. They all live within it. There are sixteen of them! He lost fewer animals than most for they are housed beneath his living quarters." He smiled, "His wife has agreed to make butter and cheese for us. I said we would pay and two of his daughters will be paid as servants. They will not live in my hall but come each day!"

"And so you become lord of the manor. This is good."

He turned to Matthew and John, "Take the pups to the keep. We need to let them know this is their home. We do not want them running back to the bitch."

As they took them away, I said, "What did you think of your courser, Eagle?"

"He is magnificent. I am grateful to you and Alan Horse Master. It will make my life easier. There is so much to occupy the mind of a lord of the manor."

I nodded, "Aye, son, I know!"

Just then I saw David of Wales approaching. He had with him Walther of Coxold and one of the new archers, Garth Red Arrow. He looked at us both and said, "Could I have a word, my lords? I fear I have made an error of judgment."

Garth Red Arrow hung his head. I saw that he was young, perhaps eighteen summers old. When he had been brought to me, I had noticed how powerful he was. I deferred to William. Technically he was one of William's men. William nodded, "Speak, Captain."

"Garth Red Arrow only arrived at the castle two months ago. He has great skills. I thought him a good addition to the garrison."

"I hear a but in your words."

"We have discovered that he was an outlaw. Wilfred of Sheffield told us. The two had conversations and it transpired that Garth Red Arrow came from the forests which lie close to Sheffield. When we questioned him then the truth emerged. He was an outlaw."

William looked at the young warrior, "It is true, Garth Red Arrow?"

"Aye, lord. I did not mention it for I wished for a new beginning. I was born an outlaw. My father was the leader of a band. We robbed on the road from Sheffield to York." William nodded. The punishment for robbery was harsh. It was blinding or maiming. William nodded for him to continue. "I never slew any. I did not wound any save those who hunted us. My father was caught and hanged a year since along with most of the other men. The others left and I was left alone in the woods with my mother. She died six months since. When I buried her, I decided that I had been punished enough by God. I would reject the life my father had chosen. My mother had come from Durham and so I went to the cathedral to pray at St Cuthbert's grave. It was while I was there that I heard a voice in my head. It told me that the only way to redeem myself was to serve those who defended the land. When I came from the church a priest saw me and witnessed my distress. He took me to a confessional and I confessed all of my sins. He told me that I would be forgiven and I could begin anew. I had to bathe naked in the river by the cathedral and then serve the knight who had saved Durham, Thomas of Cleveland. I came south and I joined your men, lord. That is the truth of it."

This was William's dilemma. If he chose to reject Garth Red Arrow then it would become mine. It was a test. I saw him looking from the archer to me. "Father, did you not tell me of the archer who was buried in the church, Dick?" I nodded. "Wasn't he an outlaw and yet the Warlord knighted him?"

"Aye son, that is true."

"Garth Red Arrow, look me in the eyes so that I may see into your soul." The archer did so. He looked fearful. "Do you swear that the tale you have told me is the truth and not a story to help you inveigle your way into my home?"

"I swear, my lord. I bathed in the river and the priest told me that my sins were washed away!"

I asked, "What was the name of the priest?"

"Brother Paul."

I nodded, "He was one of the priests who came with us to Jedburgh. He is a good man."

My son nodded, "Aye I remember him. Swear that you have given up your former ways and all will be forgotten."

Walther of Coxold shook his head, "This is a mistake, my lord."

My son shook his head, "It is not your place to say so, Walther. I have looked in his eyes and I see a redeemed man. Christ told us to forgive. If Brother Paul has done so then so shall I. If Garth Red Arrow is foresworn then he has made an enemy of God and will rot in hell for it. I do not believe he will."

I could see that Walther of Coxold was not happy but my son was Lord of the Manor and his word was law. They left us, "You handled that well and I do not see that it can hurt you here."

By the end of the day, we had timber posts in the holes but that was all. We had yet to ram in stones but we had made a good start and we enjoyed our fresh bread with butter and fresh cheese. As we ate, in the open air, William spoke to his men, "And you will be pleased to know that Rafe's wife is an alewife. She has agreed to sell us the barley beer she makes."

The men cheered. To a warrior such things were important.

The next day, I joined my men, stripped to the waist, to begin to build the hall. David of Wales and his archers fashioned barrows and wheeled the cow dung from the farm of Rafe of Elsdon. Then they dug and wheeled barrows of clay from the riverside. Meanwhile, the rest of us packed stones around the base of the timbers and tamped them down hard. We gave the squires and pages the task of collecting small stones and using a hammer to render them as small as possible. Dick and his archers wove the willow into panels to fit between the posts. It took us all day to embed the posts and finish the willow panels.

Sam was asleep as soon as he had eaten. William put his own cloak over his nephew. "He worked hard today. I hope he does not regret asking to be a page. It was easier for me. We were on campaign most of the time."

I nodded, "This is the real work of a page or squire. This is the work which lacks glory but is necessary."

Alan of Bellingham had joined us in the work and I had noticed that his back was crisscrossed with scars. Just before I headed for my bed, I asked him about them. "Flagellation was a regular part of life as a Hospitaller. I am not sure of its value, lord, and I am glad we no longer need to do it."

"I just wondered."

"You and your men are not afraid of hard work, lord. Brother knights worked as hard but since I have returned to England then I have not seen knights dirty their hands."

"For me it is necessary. I share the burden of toil with my men. It helps me to understand them."

"Then you are a rare lord indeed."

The next day was the start of three days of mess. We tied in the willow panels and then mixed animal dung, straw, clay and crushed stone to make the daub. There was no way to apply it without getting dirty. We had enough of us to apply the daub all around the walls. In that way, we built up the layers. William had plans for a second floor so that on the third day of daubing we began to lay the cross beams for the second floor. We split logs and then hammered nails to hold them to the beams. We used cross beams and diagonal beams for strength. After five days the ground floor was finished and we began on the second floor. We split timbers to make rough planks. We left a hatch to enable entry and then we repeated the process of willow and daub. The roof took two days to build. We used a turf roof. We had no way of firing tiles and there was no slate. William could always add a better roof later.

Rafe's daughters had begun work for us and we left Alan and the girls to make the hall habitable while the rest of us went on our first ride around Elsdon. William knew the four farmers from the village: Rafe, Tom the Miller, Harry Sourface and Dick Jameson. The village held just thirty-two people. The four farms were the village. The four farms were astride the beck and the roads. Tom the Miller's farm had been the mill but a lack of grain and damage from the raids meant it no longer functioned as a mill. The leat had become filled with rubbish. That was a task for the future. The other farmers, there were four of them, were more isolated. They were the ones at risk. Cedric Sheep Man and his wife lived with their sons and daughters on the fells closer to Otterburn. They were a big family. None lived close by. They had had their flock decimated many times but Cedric was an old soldier. He would not let the Scots beat him.

He was delighted to have armed men who could come to his aid. He went into his house and fetched forth a cow horn. "If the barbarians come again, lord, I shall sound this cow horn three times. That way you will have a warning."

"Aye, Cedric but save yourself."

"I am a hard 'un to kill, lord. The French found that out!"

We headed east to the farm of Phillip the Priest. Alan of Bellingham had already told us of this farmer. He had been a priest and he and one of his flock had fallen in love. It was forbidden for a priest to marry and Peter would not contemplate doing as many priests did and having a secret liaison. They had run away and found the farm high in the hills. He was a good man and the manor hid his identity although calling him Phillip the Priest seemed to be the wrong thing to do. They had four children and all were young. He had a few goats and a handful of sheep. My son asked him about his name. He smiled, "The church from which we fled is far from here but only those in Elsdon call me Phillip the Priest." His face fell. "The Reeve said that you were a good lord who would understand…."

My son held up his hand, "I will not judge. You have committed no crime." I saw relief on the faces, not only of Peter and his wife but also Garth Red Arrow.

Old Will lived alone. His wife had been taken as a slave and his sons had died when they attempted to rescue her. He lived by trapping animals and growing vegetables. "If you wish to punish me, lord, for hunting your rabbits then take my eye, as is your right. I have lost all else besides."

My son shook his head, "You have lost too much already. Hunt them. My father allows those in Stockton to do the same."

"Then he is rare, lord, for east of here there are many one-eyed men!"

The last farmer was the youngest and the one who had arrived most recently. David of Amble had had a falling out with his family. His father was the captain of a ship and when David had married the daughter of a swineherd, he had thought his son had married beneath him. David and his young bride had arrived a year since and they farmed a hill farm to the east of Elsdon. They were the most impoverished of the farmers.

"I am lord now, David. Your farm is just a mile and a half from the castle. If your wife would come and bake our bread for us and prepare a meal, I will pay her either in coin or in kind. I intend to go to Morpeth market to buy animals for the castle. You could begin your own herd or flock."

And so my son found his manor and made himself known to his people. As much as I might want to stay, I would be undermining him. Already some of his men looked to me. We had repaired the gates and ditch. Ridley and his men had added two wooden towers to the gates. It was now up to William. He would become the lord of the manor.

**Part Two
Sir William of Elsdon**

Chapter 5

My father embraced me and he hugged me tightly. He said, huskily in my ear, "God speed, my son. I am confident that you will do well but I do not like to leave you. I am but two days hard riding from you. Send to me if you need aught."

"I will and thank you for all that you have done for me."

"You are my son and that is what a father does."

He mounted and I went to Sam. My nephew had changed since he had become my father's page, "And you, young Henry Samuel, I expect great things from you. You are your father's son."

I saw him sit straighter in the saddle, "I will try to emulate him but also you. None of us can ever hope to achieve that which the Earl has done."

They turned their horses and headed out of my gate. I watched them disappear down the road. The men at arms and archers who rode with my father were solid men. They were men with experience. I had had their reassuring presence my whole life and now they and my father were leaving. I was alone.

I watched them ride away and, closing my eyes, I remembered the vision I had had when I had undertaken my vigil. Others, had I confided in them, might have said that the vigil was the result of a dream but I swear that I saw and heard something which will live with me forever. There had been two candles lit on the altar. One sputtered and died. As I rose to relight it, I heard a voice. I still do not know if it was in my head or in the church

The Bloody Border

but the voice said, '***Stay, William.***' Even as I looked, I saw something which could have been smoke from the sputtering candle or maybe it was a spirit. As it rose from the stone tomb of the Warlord, I assumed it was a spirit and I gripped my sword tighter, holding the crosspiece close to my lips.

'*William, you are destined for greatness. Men will try to compare you to me or to your father. Ignore such comparisons. We are all of the same blood. We are of the blood of those who lived in this land before the Normans came. You are English. Like your father, I began with nothing. We both moulded our world to suit us. Use that which you have. Do what your heart tells you is right and you will do your duty. Listen to the voices in your head for they will speak from beyond this world. William, you are the future of this family and it will be safe in your hands.*'

The spirit disappeared. Miraculously the candle had sputtered into life again. I knew then what my life's work would be.

As I opened my eyes to survey the castle that was Elsdon I began to see the size of my task. Matthew was improving as a squire but he and John would need much work. I did not know my archers and men at arms. I suppose that Alan of Bellingham was the closest thing to an adviser that I had. I heard the Warlord's voice. I had to make a start somewhere. I turned and rubbed my hands. My men, all of them, were standing expectantly behind me with Alan of Bellingham, "Let us begin as we mean to go on. I intend to make a rota. We will have an archer and a man at arms in the keep at all times. Each will be there for twelve hours. During the hours of darkness, we keep the gates of the castle and the keep locked and barred. The best horses will be stabled in the lower part of the keep. That leaves one spare man. It will enable us to rotate the pairings. I am keen that you all get to know one another." I turned to Alan, "Reeve, make the rota. Do we have an hourglass?"

"No lord."

"Then that is something we shall need. Make a list of all that we require. Tomorrow we ride to the market at Morpeth. I promised David and Alice that they would have animals for recompense and they shall."

The Bloody Border

My mother had sent beakers and jugs as well as cooking pots. My father would not have thought of those. There were other things we needed which would make life better. We needed tools so that we could make our own furniture. Mother had not thought of them.

I gave a series of tasks which needed to be completed and then went with my squire and page to our hall. "Tomorrow we might be seeing another lord. We wear our best in case we do. Your task today is to make our quarters organised. When that is done you can clean and sharpen our weapons. This is the quiet time. Come harvest and winter then we shall be hunting bandits."

Alan had told me that it was from September to December that the bandits and raiders were most active. They raided the grain that men grew and the fattened animals which were intended to feed the farmers through the winter. My plan was to be as secure as we could be before then.

Alan came in and I said, "Come, Reeve. I have put it off long enough. Let me see the accounts of the manor."

I did not like having to pore through numbers and accounts but it was necessary. By the time we had finished Alice, wife of David, had cooked our meal. The men were also exhausted but that was the physical labour of improving the ditches. My father and his men had cleaned them. My men had sharpened them and begun to embed stakes. After we had eaten my men lay on their sleeping furs. We had yet to build our beds. We had made a table and bench but that was all.

I took out my crowd. Most knights did not pick one up once they had their spurs. I enjoyed playing and singing. I began to play and sing. The men seemed to enjoy it. When I had sung three songs, one serious and two bawdy, Matthew asked, "Do I have to learn to play one too, lord?"

"I am afraid so but it is not hard. We will first have to make one. That will not be hard for you as you have skilled hands. Copy mine. It will keep you occupied during the long winter evenings. They have more snow here than in Stockton."

I took Roger Two Swords and Idraf of Towyn with me when I went to Morpeth with John and Matthew. The archer and the swordsman just happened to be the closest ones to me as I mounted. We took two sumpters only. I was not certain of the

The Bloody Border

prices nor of the range of goods the market would offer. The journey, as the crow flies, was just seven miles but it was thirteen miles by horse. We would no sooner get there than we would have to turn around to come home. I noticed that the closer we came to Morpeth the more prosperous grew the land. The fields were bigger and there were more animals which grazed upon them. When we neared Morpeth, I saw why. It was a solid castle with a good wall around the town and a fine position over the river. This town could defend itself if a raid came. If we had the farmers they had, then I could make Elsdon as strong. I should have introduced myself to Sir Ranulf de Merlay, the lord of the manor, but I had no time. I had arrived at noon. I went directly to the market. I had a long list of items and I began to buy them as soon as I was there. I was late. The better animals had been sold and I only managed to buy a ram and four ewes and four milk cows. They would have to do. Leaving them with Roger and Idraf we then bought the other supplies. I was lucky. I found an hourglass. It cost a pretty penny but it was worth it. Men would know that they had all worked the same length of time when they watched my walls. Fairness was all.

When those around me began to bow I looked up. I saw a knight with half a dozen men at arms approaching me. He had a face which suggested he was not happy with my presence. "I see, sir, that you are a knight. You wear the spurs but forgot the manners. Why did you not present yourself to me? I am Sir Ranulf de Merlay and the appointed Lord of Morpeth!"

"I beg your forgiveness, lord. I am Sir William of Elsdon and I am the new lord of the manor there. I have recently taken over the manor and I have left my handful of men to guard my hall. I would have spoken with you had I had time but…"

His face changed in an instant, "My dear boy! Forgive my manner. I should have recognised your surcoat. It is like your father's. I did not know that the Bishop had found someone to take it over." He lowered his voice and spoke conspiratorially, "It is the most dangerous manor in the Palatinate! At least Norham has walls! What is it that you wish?"

"We have little there and I came to buy sheep and cattle." I smiled, "If you have those who need a farm then I have land."

The Bloody Border

"Whatever you need I shall provide. I will try to call upon you in a week or so. I have Sir Eustace and he is a reliable knight and now I have you. The blood of the Warlord courses through your veins and you have given me hope."

As we headed back to Elsdon I did not feel hopeful. I felt hopeless. I had a handful of men to defend a river crossing. I was not up to the task! Sir Ranulf seemed a good man but he was not close to me. We would reach home at dusk. If danger came, we would be alone.

As we rode, Matthew said "I am honoured to serve you, lord. Mighty lords seem in awe of you!"

"It is the reputation of my father and my family. I have much to live up to. But we have made a start."

"I know that John and I come from humble origins but know that we will not let you down. We will learn. Platters and dishes may confuse us but put an enemy at the end of our swords and we will show you that we are warriors. Alan of Bellingham has promised to show me how to ride. I like him. He reminds me of my grandfather; God rest his soul."

The words were probably insignificant, but they showed me that we had the kernel of a body of men that could fight. If an untried youth could feel this way then what could we not achieve?

Four days after we returned Walther of Coxold, who was on duty, sounded the alarm. It was in the late afternoon and if there were men trying to attack us then this would be a good time. Riders were heading from the south. I hurried up the keep and shaded my eyes. I felt my anxiety subside. It was not a rabble of bandits racing to overwhelm us. There were wagons and animals. It had to be the Bishop keeping his word.

I hurried down to the gate and ordered it open. Alan, Matthew and John joined me as did the other men who were not on duty. I recognised Brother Paul who was in the leading wagon. He jumped down and bowed, "I am sorry we are late, my lord. We are not drovers and the animals seemed unwilling to move. We have wheat, barley, and oats as well as beans and vegetable seeds. We have three firkins of ale and one amphora of wine. There is a bull and, with him, two cows. In addition, the Bishop sent a pair of breeding pigs and fifteen ewes. The bishop would have sent more but the winter last year was hard and we did not have as many surplus animals as we would have hoped.

I clapped the priest about the shoulders, "Brother Paul, it is good to see you again! This is manna from heaven. You must stay the night."

He gave me a wry smile, "The thought of returning south never entered my head, lord."

"The Bishop is a generous man."

Brother Paul lowered his voice, "It is an investment, lord. Sir Robert lost all because of a lack of support. The Bishop knows that a strong Elsdon keeps the rest of his lands safer."

I turned, "Put the grain in the granaries, the ale and wine in the kitchens and put the animals in our pen." Alice, the wife of David, had prepared our food and gone. She was a generous cook and there would have to be enough for the carters. "Matthew, go to Rafe and buy some bread and some cheese."

"Aye, lord."

As we headed up to the hall Brother Paul saw Garth Red Arrow, he gave a smile and a nod. "Brother Paul, Garth told me his story. You forgave him?"

"He was a troubled youth but, aye, it seemed to me that he was speaking the truth. I saw no lie in his eyes and his words came from the heart. I am pleased you believed him. I can think of many lords who would have chosen to rid themselves of him. He is raw clay but I see a nugget of gold within him. If you are aught like your father then you can work miracles and redeem the prodigal son."

I laughed, "I will try." I waved a hand. "This is my manor."

"And you have a hard task ahead of you. Still, the Good Lord rewards those who take on such challenges. At least I hope so." I cocked an eye at his enigmatic words. He smiled, "I am your new priest of the manor."

My heart soared. I had Alan of Bellingham and now I had Brother Paul. I was young but they were older men. I would have sage advice. I took my sword from its scabbard and kissed the hilt, "Thank you, God!"

I delivered on my promises and David and Alice were given a ram and two ewes. We had a small flock. Our cows would give us milk. The bull, although small, was an unexpected present

The Bloody Border

from the Bishop. Brother Paul confided that he came from the Bishop's own herd and he had hoped for a bigger beast. I did not mind the small bull. So long as his seed was hardy then it would do. Rafe's daughters who helped us were augmented by his only grandson, Brandon. He had seen six summers and for a penny a week he watched our animals for us. His grandfather was grateful for the income. This was a manor where the farmers knew that success or failure could balance on a single penny or animal.

Now that we had grain, we had to improve the granary. Alan of Bellingham suggested that we build a new one and use the old one as an animal byre. I agreed as it would not require much work. He had the idea of making them close to each other so that we could defend them.

As well as work in my castle I needed to get to know the land. Leaving my men at arms to toil I took my archers and squire to explore the woods which lay to the north of us. We followed the beck north of us. It was not deep for it was summer. Alan had told us that in winter when the rains came, it could be an impassable torrent. Now, at the end of summer, it was almost a trickle.

I waved forward Garth Red Arrow. He and Walther did not speak to one another. It was a problem to which I would have to find a solution. Walther had served my father for many years but Brother Paul's words showed me that there was hope for the former outlaw. "Garth, here your experience and your life will be valuable. I want you to look for signs of bandits." He looked up at me and I saw the hurt on his face. "Garth, we cannot hide your past. You are forgiven but your past is still a part of you. You were sent to me for a purpose. If there are no signs of bandits hereabouts then good. We will sleep easier this winter, but if you do find signs of them then we can be prepared."

"Aye lord. I will ride just ahead. Their signs will be most subtle." He kicked his horse in its flanks and they headed up the stream.

My archers watched the woods which flanked us for danger and I studied the trees. They were good timber. If we needed more buildings then we could hew them from these woods. There was a wide variety of types. Perhaps that was as a result of the banditry. There had been fewer men to thin them. They had been allowed to grow and proliferate while farmers just defended what they had.

Ahead of us, Garth suddenly stopped and dismounted. He tied his horse to a willow branch. He neither drew his sword nor nocked an arrow. There was no danger. He disappeared into the woods. Walther and the rest of my archers had each nocked an arrow. A short time later Garth reappeared and he untied his horse. "I have found their signs, lord." He mounted and clambered up the bank. We followed.

It was not a path we followed. Garth had seen evidence of men but this was no regular trail. Garth's horse's hooves had obscured any sign there might have been there. We climbed a small slope and then the ground fell away to our right. I saw a natural dell. Garth dismounted. Leading his horse to the lowest point he stopped. He gestured to the ground as he moved last year's dead leaves, "This was where they had their fire, lord."

I dismounted and saw, beneath the old leaves, blackened earth. The fact that last year's leaves covered it told me its age. "You have good eyes, Garth."

"A bandit needs shelter and water." He pointed to what appeared to be branches broken from the trees. "They used those to make hovels. They were careful and they scattered them, when they left, to make them look natural." He picked two up. "See, lord, they have been cut with a blade. They were not broken."

There was more to Garth's words than he was telling me, "Speak your thoughts, Garth Red Arrow. What is it that you are thinking?"

"If the bandits hid this camp then they intend to return to it. They have not been here for almost a year. The wood they cut has not yet rotted. If you asked me to put my wages on it then I would say they will return when we harvest."

Walther of Coxold shook his head, "Conjecture, lord, what does this cockerel know?"

I stared at Walther. He was one of the oldest men I commanded. I had known him since first I went to war. He was talking to me as though I knew nothing. "Let him speak,

The Bloody Border

Walther. He can give us an insight into the minds of these men who may return to do us and our people harm."

Emboldened Garth spoke more confidently. He became animated, "Bandits are lazy men. Most of the year they need to do nothing save live off the fruits of their robbery. In the forests of Sheffield, we had travellers on whom we could prey. Here there are no travellers. The gold they mine is from the crops and animals of the farmers. They cannot take the crops until they are harvested and the animals are safe until they are full from summer grazing. If they come south at harvest time, they can take what they need for the winter."

I nodded, "And that makes perfect sense to me." I looked up through the trees. It was almost noon. "We will return to the castle. I will speak with Rafe and Alan of Bellingham."

Once back at the castle I took Walther of Coxold to one side, "Walther, you are a good man. I have seen you in battle and there is none braver." He nodded, "Yet you do not seem to trust Garth Red Arrow. We both know that is not a good situation. You volunteered to be here. If you cannot serve with Garth then return to Stockton. My father would have you back in the blink of an eye."

His face looked as though I had slapped it, "Lord, you would choose a bandit over me!"

"He was a bandit. The Church has forgiven him. My father has forgiven him and I have forgiven him. He has skills. Tell me, is he a poor archer?"

"No, lord, he can send an arrow further than any save me or David of Wales."

"And he found the camp today?"

"Aye, lord, but that is my point! He is a bandit! Scratch his skin and he will bleed bad blood. He told us his father was the leader of the bandits."

I shook my head, "And is that not a reason why he stayed a bandit longer than he wished? When his father died, he left. That speaks well of him in my eyes for he was loyal to his father. You have until we harvest the fields to make up your mind. We cannot have a divided camp when we are fighting bandits. I would rather be light by one man than have a division amongst my warriors."

He left. I had hoped that my words would make him change his mind but I was wrong. For the next month, he continually tried to find fault with Garth Red Arrow. Matthew came back from stabling my horse. "Lord, Garth Red Arrow is a good man. The other archers like him."

Matthew had grown. Since his brother had left with my father he had grown into his role as a squire. The two of them had been competing against one another, now he was not only watching over me but also helping John. That day saw a change in our relationship. A good squire is also there to help his lord with problems. "And Walther?"

"Less so, lord. The other archers are all young. Walther orders them around. They do not mind taking orders but…"

"But it is his manner." He nodded. "I thank you." I put my left hand on his shoulder and swept my right one around the upper bailey. "What think you to our home?"

He grinned, "I think, lord, that if bandits came, they would bleed upon our defences."

"Aye but if an army arrived then my father would find our bones inside burned walls. Let us pray the Scots heed the King's words."

"Lord?"

"Nothing, Matthew. I was just being as Walther of Coxold and seeing the beaker half full."

Now that we had a priest, we could have a real service on Sunday morning. We had repaired the church. There was no bell to summon the parishioners but most lived close enough. Brother Paul waited until Phillip the Priest and his wife arrived. Only Old Will did not come to the Sunday service. The little church was packed but that was because of my men. Two remained on watch in my keep. Alan of Bellingham had done his best but a real priest gave the folk of my manor security. Life was parlous enough. If they died then they were more confident about going to heaven. They could be shriven by a real priest and not a warrior monk.

My archers set up the butts after the service. The farmers knew the importance of archery practice and now they had experts to help them. Phillip the Priest needed all the help he could get. He could barely pull back the bowstring. I saw that

Garth Red Arrow was very patient with him. I stood with Matthew, John, Alan of Bellingham and Brother Paul.

"What of Old Will? Why did he not attend?"

Alan of Bellingham shook his head, "He blames God for the loss of his family. He is a bitter old man. He has lost his faith, lord."

Brother Paul said, "Then I will visit with him. It is my duty to serve all of Christ's flock. If I might borrow a horse, lord?"

I nodded, "Matthew, John, go with Brother Paul. You know the way to the farm and you can be his escort."

"I need no escort, lord."

"You remember the road to Jedburgh, Brother Paul? Three men on horses may deter a bandit!"

John and Matthew were now wearing their leather and their mail all the time. John had no helmet yet but Matthew's father had sent hide and he had made himself a leather helmet. It was some protection. Both had daggers and Matthew had his short sword. Roger Two Swords had been showing the two of them how to use their weapons.

I had so much to occupy myself that the days were never long enough. The manor had been without a lord and that had hurt it. Alan of Bellingham and I pored over the accounts while my men continued to improve our defences and Brother Paul tried to save the soul of Old Will. At the end of four hours of my life I would never have back I poured us both some well-deserved wine. "So, what you are saying, Alan, is that if we had not had the supplies from the Bishop and if he had not paid me a subsidy then we would all starve and the manor would not be viable."

He smiled, "That is about the size of the problem, lord."

"And there is an answer?"

He nodded, "Have more farmers come to farm the abandoned ones and have our own farmers clear more fields. There is a demand for wool. Sheep are easy to raise. It is just that they are hard to keep hold of when there are bandits."

"We have two years of grace then. We must clear the bandits and make it more attractive to men seeking land."

"Aye, lord. You have made a good start by helping David of Amble and his wife. They are young and they are eager. I will ask Rafe if he wishes one of the other empty farms for his sons.

He was loath to do so while there was no lord of the manor." He smiled at me. "You have brought us hope, lord. Do not fall into melancholy. It destroys a man from within."

When Brother Paul returned, he was down hearted. "The man has truly lost his faith and lies in a pit of despair. Perhaps God sent me here to redeem him. With your permission, lord, I will visit with him each Sunday while the men practice with their bows."

"So long as my squire and page ride with you, aye."

When the days became shorter and the mornings had a chill in them, I initiated patrols around my manor. I had four men in each patrol. There were two archers and two men at arms. I went along with one every other day. John and Matthew came with me. We rode the boundaries of the manor. That encompassed a larger area than was actually farmed. We went to each deserted farm to ensure that there was no occupation. We also visited the camp Garth Red Arrow had found in the wood. When it continued to be empty that gave us hope. One Sunday, while the men were practising their archery and Brother Paul was at Old Will's, I spoke with Rafe.

"So Rafe, what do you think of Alan of Bellingham's suggestion that your sons take over two of the fallow farms?"

"I confess, lord, that I am pleased and reassured by your presence but I was equally impressed when Sir Robert was lord and we both know how that one turned out. May I speak openly, my lord?"

"Of course."

"When April comes and the land becomes warm, if you are still here and we are all above ground then we will look at the farms which are fallow and, if they are viable, we will take them over. Does that answer suit, lord?"

"It is an honest answer so aye."

Two Sundays later, while Brother Paul, John and Matthew were at Old Will's, David came to me with his wife. "We have news, lord, Alice is with child."

"And that is truly good news!"

David's arm around his wife told me how much it meant to them. "Until the babe is born Alice can continue to cook for you."

The Bloody Border

I had not even thought of that. I smiled, "Of course. I can make other arrangements. Rafe's daughters are growing and they may be able to do as you do."

"I shall miss the payment, lord. We now have a flock and like my wife, they have young within them. We will prosper."

I went over to the butts. The farmers, especially Rafe's sons were improving. A mixture of regular practice and expert advice from my archers had wrought a much-needed improvement. "That is better Rafe son of Rafe. You almost hit the inner." James was a good teacher. He had been with my father almost as long as Walther of Coxold but he had an easier, less abrasive manner about him. Walther was the one who found the faults and James was the one who corrected them. They were a good team.

"My lord! My lord! Riders!" Wilfred's voice made me start.

I turned and saw Brother Paul, Matthew and John galloping towards us. Brother Paul lagged behind. Matthew reached us first. He leaned down and said, "There are bandits at Old Will's farm. I fear he has come to harm!"

I did not hesitate, "John, you stay here with Alan of Bellingham. Men at arms and archers, to your horses. Farmers, fetch your flocks within the bailey and guard my walls." We were going to have to fight together for the first time!

Chapter 6

It took longer for us to arm and then ride out than I would have liked. Later I realised why. We had not been mailed and it was Sunday. In future, we would be mailed all of the time. I did not bother with my helmet. I wore my mailed hood instead. As we rode Matthew told me what they had seen. "There were men at the farm. We must have surprised them. Brother Paul had kept us at a slow pace and we did not gallop. We counted at least twenty men. When they spied us, they prepared to fight. Brother Paul told us to return."

"And right glad I am that he did so." The idea of losing two untried young men did not bear thinking about.

When we reached the farm, the bandits had departed. Old Will lay in a pool of blood. Brother Paul would no longer need to minister to him. He had fought hard. His dog also lay dead. We looked in his home. The old man had had little to take but what he had they had taken. I turned and spoke to Garth Red Arrow. "If you were the bandits what would you do?"

"I think they may have already done it, lord. See the tracks, the bandits came from the north and the west. When they left they headed towards the road and their camp. There are other tracks leading here to the farm. I think they came from Phillip the Priest's house. They must have raided that farm first. It would be empty for the farmer and his family were in church."

Walther's face had a scowl upon it but I knew that my young archer was correct. "We will ride towards the camp but not follow the warband of bandits. We will head to Phillip's farm."

Wilfred of Sheffield had a wise head on his shoulders, "A good plan, lord. They will be watching their back trail. They will be moving at the pace of the animals they took. We have a chance to catch them."

I shook my head, "The aim is not to catch them but to hunt and kill them. We make the experience of raiding this valley so unpalatable that they seek somewhere else."

When we reached Phillip the Priest's farm, we saw that it had been ransacked. He and his family were at my church. Thank God that they were unharmed. His goats and sheep had been taken. We hurried to the road and then the river. We would be travelling faster than men on foot who were driving animals before them. I intended to use the fact that we knew of their hideout to our advantage. We rode around the woods to approach from the north. That was the one direction they would feel was safe. We left our horses more than a mile from their camp. We tied them close to the water where they could drink. I had too few men to leave horse guards. I let Garth lead. He was the woodsman.

"Alternate archers and men at arms. Await my command to release your arrows. Spread out in a line. We are hunters and we will drive our prey."

I drew my sword and my dagger. Matthew was on one side of me and Garth on the other. Roger Two Swords flanked Matthew. We moved slowly through the woods. The ground was firm and we watched for branches. We needed to be silent. We heard the animals before we either smelled or heard the men. The goats and sheep did not enjoy being moved and they were bleating. Having been here before we knew that the ground rose up a bank and the dell would be below us. The bandits would be expecting danger from the southeast. When Garth reached the top, he nocked an arrow. I was next to him a heartbeat later. We used the trees for cover. Below us, we saw their camp. We spied the bandits and our animals. There were just fourteen men. I saw that three had been wounded. Old Will had died hard. They were facing away from us. I think they were selecting an animal to slaughter. This was one direction from which they did not expect danger. It was too good an opportunity to miss.

I shouted, "Release!" As six arrows flew from bows the rest of us ran towards them. Six arrows found flesh and another six sped on their way even as we ran towards the bandits. I saw one bandit who looked to be a leader. He was wearing a leather jerkin and had a helmet on his head. He attempted to rally his men. I ran to him and even as he brought down his sword to take my head, I blocked it with my own. His sword buckled but it mattered not. My dagger drove up into his throat. I ripped it sideways and he fell in a spraying arc of blood. The archers targeted those who were not close to us. The ones who tried to flee fell with an arrow in their backs. Roger Two Swords wielded his two weapons better than I had seen some men wield one. Even Matthew managed to gut a bandit who swung his axe at my squire's head. Matthew ducked and rammed his sword into the man's chest. It was over so quickly that I had to scan the dell twice to make certain that none lived. I saw my men kicking over bodies to ensure that the men were not feigning death.

"Collect the animals and then strip the bandits." I turned, "Roger, pile the enemy bodies on their fire. We will let the fire consume them." I had planned on leaving their heads as a warning. I decided that burning their bodies would be as effective. When the camp began to smoke and acrid smoke made us cough, we left.

We drove the animals back to Elsdon. The pall of smoke rose behind us and the smell of burning death filled the air. Matthew looked a little green. Roger Two Swords rode next to him. "You did well today, Master Matthew. You killed your first man. He was a wild Scottish axeman and they make many grown men shake with fright. You will do well, Master Matthew."

It was almost dusk as we reached our castle. Alan and Rafe opened the gates. The men of the outlying farms looked at me expectantly and I gave them the bad news immediately, "Old Will is dead, as are his killers. Phillip, we have recovered your animals. Stay the night in the castle just in case there are enemies abroad. It is better to be safe than sorry. Tomorrow I will take my men and ensure that the enemy, these bandits are, indeed, destroyed."

There was sadness at the death of Will. Brother Paul felt especially bad for he had not redeemed him but there was also joy. The raid could have been much worse. My men had done all that was asked of them. We had a beginning.

The next day the people returned to their homes. Leaving just Brother Paul and Alan of Bellingham to watch my castle we rode back to backtrack the Scots. We discovered that they had passed by Otterburn. We saw that they had destroyed farms along the road. We reached the tower and Sir James emerged. He was no longer a young warrior.

"Sir William, were you attacked too?"

"We were. We destroyed the bandits who sought to take from us. They killed Old Will. And you?"

"They struck quickly. I brought my folk into my tower but we have lost farms and animals. Your losses?"

"One farmer was killed and we recovered the animals. Sir James," I lowered my voice, "we need a system to warn us. You have a tower. If you light a signal then we will know of an attack. It can aid you. We have good men and between us, we can make this a killing ground."

He shook his head, "Once I was like you. Then I lost my wife and my sons. These barbarians grind you down. They are like the tide on a seashore. Eventually, our defences will crumble as will I."

We went into his castle and spoke. It emerged that there had to have been a large warband which split into two. Sir James' men in his tower had seen them driving animals towards the border. I left Otterburn feeling subdued. We had had a victory but it did not feel like one. I was on my own. Sir Eustace could guard one flank but Otterburn would merely slow down an attacker. We needed a different strategy.

Riding home both Roger and Garth spoke to me. "Lord," said Garth Red Arrow, "our men destroyed those bandits so quickly it terrified me. You should be pleased rather than looking as though the dog has stolen your dinner!"

Roger smiled, "And we all fought together for the first time. Your squire showed great skill, lord. We have weapons to melt to make arrowheads. All is well."

"Roger is right, lord. We destroyed half of the band of bandits. The other half will wonder what happened to them. Uncertainty is an enemy."

They were right but I had a nagging feeling in the back of my mind that we could have done more. I just did not know what!"

The Bloody Border

The attack acted as a spur. My farmers built stronger enclosures. Our dogs were now ready to be used as guard dogs. I gave a couple to those farmers who had no dogs. Our own would patrol the baileys at night. I asked, in the village, if anyone was a smith. They were not. We would need one. The horses would need shoeing and our mail would, eventually, need repair. I spoke with Tom the Miller. "Do you still mill?"

He shook his head, "The mill worked until the last raids and then the leat filled. It could be repaired but we do not produce enough grain to warrant working it. We send all of our grain to Rothbury. It costs coin. Most of the women grind by hand and it takes time."

"Then we will begin the mill again. I will make it worth your while. Money should stay in the village. Does Otterburn have a mill?"

"No, lord, they send it to Rothbury too."

"Then we let them know that we mill. We will make Elsdon more attractive!"

The next day I rode with my squire and page to Morpeth. They had a mill and they had a blacksmith. We took a sumpter in case we could make purchases. After speaking with the lord of the manor and receiving his approval for the request I would make, I rode to the smith's forge. Sir Ranulf apologised for not visiting with me. I think he thought it unnecessary. To him the border was quiet. He had not been raided. The smith, Black Bob, saw my spurs and thought he was in for a good commission. I saw that he had two forges and three anvils. Six men worked in the smithy.

"My lord, what can I do for you? A sword perhaps?"

I took the bull by the horns, "No, smith, I seek a blacksmith to work at Elsdon!"

He laughed, "Then you have come to the wrong place. My men are happy working for me and, to speak plainly, lord, why would any choose to work in a manor where they could have their throats cut!"

I raised my voice above the sound of hammers, "I seek a smith. He will work inside the castle of Elsdon and I will pay him two shillings per week. Any work he does for the village will be on top of that pay."

The Bloody Border

Black Bob's face darkened and he said, "I told you, lord, that none will work for you. The lord of Morpeth would not be happy."

I turned, "And I have spoken with the Lord Ranulf. I have his permission." I turned to the smiths. All of them had stopped working, "I will go for some ale at the Black Swan. My men and I will eat. If any choose to speak with me there is ale for them." We left and I wondered if any would come.

As we sat at the table John said, "I could smith for you." I have grown much and I watched my father.

I nodded, "I know but then who would be my page? If you had wished to be a smith then you would never have left Stockton. You wish to be a warrior. When the smiths come and come they will, then it will be your questions and their answers which determine the one we choose."

"You are right, lord, they will come if only because no man likes to be told he cannot choose his employer. If any man wished to leave my father he would happily allow it for he would not wish a man working for him who was unhappy. Black Bob had a scowl on his face. It looked to be a permanent feature. I would not like to work for him." John had the innate common sense often denied nobles of the same age.

In the end, only one came and he sported a bruised face. He looked to be young, perhaps eighteen summers but he was well muscled. I called over the alewife and ordered another beaker of ale. "You wish to be a smith?"

He smiled, "I am a smith, lord, but I would like to be one who does not have to endure slaps and punches from a master smith."

"He hit you?"

"Aye the others fear him but I told him that if he hit me again then I would return the blow."

The ale arrived and the alewife nodded as she said, "Black Bob has a fearsome temper, lord. I have had to call the watch to him on many an occasion. His wife died in childbirth and it changed him. It made him a bitter man."

I nodded my thanks, "What is your name?"

"Tam of Alnmouth."

I looked at John. If we only had one candidate then questions were redundant but I could see by my page's face that he was keen to ask questions which would test the young smith's knowledge. He began an interrogation of Tam. It soon became obvious that Tam knew his business. When he had finished, my page nodded.

Tam smiled, "Your page knows his way around a workshop, lord."

"He is the son of a smith and the tradition goes back to the time of the Conqueror."

I saw his mouth open in amazement, "And he will be a knight?"

John grinned, "That is a long journey, Tam of Alnmouth. I have learned to sit astride a horse without falling off and I have fought my first enemy. It is baby steps I take!"

"So, Tam, will you be the smith at Elsdon? It is a wild place but I hope to tame it for I have good men."

"I will, lord, but it is more than just me. I have a wife, Anne."

"Can she cook?"

He nodded, "Aye lord, plain enough fare but tasty. Why?"

"The woman who cooks for us is with child and soon we will need a cook. I could pay her."

"Then that is good. Do you have a smithy?"

"We would need to build one but we have metal to make an anvil. Have you your own tools?"

"I am a free man and I am a smith who served his apprenticeship. They are back at the workshop."

I took money from my purse and placed it on the table. "Finish your ale and we will return hence. I have to see the miller."

As we rose and after he had drained his beaker, Tam said, "Then you will need someone who can talk to the dead. Much the Miller died a month since."

"Where does the manor mill its flour?"

"They use the mill themselves. It takes time and they do not have the skill. His lordship seeks a miller. Why do you ask?"

"We have a mill but not enough grain to warrant its use. Before we return to the smith let us go to your house. Your wife will need to know her new circumstance. Will you need a cart or wagon?"

"Aye lord. We have little enough but all of it is precious to my wife and me. Our parents are dead and the items we have remind us of them."

"Then we will buy a small wagon. The manor needs one."

Tam pointed to a wheel hanging above a workshop. "Jacob the Wheelwright is a good man. He will not rob you."

Jacob was, indeed, a good man. He was happy to accommodate a new lord and he gave me a fair price, "I can have a wagon ready for you by tomorrow, lord."

That meant we would not be returning home any time soon. We negotiated a price and left. Anne was of an age with her husband. Her plump features confirmed that she not only liked to cook but to eat too. She was more than happy to come to Elsdon. I advised her of the dangers. She nodded, "The Scots are dangerous, lord, but so are some masters. Black Bob is a bad man. My husband is unhappy with him as a master and from what you say we will be living in the lower bailey. If we are not safe there then we are safe nowhere."

I turned to Tam, "We will leave with you on the morrow, I would speak with Sir Ranulf before we beard Black Bob! Matthew and John, stay here. I am sure Tam and his wife will need help to pack."

I returned to the castle. Sir Ranulf was in his upper bailey practising with his squires. "Did you conclude your business, Sir William?"

"Almost but I need to speak to you first."

I told him of Black Bob and his attitude towards Tam. "Aye he is a little free with his hands but he is a good weaponsmith. I will come with you when you speak to him. Do you go now to speak to him?"

"Aye for the wagon we have just purchased will not be ready until tomorrow. My new smith will need to pack up his home."

"Splendid! Then you and your squire can spend the night at my castle. I shall enjoy the company. You and your father are privy to the King's dealings. I would know more about this young King."

He turned to his squire, "Henry, fetch our cloaks. We go abroad."

The Bloody Border

When we were alone, I said, "And there is another matter, Sir Ranulf. We have an idle mill. I was going to repair it but I am aware that your mill and therefore your manor profit from the manors who do not have a mill."

"It is good of you to ask and shows that you are, indeed, from noble stock. I am more than happy for you to mill. I seek a miller. Would yours come to work here?"

I smiled and shook my head, "I doubt it for he is a farmer and if the Scottish raids could not induce him to leave then I doubt that an offer to become a miller alone would work."

"You may be right but I had to ask."

We left the castle and headed to Tam's house. Leaving Matthew to help Anne with her packing we went to the smith. When Black Bob saw us approach his scowl became so severe, that I thought his face might crack. Tam said, "I have come for my tools, Black Bob."

"Aye, and you have brought others to help you!"

Sir Ranulf said, sharply, "You are a good smith, Bob but do not test my patience. Speak gently in the presence of this lord or you will be punished."

Tam said, "And I am not afraid of you. The blow you struck before was the last one. If you wish to fight me then I will show you that I can handle myself."

Silence fell. I saw the three other smiths all looking from Black Bob to Tam and back. It was Black Bob who backed down, "Take your tools. I am glad to be rid of you!"

Tam went to his bench. I saw that it was neat and ordered. He took his tools and carefully placed them in the leather satchel. He hefted them on his back. He turned to the other smiths, "I say goodbye to you fellows. I have enjoyed your company. Should you ever decide to free yourself from the serfdom of Black Bob the bully, then I can offer you a place with me at my new home and smithy in Elsdon!"

We left. Sir Ranulf laughed, "I have never seen Black Bob back down before. There is more to you Tam the Smith than meets the eye."

We left the next day. Before we left, we visited the grain chandler. Thanks to the demise of the miller he had surplus barley, oats and, best of all, wheat. I bought four sacks: two of wheat and one each of barley and oats. I also bought seed barley. I had an idea to plant a crop of winter barley. As well as the wagon we also purchased some scrap metal from Sir Ranulf. Like me, he had dealt with bandits and their weaponry, from helmets to swords was too poor to be used. He was happy to allow us to use it although we paid him a fair price. I was spending the Bishop's money at an alarming rate. We loaded the wagon and hitched the sumpter to it. Tam let his wife sit on the wagon and he walked the horse. It made for a slow journey to Elsdon but that was no bad thing as it allowed us to talk. It soon became clear that Anne knew about cooking. Her family had been a large one. She had inherited her mother's pans and cooking utensils. The wagon was laden. The fact that only Tam had chosen to work for me was now a blessing for it had brought his wife. The castle needed the presence of a woman. As we neared Elsdon I asked her if she would become a housekeeper as well as a cook. I knew that I was out of my depth when it came to furnishings. My mother or my sisters could have advised me but they were a lifetime away. She agreed and I saw order entering my life. I could concentrate on being the lord of the manor and a knight once more.

We set to building a house and a smithy. A smithy was a fire risk and so we built his smithy close to the bread ovens. His house we attached to the kitchen. It meant we only had to build three walls. When we had cleared the ditches, we had found a great number of stones. They were not good stones but they would give Anne and Tam stone walls rather than wattle and daub. I saw that Anne was pleased. In those first days, my men at arms and archers worked as hard as thralls. The food which Anne cooked was motivation enough. She was a good cook.

When she came to the keep her critical eye showed her disapproval. "These are not the quarters for a lord!"

"I do not live here. I live in the lower bailey."

She shook her head. Her voice reminded me of my mother, "Sir William, you should live here. You are lord of the manor and should not squat with your soldiers. When next you visit Morpeth, I will come with you and we will buy some decent material to make wall hangings. These quarters are little better than the stables beneath! My husband will make some tools and then you can make furniture!" She shook her head.

"It is too far from the kitchens, Mistress Anne. The food is cold by the time it reaches here!"

"I am sorry, my lord, but that does not need to be so. You have a fire and it is not beyond the wit of man to build a warming block next to it. I will speak with the Reeve."

She was a force of nature and poor Alan found himself working under a second master! Tam knew his business as did John. With Matthew to help them, they hewed a huge oak and sawed the trunk so that they could embed the anvil which they made. The two of them melted great quantities of metal and carved a mould into the oak stump. They did that before they began the roof of the smithy. It was getting on to Autumn but the weather had not changed. Working outdoors was not a problem. We even managed to clear the leat and repair the mill wheel. Abel Millerson showed that he had not forgotten the skills taught to him by his father. He helped Tom the Miller. The mill began to grind once more. The first sacks Tom ground were mine. I allowed him to keep a tenth for his work. I distributed two-fifths to my farmers and kept half for myself. It was not a selfish act. I stored it for the hard times I knew would come. When next I visited Morpeth, Anne showed her skill. She negotiated good prices and our small wagon was laden when we returned. My keep became a home!

By October the house, smith and the changes to my keep had been made. Matthew, John and I had beds in the keep. It meant we no longer needed two men to spend the night in the keep. My squire, page and I barred the door and we were our own sentinels. The two of us and the dogs we kept would guard my bastion! As we lit our bone fires and celebrated the end of the harvest, I was content. We had survived our first attack and my manor felt a little more like Elton and less like a wild outpost surrounded by enemies. Of course, that was an illusion. Enemies were in my land.

Chapter 7

We had neglected our patrols. My farmers had become our watchers. They were the ones who looked for footprints which were alien. They sniffed the air for fires. They counted their animals to ensure that they were all accounted for. It was Cedric Sheepman, my most isolated farmer, who alerted us to danger. It was while he was at the butts practising with the others. "My lord, it may be nothing but my sons were out with me collecting a couple of strays on the Yalesham road yesterday eve." I smiled. The Yalesham road was an old drover's trail. There had been a time, probably when the Romans were on this island when cattle had been driven through the manor to the land to the north. Now it was little more than a wide greenway which was largely overgrown. It was what passed for a road in these parts. "My dog sniffed for longer than normal and that is not like her. I investigated. Someone had emptied their bowels. It was not me and, as far as I know, none had used that road. It should not have worried me but after Old Will it did. Men had used the old road recently."

"You think cattle thieves?"

"We have had the bone fire. Winter will be upon us. These bandits seek food for the winter. We have obliged them by bringing our animals into our byres. If I was a bandit then now would be the time I would come to steal. Aye lord. I think the scouts have been sniffing around our lands."

"Then tomorrow I will take my men to the Yalesham road. Let us scotch this threat before it can grow. I have lost one farmer and I would not lose another."

The Bloody Border

I left John along with Wilfred of Sheffield to help Alan of Bellingham and Brother Paul to guard my castle. Now that Tam the Smith lived within my walls then we were better off in terms of men who could defend it. We rode to the farm of Cedric Sheepman. His sons, Abelard and Cedric came with us. They knew the precise place he meant. They jogged easily by our side. This was not horse country. One of their huge sheepdogs came with us. Like the dogs we had at the castle this was a northern-bred dog. Although they were rare, we still had wolf attacks. Our dogs were capable of deterring wolves and foxes.

Yalesham was in the manor of Otterburn. As such it was the responsibility of Sir James of Otterburn but I could not ignore the threat. They might come through Yalesham and over the trail to get at us. Cedric and his family would be in danger. We followed a track which twisted and turned with the contours of the land. It rose and fell over small ridges and shallow valleys. Cedric's dog was better than any scout. If there was danger then his hackles would rise. I knew that Yalesham was an isolated community of half a dozen homes. The River Coquet bordered one side of the village. There was no crossing of the river. If you had business there then you visited the hamlet, otherwise, you would never need to go to it. Cedric showed us where he had found traces of intruders. Garth Red Arrow used his skill to find footprints that were not Cedric's. He pointed to tracks made by someone with smaller feet than Cedric or his sons.

It was as we neared the village that the smell of death came to us. The dog's hackles rose. "Draw weapons!" My archers had bows strung already and they each nocked an arrow. The track led to the hamlet. There was a road, of sorts, which went from Yalesham to Alwinton but that was north of the river. It could only be forded when the river was low. We stepped onto the rough track and headed into the houses. The dead were still where they had fallen. There were eight men and youths. All were naked. Their bodies had been mutilated and their heads removed. The dog hung its head. The enemy had fled but I was taking no chances. "Search the houses."

It soon became obvious that this attack had happened perhaps ten days earlier. Animals had begun to eat their bodies. Sir James would not have known of it. There was no need. There was no church in the hamlet. It was a long walk to Otterburn. Often such folk gathered in the open for prayers. They had a place filled with their ancient dead. Crudely carved stones and crosses showed us where they interred them. We buried them in that cemetery. The bodies we buried almost doubled the number of graves. Garth Red Arrow saw that the tracks led northwest. The Scottish bandits had been foiled by us but the folk of this hamlet had not been so lucky. We headed to Otterburn. Cedric and his son returned directly to their farm.

Sir James had aged considerably since last I had seen him. The men he had lost in the short war had not been replaced. He looked to be in poor health. When I told him of the tragedy, he was distraught. "It is my fault. When I was a younger knight I rode abroad and the Scots feared me. Yalesham was a small community. They were good people. They kept to themselves. It will die now." I did not like to say that it was a place of the dead already. It was a ghost settlement.

This melancholic outpouring would do nothing for the farmers who remained, "My lord, we must act. I will send to Sir Ranulf and Sir Eustace. We must mount men and respond to this. They took the women and children. They cannot have gone far. How many men do you have?"

"There are just four of them and they are as ancient as I am."

"Then send the four to your farms and warn them of the danger from the Scots. We need more men. Rothbury and Morpeth are well garrisoned. With their help, we can quash these incursions. If we strike sooner rather than later then we may prevent more losses."

When we reached my castle, it was dark. I was exhausted. It was not just the ride which had done so it was inner exhaustion. While I had been making my castle stronger, other Englishmen were suffering. I wrote letters to Sir Ranulf and Sir Eustace. "Alan, I would have you and Brother Paul deliver these letters. I intend to ride tomorrow to the northwest. If Sir James has not been patrolling the Roman road from High Rochester then who knows what mischief there may be."

Before I retired, I went to the smith's house. "I fear that I must leave you and your wife alone in the castle tomorrow. I will speak to Rafe, Tom and Harry. They are all close enough to come to your aid. Keep the gates barred until we return."

He nodded, "You need not fear, lord. We will keep your home protected. Anne and I could hold off an army from your keep."

I had been lucky in the people I had chosen.

We left before dawn for we had many miles to travel. We were mailed and we had both spears and shields. We were going to war. Tam dropped the bar into place as my last man clattered over the bridge. I realised that if I made the bridge into a draw bridge then they would be even safer.

There was a road to Otterburn. We made faster time there. Sir James' men told us that they had found the tiny hamlet of Byrness destroyed. It was not a recent event but had happened since my father had defeated the Scots. So much for their peace. Otterburn was now the last English settlement before Scotland. "Sir James, I will ride to the high pass at Redesdale. We will look to see if we can find traces of these bandits."

I knew it was hopeless. Yalesham had been destroyed many days ago and Byrness many months since. Even allowing for the slow progress the bandits would make taking their animals and captives north they would now be safe in Scotland enjoying English mutton and beef. Even so, I had to ride the road to the border for my own peace of mind.

The Roman road ran along the River Rede. It undulated. We passed the old Roman fort. High Rochester had been a thriving village but raids over the years had made it a place of ghosts. We stopped at the fort to water our horses and eat. It afforded a fine view to the northwest towards Scotland. It was as Matthew, John and I were enjoying bread and fresh cheese that my sharp-eyed squire, leaning against the gate, spotted men approaching.

"Lord, I see a horseman leading men on foot. They are coming down the road. They come from the Scottish side of the fort."

"Climb a little higher and ascertain numbers." While he did so I shouted, "Stand to!"

Matthew had clambered up to the fighting platform, "It is a knight, by his mail and he has two more men on horses. I guess there are twenty men in total."

This was not an English knight. He was Scottish. Had we not had attacks on villages and hamlets then his intentions might have been peaceful. I would take no chances. "Walther, line the wall with our archers. Wilfred, have the sergeants mount. John, you stay here with the archers." I hurried to my horse. I was riding Eagle. I had not ridden him much of late. I now saw that my choice of horse was fortuitous. "Matthew, unfurl the banner. We will let these Scots know who we are. Perhaps it will make them withdraw and we can avoid bloodshed."

We left the fort and headed through the south gate to the road. The fort and the ridge hid us from view. Once on the road, we trotted towards the Scots. As we crested the ridge we were seen. They were two hundred paces from us. My archers were hidden and they saw just eight men. We might have been mounted but we were outnumbered. If they continued approaching in a loose column then their intentions were peaceful. They halted and it soon became obvious that they were belligerent. The horsemen donned helmets and the men on foot spread out.

I shouted, "Walther, choose your moment well to send your arrows."

"Aye, lord!"

"Matthew, stay behind me and watch my back."

"Aye, lord."

I did not recognise the surcoat of the Scottish knight. Now that they were closer, I saw his spurs. He had a squire but no banner. Only the knight wore mail. The others wore studded leather jerkins. They had open-faced helmets. They did not gallop. They were keeping pace with their men on foot. The ones on foot were all dressed differently. None wore a tunic to identify them. They had a variety of weapons. None had a bow. Half wore helmets.

Roger Two Swords observed, "If you wish my opinion, lord, then I would say these are farmers who come with their lord to steal English animals." I heard a murmur of agreement from the others. He was right.

"They have shown their intentions. We wait until Walther has sent his arrows and then we charge at the knight."

I wondered if Walther had left it too late for the Scots were just one hundred and fifty paces from us when he began to loose his arrows. I need not have worried. He knew his business. The six archers sent eighteen arrows in quick succession. I yelled, "Charge!" as the first of the arrows hit. One struck a horse and unseated the rider. Three others hit the men on foot. We had taken them by surprise. It would not last. I saw more men fall, including the squire. Nine of the men on foot suddenly took off towards the fort. That left two horsemen and five men who could fight. I rode for the knight. He had a spear, as did I. I hefted my shield around and spurred Eagle. I had the advantage for mine was a war horse. The Scot rode a palfrey and a small one at that. Eagle had power and managed to gallop faster than the others around me. The mounted man at arms came at my shield side. I concentrated on the knight. The spears of the knight and the man at arms struck at the same time. One spear hit my shield while the other, the knight's, slid along my helmet. I pulled back and stood in my stirrups as I rammed my spear at the knight's middle. Although he managed to pull his shield around it did not stop my spear which punched him from his saddle. He was dumped unceremoniously on the ground. Matthew rammed my banner into the side of the head of the man at arms. He fell unconscious at the side of his horse.

When Roger led my men at arms to hack and slash at the remaining five men at arms close to us then it was over on our side of the field. I wheeled Eagle and pricked the throat of the knight, "Yield or die! I care not which it is!"

"I yield!"

Then I heard shouts and cries. My six archers and John were being attacked by the nine men who had been on the left of the Scottish line. "Matthew, guard the prisoners. The rest, with me." We wheeled and galloped towards the wall. The ditch had long ago been filled in and was now just a hollow. I saw men fighting. My archers could use swords but they were better as archers. I galloped through the north gate. I saw, to my horror, two Scots fighting Walther of Coxold. He had John behind him. The rest of my archers were engaged in mortal combat and could not go to his aid. I did not hesitate and I rode towards the backs of the two Scots. Walther blocked one sword with his own and then the other sword with his dagger. John's hand darted out with his dagger and he stabbed one of the Scots in the thigh. The other also had a dagger and he ripped it across Walther's throat. I reached them just a lifetime too late. My sword split open the

The Bloody Border

head of one Scot and then backslashed the wounded one across the neck. They both fell dead.

It was over. None remained alive but we had lost an archer. It had not been a good trade. I was angry. I turned to Garth Red Arrow, "See to Walther's body. We will take him back with us. I will go and have words with this knight." I dismounted and handed my reins to John. He looked shocked and with good reason. A man had died to protect him and he had come within a sword strike of death himself. "Watch Eagle." Having something to occupy his hands would take his mind off the event.

The man at arms who had fallen from his horse and the squire were both sitting upright as was the knight. They were both bruised and battered from the fall but they were not wounded. I strode towards them. Walther was the first of my men to die and I was angry. "What is your name?"

"Sir Duncan Eliot."

"Why did you break the peace?"

"I did no such thing. You attacked us!"

"This is England. You passed the border seven miles ago."

"We dispute that! This is Scotland."

He sounded petulant. There was little point in arguing with such a one. "I hope your family values you for the ransom has just doubled. Annoy me again and you may rot in my castle until you are both old and grey!" I pointed to the squire. "You and your man at arms go to your lord's home. The ransom is one hundred pounds of silver!"

The knight said, "What? That is a fortune!"

"And it will teach you to honour the border."

"And if they cannot pay?"

I smiled, "Or perhaps they will not! It is no matter to me. If they refuse to pay then you shall work the bellows for my blacksmith!"

"I am a knight!"

"Then pray that your family values you. Now you two, go!" They went to the horses. I shook my head, "No! You walk. It is but six miles to the border! Walk!"

We took what little the men had on them and left their bodies. We slung Walther's body over his horse. We would bury him in our village. He deserved a grave where he could be mourned. We reached Otterburn where I told Sir James what we had discovered. He looked at the knight with hatred, "Your people slew innocent villagers. If you were my prisoner then I would hang you!"

I smiled, "And that may well be his fate, Sir James, but for now we will return to my home."

The meeting had upset the knight. Sir James looked like a kindly old man but there had been pure hatred in his eyes.

The young knight looked confused. "Why are you both so angry?"

"You honestly do not know?"

"We were coming to raid cattle and sheep. Our people have done so since before men recorded life in these parts."

I so wanted to strike him but I knew I could not. "And what of the women you enslaved? The men you butchered?"

He looked down, "The women will be looked after."

"As slaves or concubines. You have spoken enough. Speak again and I may take your tongue."

We had taken the weapons from their dead. Now we had a smith we could either repair them or melt them down.

Brother Paul and Alan of Bellingham had returned by the time we reached my home. They saw the body of Walther and Alan shook his head, "The first death, lord."

"Aye, and there may well be more. We have a prisoner. Reeve, I put him in your charge. If he causes trouble then the smith can shackle him. Brother Paul, we have a warrior to bury."

"We will inter him tomorrow, lord. I can see that you are angry. It does not do to bury a man with anger in your heart."

"You are right. And what of my messages?"

Alan of Bellingham shook his head, "Both lords said that they were unable to come to your aid at this time and they asked you to deal with the incidents at Otterburn and Elsdon."

I was disappointed. Had we acted in concert then we might have had success. Coming back, we discovered that the knight's family had a manor not far across the border. With two more knights and their men, we could have rescued the ones my men called the lost women of Yalesham. I saw now that it was up to me alone "Thank you for your efforts." I looked up at the sky. It was turning black. The weather was suiting my mood and I

The Bloody Border

wondered the effect it would have on the security of our manors. I could not bear to eat with the knight. He shared his meal with my priest and Reeve.

I ate in my keep with John and Matthew. John had been silent. I looked at Matthew as John moved his food around his platter. I decided to be harsher than I might have been if we had been in Stockton. "John, there will be more days like today. You will see more men die. If this life is not for you then there is no shame in returning to your father."

He shook his head, "If anything, lord, it has hardened my resolve. It is just that a man gave his life to protect me today. He was a good man and a respected archer. Am I worthy?"

This I understood. "You make yourself worthy. Each day, from now on you ask yourself if what you have done that day was worth the life of a man. You live the best life that you can."

"Then I shall do that and I will become a worthy warrior."

I looked at Matthew, "You were behind me today. I need to know who led the sergeants. I have an idea in my head but you saw more and I need to know what you saw."

"Roger Two Swords, lord. He is not as old as Wilfred but it was he who was the closest to you. It was he who protected you from the attack you did not see."

"That is what I thought. And now with Walther dead, I need a captain of my archers too. I will sleep on this and then make my decision on the morrow."

When I woke, I had made my decision. Brother Paul spoke over the grave of my archer. He was buried in a good spot in the cemetery. I knew that my archers and men at arms would tend it. He had neither wife nor children to do so. After he was buried, I had Alan of Bellingham broach a barrel of ale. Anne had baked some honeyed oatcakes. I know not why they went so well with ale but they did. Anne was helped by Alice. She was not yet too large and she had liked Walther. It felt like family. The weather had turned and the grey skies when we had put soil in the grave had turned to rain. Alice said it was God crying. Brother Paul shook his head. It was an old superstition. We gathered in the hall in the lower bailey.

"While we are all here, I have to tell you that I am going to make Roger Two Swords captain of my sergeants and Garth Red

The Bloody Border

Arrow captain of archers. They will each receive an extra six pennies a month for their trouble."

The faces of the men told me that they were all happy about the decision. "We thank you, Sir William!"

Alan of Bellingham asked, "What about our Scottish friend?"

"He can stay in the keep for a couple of days. It might do him some good. He seems arrogant."

Alan of Bellingham nodded, "I spoke with him last night. He lives not far from the border. I am guessing that the other animals which were taken could be found there. The captives too, perhaps."

"And where would that be?"

"Branxholme, many miles west of here."

Brother Paul shook his head, "The last time we had raiders the animals were taken to the lands of Fife."

"This is not Fife. It is the land of the Mormaer of Teviotdale."

The seed was planted. Could I engage in a raid across the border? I looked at my men, I had too few. It was, however, tempting. I had not received news from either Sir Ranulf or Sir Eustace. Now it was too late for my sergeant at arms. Next time I would not bother to ask them for help.

Sir Duncan's squire arrived with the ransom ten days later. The rains which had begun on the day of the funeral had not relented. The newly cleaned ditches kept us dry although the river was close to bursting its banks. The squire had an escort of six men. We held them in the lower bailey. My archers had their bows strung in case of treachery. They had brought a spare horse for the knight. The squire dismounted. "I have the ransom."

I nodded to my Reeve and Brother Paul. "Take it to my keep and count it."

The squire looked offended, "It is all there, my lord!"

"Good, then when it is counted you can take your lord. Roger, fetch the prisoner." I smiled, "I hope you have brought a cloak or he will suffer in this rain."

"I have, my lord."

Brother Paul came from my keep with Roger and the Scottish knight. Brother Paul nodded. "You are free to go, Sir Duncan, but I give you a warning. The days when Scots could use England as their larder are long gone. Despite what you think this is now England. King William admitted that when my great grandfather captured him. I have been lenient this time. Next time I will be less generous. Next time I will not give you the chance to yield."

"You have eleven men and two boys! Do you think that we could not walk in here and take this land if we chose?"

I shook my head and spoke to Brother Paul, "I was too lenient. I should have asked for twice the silver. Sir Duncan, the next time you are within a sword's length of me you will die. I can speak no plainer than that." I allowed the words to sink in. "If you wish to make your life a little easier then I suggest you send back the captives and animals you took. It will not save your life but it will be less likely that I will exact full vengeance for the atrocities committed by the barbaric Scots! Now leave."

The money would allow me to hire more men. The problem was there were none to be had. I wrote a couple of letters. I had promised my mother I would write and I had yet to do so. I penned a letter telling her about my new life. I told her about Anne and Alice. The letter I wrote to my father was longer and had the details of the trials and tribulations we had had to endure. I asked him for more men. I told him that I could pay. The Bishop of Durham had riders who rode north to Norham. They called at the major castles on their way north. I sent Alan of Bellingham with my letters to Morpeth. It might take a month but I would have a reply. He also took two men at arms for he had coin to spend on goods we would need. Winter would be upon us soon and the roads would be impassable. This would be a test for me.

Chapter 8

The snows came two days after Alan of Bellingham returned with the goods he had bought for the winter. We already had grain which meant we had beer and bread but we needed beans and vegetables. He also bought more fowl to keep us in eggs. When time allowed, I would build a dovecot. We knew that all work would have to cease when we saw the depth of snow which soon fell. Each day it took half a morning to clear the fresh fall and make a path through the bailey. I was pleased that we had managed to lay in so much hay and feed for the animals. Rafe had been invaluable. He knew what the winters could be like. The days were increasingly short. My archers fletched arrows and my men at arms practised with John and Matthew. Both had improved. They had an advantage in that they were both big anyway. Their fathers were strong men. They had the strength and it came down to skill.

Tam the Smith was able to work. The weather meant nothing to a man who had a forge which burned red hot. He made arrowheads. He made heads for spears and he made darts. The quality of metal for the darts did not matter. He could produce many of them quickly. He also started work on a helmet for John but mainly he worked on tools for my farmers. David of Amble now had sheep and he needed to be able to shear them. I had brought seed back and we needed a ploughshare. With more animals generally, we needed scythes. He made an adze and a spokeshave. We worked on the furniture we had started to make. With the new tools, we could give them a smooth finish. He was

The Bloody Border

kept busy and he was paid with coins as well as goods. He would not make a fortune but a man likes to be rewarded for his work.

When it was too dark and too cold to be outside, my squires and I retreated into our keep. Sometimes Alan of Bellingham would join us for John and Matthew needed to be taught to read. We carried on making furniture. We had plenty of seasoned timber and now we had the tools. Both John and Matthew were skilled with their hands and they helped to teach me. We celebrated Christmas with the villagers. My outlying farmers, Cedric and Phillip, made their way with their families through the snow to my church. The death of Old Will had brought them closer together. Then, when they had returned home, we waited for the days to lengthen and the snow to disappear. In this way, winter passed

It was February before we had a thaw and the inevitable flood which followed. We worked to clear the debris from beneath the bridge. We laid stones to give us paths and all thought of martial action was driven from us. I had not had a reply to my letter to my father. I knew that he would have sent one. If men could not travel the roads then letters certainly could not. Even though the roads were not the best I went with Matthew to Morpeth. We left well before dawn and travelled on roads which were slick with mud. When spring proper came, we would need to have more surcoats made. We had travelled but two miles and our surcoats were bespattered and besmeared. Being lord of the manor was expensive.

Morpeth had suffered as had the outlying farms. We passed two without smoke. Either the families had taken shelter with others or, more likely, they had died during the harsh winter we had endured. Sir Ranulf was ill as was his wife and it was his priest who spoke with me. "His lord and ladyship were both laid low with winter fever. I pray to God that they will recover. He handed me two letters. "These came at the start of December. I am sorry we could not send them to you but the roads…" he tailed off lamely. I was disappointed. While it was not important to those in Morpeth, it was to me.

I nodded and we left. I had coins and we bought a few items while we were in the town. I would leave the letters until I reached home. I had seen the hand and seal of my father. It was as we headed back, I realised that I needed a seal too. King Henry's sudden decision to give me the manor meant that there were many ceremonies and customs which had been overlooked. I would have Tam forge me a ring and I would have a seal made.

It was dark when we reached the haven that was my castle. Anne had food prepared and the cosy keep welcomed Matthew and me. The snows might have gone but the icy blast from the east had chilled us to the bone. Our horse's hooves had crunched on frozen mud when we had ridden the last few miles. I saved the letters until after I had eaten, I would savour them. I still had some wine left and I poured some to accompany the letters. It was strange reading my mother's letter for it had begun in October. I could see the part where she had received my letter. It was full of a mother's worries that I was managing. It spoke of a Christmas which promised to be joyful with her increasing number of grandchildren. It made me realise what I had missed. At the end, she chided me for my tardy missive. She was right to do so. I should have written more frequently.

My father's letter was more functional and informative. He spoke of matters beyond Stockton's walls. He told me of the King in Gascony and the alliances which were emerging. Like my mother's missive, I saw the change in tone after he had received my letter. He promised to go to York and see the Sherriff there. Sir Ralph had been his squire. That gave me hope. York had many more men seeking a master. There would be men coming north but the question was, when would they arrive? The fact that I had been able to ride to Morpeth told me that bandits and the Scots from across the border would also be able to move. Our foresight meant that we had not lost any of our people. The Scots would have eaten the few animals they had stolen. If they sought more then our lands and those of Sir James were an obvious supply. We would need to ride abroad. We would need to look for signs of enemies.

We woke to a frozen landscape. The snow had melted and the skies were blue but the ground was solid. I summoned my men. "Prepare your horses and your war gear. Tomorrow we ride to Otterburn. If that is safe then the next day we ride to the Roman fort. We will not be caught out again by these bandits who prey upon us."

"All of us, lord?"

I nodded, "Aye John, you too. I believe you have grown a handspan over the winter. Mistress Anne's food seems to suit you." My men all laughed for it was true. He had grown. Soon he would need a full-size horse. As I looked at him, I wondered about my nephew, Henry Samuel. Had he grown too?

That done I left to visit the four farmers of the village. It was as I spoke to Rafe that my spirits were lifted. "It has been a hard winter, lord, but one result has been that my two sons wish to take you up on your offer of farms. All of us living so close brought us perilously close to blows. Young Rafe and Harry are happy to leave my home. They have their own coin and animals."

"And I am glad that they do so. Your farm produces all that it can. If they take two more farms then we increase the produce of the manor. There is Old Will's farm and the derelict one southwest of Tom's Mill."

"Aye, lord and that would suit. Harry likes animals. I can let him have the start of a flock. Rafe prefers to grow. Being close to the mill will be handy. I will tell them."

"And I will have Alan of Bellingham write out the deeds of tenancy."

I spoke with the other three farmers who lived in the village and they were equally pleased. One reason was that with farms occupied further out then the chances of being surprised by raiders and bandits lessened.

It was the first week of March when I took my patrol out. The harsh winter had also affected Otterburn. There were two more empty farms to be seen as we neared the tower and when we spoke with Sir James, we discovered that four villagers had died in the winter. The old man shook his head, "This is a harsh and unforgiving land. I am glad that my wife is no longer alive to witness this. Between the snow and the Scots more than half of my people have perished in the last three years." He lowered his voice. "I have a nephew. He serves the Sherriff at the New Castle. He has recently taken a bride. I thought to invite him to take over my manor. It is too much for me. You have shown me that. Your actions last year were the actions I should have taken. Had I done so then how many of my people might still be alive?"

The Bloody Border

"He may not wish to come, Sir James. I am lucky. I have no wife. Had I a wife then I might think twice about taking on such a challenge as this. He would need men at arms and archers. They are expensive."

He nodded, "I have money. I know I do not have many men but I am of an age where I like the comfort of familiar faces. There will be enough money to pay for men."

"And has there been any signs of enemies in the land?"

He shook his head. "Old Peter the hunter walked my woods this winter hunting game for my table. He has good eyes and he saw no sign of men in the woods."

"Then tomorrow I will take my men beyond your land towards Byrness. We will not be taken by surprise again."

I spoke with Brother Paul and Alan of Bellingham when I returned to my castle. I spoke of my fears for Sir James and, more importantly, the people of Otterburn. Brother Paul nodded, "It seems to me, lord, that I ought to ride to Durham when the weather is more clement and speak with the Bishop. This is not a matter to be written down. The Bishop is a tactful man. He might choose Sir James' nephew but, on the other hand, he may not. The King may have suggested another to him. That was how your name came up, was it not, lord?"

"Perhaps, more likely it was that I happened to be in his eye line and he thought to use my family name. We will ride to the border and see what we can see."

The cold and icy wind continued. My farmers would not be ploughing fields. Our crops would be delayed. We had barley to harvest but the crop would not be as good as might have been expected. The good news would be that we could allow the pigs into the fields to clear the barley stalks once we had harvested the crop.

We wrapped up well, as we rode north and west. I was grateful for my arming cap and I even wore my helmet, albeit with the visor raised. My cloak had fur lining. When I lived in Stockton, we had trapped some weasels and stoats. Their fur was warm. I did not wear my mail mittens but leather gloves which Matthew had made over winter. He knew how to work leather. The gloves were warm too. We passed Otterburn without stopping. Once we reached the fort, we did stop. This was higher ground and there was still frozen snow. It hid the blackened soil where we had burned the raiders.

Garth Red Arrow said, "There has been no one here, lord, since the battle. They have not ventured down this road yet."

"We will still head to the border. I want them to see my banner. I need them to know that we are being vigilant and our victory will not make us complacent."

We ate and watered our horses. Then we rode down the road. John was with us. He still had his small horse and he was lower to the ground. Perhaps that was what helped him to see movement. "Lord," he said quietly, "I saw a movement in the open door of one of the wrecked houses to the right."

I trusted John, "Archers spread out to the right. Men at arms, follow me."

I spurred my horse and rode towards the door. I heard a skittering and then a shout. Idraf of Towyn shouted, "Here, lord! I have caught something!"

He rode towards us and dangling from his arm was a small boy of perhaps seven summers. He was thin and almost blue. What had we found?

I realised that the child was barefoot and his teeth were chattering. "Idraf, wrap your cloak around him. The rest of you search the buildings for others. Garth, find his tracks."

I spurred my horse and reached Idraf. He had wrapped the boy up. Idraf's cloak was not fur lined. Idraf said, "Sorry, lord, he is just a child. I picked him up by the scruff of the neck. I fear he is dead!"

I took off my own cloak and felt the icy wind. How had this child survived with just a thin piece of tunic about his shoulders? "Give him to me. It is not your fault." I saw that, although he was still breathing, his eyes were closed. "This child is dying. We must get to Otterburn as soon as we can. Matthew, fetch me the honey." While my squire searched for the honey we carried for wounds, I wrapped the child so that the fur of my cloak was next to his body. I wrapped the cloak around him a number of times. I held the cloak close to me. Mathew brought the honey over. I put my fingers in the clay pot and took a couple of fingers of the honey and I put it in his mouth. Many believed that honey had properties to heal. It was all that I could think of. "Come, we ride."

I spurred my horse with the boy cradled against me. He was either asleep or unconscious but his lips moved. Perhaps his body made him lick the honey. I knew not. Garth Red Arrow rode next to me. "He came from the border, lord. There were prints in the snow. They matched his feet. I found the bracken he had tried to eat. How has he survived?"

"God has sent us here. We must save the life of this child. You have a good horse. Ride ahead to Sir James and tell him that we need a healer or a priest."

"Aye lord."

We rode hard. I was cold now and I could only imagine what the boy had felt as he had sheltered in the ruined house. I did not know if he was Scot or English. It made no difference. He was a child and we could not abandon him. I also had the answer to my question. The Scots were still on their side of the border. I knew that we could not reach our home before dark. We would have to impose upon Sir James. There would be food wasted at Elsdon. Anne and Alice would have cooked for us. That could not be helped.

When we spied the tower of Otterburn I prayed that we had reached it in time. The boy still breathed but it was shallow breathing. We were spied from afar and the gates of the tower were open. An old monk stood there with Sir James and Garth. I dismounted whilst still holding the boy and I hurried in to the tower. There was no fire burning for this was a guard room but Sir James pointed towards a door. The guard room was still much warmer than the outside. We stepped through the door and entered a room where there was a fire. The monk said, "I am Brother Abelard, I will take the child. Your man described the symptoms. The cure is dramatic." I saw that there was a bath of steaming water before the fire. The monk took my cloak and handed it to me. He then took the icy rags from the child and laid his blue, naked body in the water. The monk put his finger on the boy's lips and then licked the ends of his fingers. "You gave him honey?"

"Aye, did I do wrong?"

"No, my lord, you did well, that, the cloak and the warmth of your body may well have saved this bairn's life. See how the colour returns to him and his breathing is easier."

One of Sir James' servants brought me a mug of ale. He put a poker in it. Sir James said, "Your men and animals are being cared for. This is a good deed you have done, Sir William.

"If he lives it is but otherwise…"

The monk kept feeling the temperature of the water. Another servant brought some clothes. They were well-made clothes. Sir James said, "These belonged to my son. He is now dead. The Scots killed him. I could not bear to throw away the clothes he had worn as a child. Now I see that I have kept them for a purpose."

The monk took some of the warmed ale that the servant had handed to him. He sipped it and then stirred in a spoon of butter. He lifted the child's head and poured some into his mouth. I was not sure if he would swallow but he did. It was a conscious act. The boy lived. The monk poured half of the beaker down his throat. He smiled, "This is not small beer. This is a potent brew. He may well sleep." Putting down the beaker he picked him out of the water and laid him on the drying sheet. When he was dried, he dressed him. I saw a sheepskin lying close by. He wrapped the child in it and after the servants had taken away the water, he laid him close to the fire. "Now we wait. If your lordships would like to eat then I shall pray for the child."

Servants brought us food. We sat at a table and ate but I kept glancing at the child. Suddenly the monk stopped praying and bent his head. I heard him murmur something then he shouted, "God be praised he lives. Sir James have your servants fetch porridge. He needs food." The monk raised the boy's head. His eyes were wide with fear. The monk said, "You are safe, my son. Sir William has saved you."

He stared around him and looked, for all the world as though he was a wild animal. When he spoke, his words were in English. "Which is Sir William? I must find him!"

Both Sir James and the monk looked at me, "What is this, Sir William? You said you had never seen him before."

"And I have not. Boy, I am Sir William of Elsdon. What is your name and why do you seek me?"

The Bloody Border

Brother Abelard shook his head. "First, Sir William, let him eat. There will be time enough for questions. We thought him dead and he lives. Let us rejoice in that."

I was impatient but the monk was right. We had time. I could not rest without knowing this story. The boy finished the bowl of porridge laced with honey and his face became filled with a healthier colour. He looked alive! Sir James said, "Now, boy, tell us your story and begin with your name."

"I am Dick, son of Harry. I lived in Yalesham. We were raided at harvest time. My father and brothers were killed and my mother and I were taken across the border. We were made slaves. When the son of the lord of the manor was captured and then returned, we were all beaten. They said it was to punish Sir William of Elsdon. The women who had been captured are led by my mother and they spoke amongst themselves and devised a plan. I was the oldest boy who still lived. They helped me to escape and asked me to head south and east until I came to Elsdon and there tell Sir William that the women of Yalesham needed to be rescued."

I sat back. Now I knew that Walther had not died in vain. I had a task and I would do it. Sir James said, "I see from your face, Sir William, that you would do this and rescue the women."

"It seems I have little choice."

"Yet if you cross the border then you will be breaking the peace. You will incur the wrath of the King!"

I shrugged, "That never worried my father. If there is something which is right then I am honour bound to do it. I will return to my home tomorrow and then prepare to…" I looked at the child, "Where is this castle?"

"It is on the main road. I counted ten Roman markers before I reached Byrness."

"Then that is Lord Malcolm's castle, Branxholme."

"A strong one?"

"It has a tower like mine but they live in a fortified hall. There is a ditch but no moat."

"Dick, where are the captives kept?"

"They are locked in a barn at night and there is a guard on the door. Lord, you must help them. Two of the girls were taken away. They did not return."

"Do not worry, Dick of Yalesham, you were sent to me for a reason. We will try to rescue your family."

Sir James nodded, "And I will stir this old body and bring my men with you, Sir William of Elsdon. Yalesham was in my manor. It was I neglected those poor people."

Chapter 9

Sir James provided a pony for the boy to ride and he had an old cloak cut down for him to wear. We left at dawn and reached my home quicker than was good for our horses. The boy was silent for most of the way. He was alone and he was parted from his mother. From his story, she sounded like a brave woman. As soon as we reached my lower bailey, I called over Anne, "This boy almost died. He was captured by Scots and his mother is still enslaved by them. I would have you care for him."

Anne was a warm woman and put an arm around the waif, "Come here, bairn, a smith always has a good fire. We will soon warm you through to your cockles!"

When the boy clung to her then I knew that all would be well and, while Matthew and John stabled the horses, I headed to my hall.

Alan of Bellingham was in the hall poring over lists. He had the accounts of the manor to prepare. He looked up, "Yes lord?" Taking off my cloak and heading to the fire for a warm I told him the tale. He shook his head, "A sad business but at least we know where they are. We can make representation to have them returned."

Shaking my head, I said, "I will take men and fetch them back!"

He turned and his face showed his concern, "Lord, you cannot do that. It might cause war. The King would not be happy about such a thing."

"Alan, you were a Hospitaller, you know that sometimes the wishes of kings are secondary."

"Aye, lord but here in England, we are ruled by a king who is precious about his power. You have done good work here and if you were removed then I fear the heart would be taken from the manor. Do not act in haste."

I was not sure what would have happened if Brother Paul had not entered. He knew nothing of the boy. "Lord, I am ready to ride to the Bishop." He stopped and stared. He could see that he had interrupted something. "What is amiss?"

Alan of Bellingham looked relieved, "There is your answer, lord, tell the Bishop what has occurred and what you intend. If the Bishop sanctions this then the King cannot harm you." Seeing the confusion on the priest's face Alan explained the situation.

"Alan is right, lord. I was going to Durham in any case. What difference will the delay of a day or so make? You are angry and this is not the time to act in haste. As you say the Scots have not yet crossed the border. They may believe that the boy has died. We have a handful of men. It would be foolish to throw their lives away."

They were right and I nodded. The relief on their faces was clear to be seen. "Ride to Durham and I will delay until you come back but with or without the Bishop's permission, we try to rescue those women.

"I will ride directly. If you let me have a spare horse, lord, I can be there in one day."

I smiled. He was not a happy horseman. "And you can ride that far?"

He shrugged, "If a small boy can survive in winter then a little hardship can be endured. Besides, Alan of Bellingham has loaned me a cushion to ease my discomfort when I ride. It will suffice."

My men at arms and archers needed no persuasion to prepare for a raid which, on the surface at least, looked hopeless. They had seen the miracle of the boy. Superstitious men, they all felt an obligation to the boy they had found and who had been brought back to life. As they came into the hall, they were all of the same mind.

Idraf spoke for them all, "When do we return to rescue the bairn's mother and the others, lord?"

The Bloody Border

"Not for a few days. Brother Paul goes to inform the Bishop and besides, the horses have had a hard couple of days. We pushed them to the limit to reach Otterburn. Prepare your weapons. We will return those women to England. That I promise you."

I left with John and Matthew. We returned to our keep. We had mail and weapons to clean. The icy, damp air did mail armour no good. They both worked diligently to clean our mail for they knew their newly acquired skills would be put to the most severe of tests soon. When we had been in Otterburn I had spoken with men who knew the manor where the prisoners were held. I now took a piece of charcoal and one of the logs we would use to burn. It had a clean axe stroke and I drew upon it to make a crude map. My mind was able to work better with a picture. When I had been growing up, I had been fascinated by my father's maps.

The tower and village lay just a few miles from the border. There was a tiny inconsequential hamlet just a mile or so from the border. That would pose no threat to us. Jed Water was close to the hall and there was a burn too. Both afforded protection to the lord and his people. Jedburgh was also less than five miles away and I could see why they did not need a castle. Jedburgh was a royal residence. The tower would be a sanctuary in case of attack. Unlike Otterburn, the hall was not attached to the tower. I guessed it was used to keep watch on the land during the day. If danger was seen then a bell would be peeled and they would occupy the tower. That knowledge determined my method of attack. We would use the cloak of night. I did not have enough men to fight a battle. My aim was to rescue the captives and gallop back across the border. If we could do so without fighting then I would be happy.

Matthew came over when I had finished my crude map. He looked at it and shook his head, "I can read some words lord but those squiggles confuse me."

I explained to him what they meant and gave him the outline of my plan. By talking aloud, it helped my thinking. "If they are on foot, lord, then the captives will be slow and the Scots will be able to pursue us."

He was right. "Then we shall have to steal their horses too."

"How many captives are there, lord?"

"From what Dick told me there are six Yalesham women who remain alive. Four are mothers and there are two young women. Then there are five children and all are younger than Dick. There are other captives there but not from Yalesham. Dick did not say how many others there were."

Matthew gave me a rueful smile, "I know how hard John and I found riding. I doubt that the women and the children will find it any easier. The children will either need to be carried by their mothers or by warriors."

I shook my head, "My men at arms and archers will be occupied." I looked at him, "You and John will have to carry a child each. Sir James can carry another." I would not risk the old man unless I had to. I smiled and poured Matthew some ale. "Thank you, squire. I now have a plan."

"But I just gave you problems, lord!"

"Sometimes that is what my mind needs."

The next two days were frustrating for me as we awaited the return of Brother Paul. The icy wind disappeared but was replaced by March squalls. As the land warmed the rain turned paths to mud. Dick son of Harry appeared to be content living in the smithy with Anne and Tam. He was well fed. Anne was handy with a needle and she had made him better fitting clothes. The ones from Sir James, while well-made were old and moths had been at them. Matthew also made him a pair of boots. The boy's feet were not large and he had enough leather left from his own to make a pair. In that way, they were occupied but I was not. The mud would slow us down. Garth Red Arrow pointed out that the rain and the poor conditions would deter the Scots too.

Five days after he had left Brother Paul returned and he was not alone. With him, he had seven men. The priest looked pained as he dismounted, "That was harder than I had thought. I have a message from the Bishop but these men were sent by your father. That is why I tarried, lord." He gestured for them to speak.

Each said his name and stepped back. "Edward of Yarum, lord."

"Peter of Hart."

I knew their villages. They were close to Stockton.

"Martin Longsword, lord. I served the Sherriff of York. My father was one of the guards slain when your brother died."

"Egbert son of Harold, lord. I too come from York. Martin is my friend."

"Lol Longstride, lord." He smiled, "I come from everywhere. I am like a butterfly! Perhaps I will settle upon this flower eh, lord?" Lol was the eldest of the men but I took to him straightway. He had humour. I later learned that he had been a travelling warrior since he had been less than seven years old. His father had been a soldier and his mother a camp follower. He had forgotten more about campaigning than I would ever learn.

The other two had bow staves in canvas bags. They were archers.

"I am Robin Greenleg, lord." I saw that he had one leg of his breeks made of green material and the other was a faded red." I cocked an eye. He shrugged, "I served the Lord of Hereford and his men wore this style of breeks. When I left his service, I continued to wear them. It gave me my name. When a man is given a name, it is unlucky to discard it.

"Alan Whitestreak, lord." I could see how he had acquired his name. He had black hair and on one side was a patch of white as wide as three fingers running across his ear. He pointed to the streak, "A bolt from a crossbow nearly took my life. It is a reminder to me to kill those with crossbows and to wear a helmet when I fight."

"You are all welcome. Garth Red Arrow and Roger Two Swords will show you your quarters. I will speak further with you." My two captains would discover all that there was to know about our new men! I turned to Brother Paul and Alan of Bellingham, "Come. Let us go to my keep. I am anxious to know the Bishop's thoughts although, I must confess, it will not change my course of action."

John hurried with a jug of wine and three goblets. We would need to buy more soon. It was fortunate I still had the ransom. Wine was not cheap up here in the north. "Well?"

"The Bishop understands your dilemma, lord. He supports you and he will not order you to ignore the plight of the captives."

Alan of Bellingham nodded, "Which is just a way of doing as Pontius Pilate did and saying he washes his hands of the matter."

Brother Paul was uncomfortable. I could see that. "I think he means that if the King hears of this and wishes you to be punished then the punishment, which the Bishop administers, will be lenient."

I turned to Alan, "The answer was the best one that I could have expected. We will rescue them but I will not do it under the Bishop's colours. We will wear plain livery. My plan means that we will be attacking at night." I decided that the experience of Alan of Bellingham and the natural wit of the priest might augment my plan. I told them what I intended. I would take my spare horses for the captives.

Alan of Bellingham nodded his approval, "You will have one sentry to eliminate. Once he is gone then, if you can steal their horses, you will be able to make a successful escape."

Brother Paul asked, "Will you take the boy?"

I shook my head, "There is no need. I know where the captives are held and I would have him safe. He is a brave soul and God has marked him for life. I will not jeopardise it. When I leave it will be you two and Tam who guard my castle. Now that I have more men it will not always be so. I can leave sentries but for this, I need all of them." I stood. "Thank you and now I will speak with my men and archers."

They were all getting to know one another. Weapons were being compared and they were sharing stories of past employment. When Matthew and I entered they fell silent. "To my new men, I bid you welcome. You have come at a propitious time. A village was destroyed and the captives were taken to Scotland. I intend to recover them."

My original men all nodded and looked pleased. "How will we do it, my lord?"

"I intend to attack at night. Garth Red Arrow, I will need a man who can hit a sentry and kill him so that he utters not a sound." He nodded. I knew that he would take on that task himself. "We also need a way to silence dogs."

Edward of Yarum held up his hand. I smiled and nodded, "I like dogs, lord. I would not be happy to kill one. I can quieten them without hurting them. I have a way with them."

"Then, Edward of Yarum, that will be your task. You new men, do any of you have an affinity with horses?"

Martin nodded, "Aye, lord, I worked with Egbert at the Sherriff's stables. We schooled the new horses."

"Then your task will be to find horses for the captives. They will not be good riders. When you have the horses for them, I rely on you two to effect their escape. You may have to ride with either women or children on your saddles too."

"Aye lord." Martin nodded confidently.

Roger Two Swords asked the most obvious question, "And how many men do we face, lord?"

"That is the one question I cannot answer. There will be Sir Duncan and his father. We know there is at least one man at arms, probably more, and squires. The men Lord Duncan led were more like bandits and farmers than retainers who know how to fight. Lord Malcolm has a tower and it is safe to assume he employs warriors. The simple answer is that I do not know." They nodded, appreciating my honesty. "This action will not meet with King Henry's approval although, as he is in Gascony, by the time he hears of it we will either be dead or the captives will be safe. For that reason, we do not wear our surcoats. We will not need shields in any case, The Scots will know who did this and it will invite reprisals but they will not be able to prove that the men of Elsdon avenged Walther of Coxold and the men of Yalesham." I looked at their faces and I did not see any dissension. "We leave tomorrow. We do not need an early start. We will meet with Sir James at Otterburn. He and his men will come with us."

Roger said, quietly, "They are old, lord."

"I know but there is honour involved. They feel they let down the villagers. I intend to have them watch and guard our horses. It will be the men of Elsdon who take all the chances."

That day I wrote a letter to my father. I thanked him for what he had done for me. Without telling him what I was doing I prepared him in case I did not return. I hoped and prayed that I would but there was always a possibility that I might not. I left the letter in my keep. Brother Paul would know what to do with it if I failed to return.

We left after a hearty meal. Anne knew we had a long day and night ahead of us. Alice was now confined to the farm. Her husband did not want her to have to travel. Anne made do with

Rafe's youngest daughters as helpers. The girls were willing and had skills. They enjoyed her company and the coin I paid helped their father. Now that her brothers were clearing the two farms Rafe and his wife had an emptier house.

We reached Otterburn at noon. Sir James was ready with his men. He would leave two to watch his tower. All were older than even Ridley the Giant and my father. I admired them for what they were doing but I would try to ensure that they came to no harm. We rested the horses and ate while I went over the plan with Sir James. We now had days and nights which were almost equal in length. We would use the length of the night to our advantage. We left Otterburn with about three hours of daylight left to us.

I had my archers out as scouts. As well as the plain livery on our cloaks we had all chosen dark cloaks. I hoped to be invisible. It was dark and we did not know when we had crossed the border. There was no moon. One of Sir James' men thought we had crossed it. Not long after we crossed what we thought was the border we passed through one huddle of huts. There were no more than three of them and none stirred. When we were through, we knew that we were not too far from the hall. We halted for we were within a few miles of our destination. The archers strung their bows. We tightened our girths and we took off our cloaks. We would need free movement. Garth led us forward. There was no frost but it was a cold, damp night. The hall kept fires burning and when the wind brought the smell of woodsmoke towards us we knew that we were close. In the distance, a dog barked. Edward of Yarum joined Garth and we followed slowly. When Garth held up his hand and then dismounted, I repeated the signal. We walked our horses.

I spied the tower silhouetted in the distance. Once more Garth held up his hand. Wilfred of Sheffield moved forward and took the reins of Garth's horse and Edward's. The two of them slipped off in the dark. We moved up slowly to join Wilfred. Sir James' men knew their task and they, along with John and a boy from Otterburn, took the reins of our horses. They would watch them. I unsheathed my sword. I chose not to wear my helmet. Sir James did. As we waited, I spied the hall, the tower and the ancillary buildings. The noise of the stream, which bubbled away close to us, afforded some protection and, although I could not see, I guessed that there was a ditch around the tower. It was a sprawling settlement and I hoped that the boy's description would lead us quickly to the slave hall. Garth and Edward would be able to find it for the only guard, according to Dick, was at the slave hall.

After what seemed like an age, Dick came back followed by Edward and two rangy-looking dogs. They appeared to be happily following him. They had not barked. My new man had not lied to me.

"We have found the hall, lord. The sentry is dead."

"Good. Edward, stay by the horses with the dogs. Martin and Egbert, find the stables and fetch the horses. Archers, wait here. When we return, we may be pursued. Deter those following. Garth, lead me to the captives."

I let Garth lead me. Matthew and Sir James were directly behind me. The tower appeared empty for there was no shout of alarm as we passed. The night was silent save for the stream. When we came to the hall, I felt the heat from the walls and heard the sound of snoring. The sentry lay dead. The arrow had struck his throat. His tunic was covered in blood. Garth carefully lifted the bar. I entered slowly. I said, quietly, into the dark, "I am Sir William of Elsdon and I am come to rescue you. I pray you remain silent. Come outside. Quickly, my men are outside and they will take you to safety."

A woman said, "Thank God!" She was louder than I had been.

"Do so silently or you will bring the Scots from their halls!" My command silenced them and I stepped away from the door. There were more than eleven who came out. Then it struck me. The boy had given numbers only of those from Yalesham. There were other captives. I had not expected so many. The die was cast. I hoped that Martin and Egbert had found horses. If we had to ride double then they would catch us.

I let Sir James and Garth lead the captives away and I waited with my men at arms and Matthew. We waited by the door of the hall. If danger was to come then it would be from within. The stables, from the smell which came to me, were closer to the river and some hundred or so paces away. I heard two things at the same time. I heard a cry and then the sound of hooves. "Stand to! They will be roused!"

There were nine of us. Roger twirled his two swords. It was his way of preparing for battle. Matthew drew his sword. The hooves of the horses taken by Martin and Egbert clattered on the stone of the yard. If those inside the hall had not been roused before they would be. The door opened and a warrior with a sword in his hand and dressed only in breeks emerged. He saw us and shouted, "Alarm!" Then he slammed the door shut. Martin and Egbert each rode a horse and led seven others. They were sumpters in the main although Martin and Egbert rode palfreys. None had saddles. That was something I had not foreseen.

As they rode by, I shouted, "Put the captives on horses with saddles. Head for Otterburn, we will follow."

"Aye, lord!"

We had to wait. When the Scots emerged, they could only come one at a time. Their bravest and best would come first. We needed to bloody their noses and then flee. "Matthew, go and fetch our horses." I slipped my dagger into my left hand.

"Aye, lord."

He had barely left us when the door burst open and five men hurled themselves at us. They had small round shields and carried short swords. I was in the centre with Roger and Wilfred. We were the closest to the five men. A man ran directly at me. I blocked the scything blow from the short sword with my own sword. The Scot's weapon was not as good as mine and I saw it buckle. I lunged with my dagger, not at his throat, for he raised his shield in anticipation but at his thigh. I ripped sideways and he fell to the ground. Roger had dealt with two of the men. He had quick hands and our weapons were better than theirs. The other two had been wounded and I heard our horses.

Even as more men poured from the hall, I shouted, "Back to the horses!"

I saw Sir Duncan in a mail hauberk. He pointed a sword at me and shouted, "You!"

An arrow flew from the dark behind me and one of Sir Duncan's men, who had stepped from the lighted doorway, fell with a red-fletched arrow in his chest. It made the Scots halt and

The Bloody Border

shields were raised. It gave us the chance to run back to our horses. Garth and the archers had brought my men's horses. Matthew held Eagle's reins. I sheathed my weapons and pulled myself up into the saddle. The archers held their bows horizontally. We were less than a hundred paces from the hall. Their arrows would not be as accurate but if you were a Scot trying to get at the men who had raided you then it would be a deterrent.

I looked around and saw that we were mounted, "Ride!" We whipped our horse's heads around. I had gone barely twenty paces when I felt something thump into my wooden cantle and the next moment strike me in the back. I had never experienced it but I knew what it was; I had been struck by a pair of crossbow bolts. It was confirmed when I felt blood trickling down my buttocks. I could do nothing about it. I would have to endure it.

Despite my command, Sir James was waiting with the captives at the small huddle of huts through which we had passed earlier. "Why do you wait! They will follow!"

Sir James was too old for this. He did not think quickly enough, "We thought to wait for you."

Just then I heard, behind us, the sound of hooves. I knew, as soon as Martin and Egbert had brought but two palfreys that the Scots had good horses and they would follow with the ones my men had not managed to bring. "Sir James, Martin, Egbert, ride to Otterburn and do not stop! We will try to slow them."

Realisation dawned and Sir James turned and spurred his horse. "Come, my people! Sir William commands this day!"

"Archers, dismount. Roger, have the men hold the archer's horses. I want three flights of arrows to discourage them. Release as soon as you see them! Then mount and we run." The warm blood, which was seeping down to my breeks, was just a trickle. I would have to pray that it was not mortal. I drew my sword.

My archers stood before their horses. I heard the creak as the war bows were pulled back. The horses and riders appeared just one hundred paces from us. The snap of bowstrings was followed a heartbeat later by cries from men and horses as they were struck. My archers were fast for the Scots had obliged us by riding down the road. They made an easier target. I saw at least two horses struck. The other riders tried to whirl away and when one fell in the road it blocked it. My archers leapt onto their horses. "Ride!" I whipped Eagle's head around and spurred him. I led my men on the road to the border.

As we rode, I saw ahead of me the faint glow of dawn. I began to plan. We had to hold them. The best place would be the Roman fort. By then our horses would be tired, as would theirs. I guessed we would arrive there at about dawn. It would be a grey dawn but if we waited there then it would give Sir James more chance to reach Otterburn.

I shouted, "Garth, take your archers. Ride ahead and prepare an ambush at the fort. We will follow!"

"Aye, lord."

They galloped past us. Without mail, they were faster. I now just had Matthew and a handful of men at arms. John was obeying orders and helping Sir James with the captives. I could hear the hooves behind us. The pursuit continued. I reined in a little. I needed Garth and my archers to set themselves for their ambush. If the Scots had sense they would be wary, having been ambushed there once before already, but I counted on their anger. We had taken their captives and we had hurt their horses. Men had died. I saw as the sun began to light the sky, the deserted village of Byrness. I wondered if the other captives came from there. We were close now. I risked turning to look behind me. It was a mistake. The bolt was still sticking in me and pain coursed through my body as the bolt caught on the cantle of my saddle. I saw that the Scots were less than four hundred paces behind me. I did not get enough of a look to identify numbers but there looked to be more than we had.

I spied the fort. I knew my archers were there but I could not see them. That meant the Scots would not see them either. "When we reach the fort ride through the north gate. Then we turn and fight them."

"Aye, lord."

Roger Two Swords had dropped behind me, "Lord, you are wounded!"

"It is nothing. Let us send these Scots hence and then we can deal with it." I sounded braver than I was. I had bled too much to be confident that I could survive a lengthy fight. I did not dare to turn around but the thundering of the hooves told me that they were close behind me.

I saw the gate. I headed for it. I heard Roger shout, "Matthew, be ready to grab the reins of Sir William's horse."

Galloping through, I saw Garth and my archers with arrows ready to fly. As soon as Wilfred had galloped beyond the shattered gates, I heard Garth shout, "Release!"

I wheeled Eagle. Matthew grabbed my reins and I drew my sword. I felt more blood trickling down my back. I watched the third flights from my archers strike the Scots. Two men fell. They knew the folly of attacking archers behind a wall. They withdrew beyond the range of my archers.

Roger Two Swords ran up to me. "Come, my lord. Let us see to your wound. Master Matthew, fetch bandages, the vinegar and honey. The rest of you get to the gate. Block it with your bodies if you have to. Garth Red Arrow, our lord has been struck by a bolt."

"Fear not, Roger Two Swords. The only ones who pass through the gate will be dead men." As I dismounted, I saw my captain of archers send an arrow towards the waiting Scots. I thought it beyond his range but it hit a horse. The horse reared and then galloped down the road dragging the man along the road by the boot caught in a stirrup.

I heard the relief in Roger's voice, "You are lucky, lord. The bolt caught in your mail and the gambeson has prevented worse bleeding but it will hurt when I pull it from you and the blood will flow."

"Just do it."

"Hurry, Master Matthew." He took off my mail coif and arming cap as we waited. Matthew arrived. "When I pull out the bolt pull the hauberk over Sir William's head. I will try to staunch the bleeding." He leaned in. "Ready lord?"

"Ready!" He pulled and the pain was so bad that I thought I would pass out. I heard him hiss, "Bastards! A barb!" Matthew lifted the hauberk. He was strong and did what many squires could not have done. Even so, the raising of my arms made the blood flow. Then I felt coolness as the vinegar soaked bandage was applied. That was quickly followed a sharp pain as Roger wiped the wound clean with vinegar. "Lord, this is a deep wound. I will need fire. Matthew light a fire! Garth we will need to use fire to seal the wound. We will need time."

Garth shouted back, "I have an idea!" I was able to see the fighting platform. He clambered up the remains of the gatehouse tower and clung precariously to it. He began to wave. He shouted, "Everyone wave and cheer. Make the Scots think Sir James brings his men!"

They all did so and Idraf of Towyn shouted, "It works! They are leaving! The two lords are unhappy, my lord. They shake their fists at us."

I nodded. I had hoped to raid and leave them in doubt as to the perpetrators. I had been seen. They would know who had done this. I had begun a war with my neighbours. This would not involve kings. It would be between the Scots from across the border and my men. What had I begun?

Chapter 10

We did not leave the fort until noon. Roger insisted that once the wound was sealed and treated with honey that I eat, drink and then rest. He sent Matthew ahead to Otterburn to have Sir James prepare a bed for me. I would have argued with him had I not passed out once the red-hot blade was applied to my skin. I awoke to the smell of burnt hair and flesh. We rode slowly down the road. My archers were the rear guard. Wilfred and Roger flanked me for they feared I might fall.

"You were lucky, lord, but the mail will need to be repaired."

Wilfred said, "The Earl, your father, has a leather hauberk beneath his mail one. Matthew could easily make you one. It would afford more protection."

"I know he wears one but I would find it too restrictive." Even as I spoke the words, I realised that it would be necessary. My archers had arrowheads which could pierce mail. Crossbow bolts were equally deadly. I was now lord of the manor. I would have to learn to fight differently.

When we reached Otterburn it was the middle of the afternoon. I saw John watching anxiously from the top of the tower. I heard his shout from half a mile up the valley. By the time we reached it Sir James and his priest, Brother Abelard, were there, "We were worried about you. You were wounded?"

"I was but my men healed me. They sealed the wound with fire, Brother Abelard, and treated it with vinegar and honey."

The priest looked relieved. "Nonetheless, my lord, I will give you a draught this night to help you sleep. In my experience, while fire stops an injury becoming worse it makes it more painful than had it been stitched."

I nodded, "The captives, Sir James?"

"They are well. Mary, the mother of Dick, is anxious to thank you."

"Who were the other captives?"

"They were the ones left from Byrness." He shook his head, "A sorry business which can be laid at my door."

"Do not berate yourself. I fear that I have begun something which will make this border run with blood."

"No, you did not. We never took captives from the Scots. They are the ones who began it. I shall be vigilant. I have written to my nephew to ask him again if he will come to the manor. I fear that his silence is eloquent. This is a harsh duty and the New Castle will be an easier place for him and his wife."

I nodded, "I shall go and speak with the captives before I dine."

"They are being cared for in the church. Even the Scots would baulk at the sacrilege of attacking a church and the captives feel safe there. They wish to thank you, Sir William."

I went with Matthew and John. I think both felt guilt that they had not managed to stop me from being wounded. Sir James had had straw brought for bedding as well as blankets and furs. I smelled food as I entered. What greeted me shocked me. In the heat of battle and in the dark I had just been aware of a larger number than I had expected. Now I saw that there were ten children and twelve women. All were thin, as was Dick. There were three young women of perhaps twelve or thirteen summers who clung to an older woman. The older woman stood when I entered and ran to me. She dropped to her knees and grabbed my hand. She began to kiss it.

"Sir William, you are our saviour. Your men told me that you saved the life of my son. He would have died had you not cared for him. I am in your debt."

"Rise, dear lady! You are in no one's debt. I did what any Christian would do."

She stood and swept a hand around her. She rested it on the head of one of the girls who looked up at me, "All of us are grateful, lord but we have a boon to ask." I nodded, "No offence to Sir James but we would not live here. The Scots will come for us. You have a castle and we would be safe within its walls."

Here was a dilemma. I was honour bound to care for them. It was my duty and yet the last thing my manor needed was more mouths to feed. I needed families who had men to work the empty farms. I needed warriors who could man my walls and repel those who would attack us. I smiled, "You are all welcome but I have to say that we are not a rich manor."

The one called Mary, Dick's mother, shook her head, "There you are wrong, my lord, for you are rich in charity and God rewards those who are pure in heart. We can work and we can toil. Just so long as we are safe then we will be happy."

When I left them, I went to speak to my men. To my surprise, Edward of Yarum still had the two huge hounds. I looked at him and he shrugged, "They seem to like me, lord. From what the women told me they were mistreated as much as the women were."

"I just came to thank you for your endeavours. The women are grateful and so am I. We are taking them back to Elsdon. I fear your work is not yet done. We will have to build homes for them in the lower bailey."

Roger Two Swords had been cleaning and sharpening his swords with a whetstone. He was smiling, "And that is no hardship, lord. How is the wound?"

"I am indebted to you, Roger. It is well and Brother Abelard is pleased with your efforts. I will see if we can manage to borrow a wagon from Sir James. It will make our journey home easier."

I was glad that Sir James was liberal with his wine and that Brother Abelard gave me a draught else I would not have slept. I awoke before dawn and I was stiff. I knew that I must have had a disturbed night's sleep for John and Matthew asked after me when we woke.

"I almost went for the priest, lord, for you cried out in your sleep."

I laughed it off, "It was probably the wine. Do not worry. I am fine." They did not know me well enough to hear the lie in my voice.

Before we left, I spoke with Sir James. "They will come. They will seek vengeance and they will ride with hatred in their hearts.

You need to take care. Send to me if you suspect any danger. I will bring my men."

"Do not concern yourself. We have been defending my tower for many years. I may occasionally take my eye from my manor but Otterburn is safe so long as I breathe. Perhaps my nephew will respond to my last letter."

I took a deep breath, "I hope you do not think that this is underhand but I spoke to the Bishop about the problem. If your nephew will not come then the Bishop might have other knights upon whom he can call."

He shook his head, "No, for I see no deceit in you. If I were in your position then I too might wish for a younger lord who could fight these child stealers."

The old knight had given us a wagon. As he said, they were his people we had saved. The least he could do was to give us a wagon. We hitched four of the sumpters we had captured to the wagon and headed home. The rains had made the roads worse and although it had not rained for a couple of days the water had run off the fields to the roads. Mud covered the cobbles and the wheels slipped. I sent two riders to warn Alan of Bellingham of our arrival and the need for accommodation for the captives. Sir James had found some clothes for the captives but not enough. The ones they had were inadequate. We had much to do. The ransom I had received would soon be eaten away. It took much longer to reach Elsdon with a slow wagon and slippery roads.

Dick knew that his mother was coming and as the wagon entered the lower bailey, he broke free from Anne and ran towards the wagon. The reunion was touching. I nudged my horse close to Anne, "Thank you, Mistress Anne. "

She nodded and linked her husband, "Aye, lord, but the trouble is that I now wish one of my own. So far God has denied us one. Perhaps my good deed will stand us in good stead."

"I will pray for you both. You are good people and deserve children."

Tam nodded as Brother Paul and Alan of Bellingham approached, "They will stay here for a while then, Sir William?"

"I think, Tam, that they wish to say here permanently. That may change once they have got over their incarceration but I do not know. I do know that I will not throw them out."

My reeve and priest had heard my words and their nods showed their approval. "Do not worry, my lord. We can cope. I have been going over the accounts while you were abroad. Thanks to the Bishop's dispensation we have more funds available this year. We have another year before we pay tax. I thought to buy more sheep." I dismounted and handed my reins to John. Alan saw the question on my face. "The inner and lower bailey can be used for all the year grazing. I saw that was possible when we cleared the snow. You have many women here and they can both milk the sheep and weave their wool. When I went to Morpeth, I saw that the woollen goods fetched a high price."

"Thank you, Alan of Bellingham. You were a warrior priest but I can see that you have a clever mind."

"I think that I was chosen to end my days here. If I can make Elsdon stronger than it was then that will be a monument. I fear that the Holy Land is lost to us and all those who died there, died in vain."

Brother Paul said, "And if you need a potion to help you sleep then ask me. They told me of the wound you suffered."

I pointed to the women and children who were climbing from the wagon. "They suffered more and for longer. The Scots will come and they will seek vengeance. I will try to visit my farmers tomorrow. I will need to explain why they will have to suffer."

"No lord, you do not. Rafe and the others know that this is the right thing that you did. They will be vigilant!"

The next days were filled with so much work that I had no time to worry about my wound. We had new dwellings to build. Alan and some of my archers went to Morpeth to buy the sheep. I wrote another letter to my father and one to the Bishop. I explained what I had done. I knew I was leaving written evidence which could come back to haunt me but I had done the right thing and that was all that counted. The worst that could happen would be if I lost the manor. The people would not suffer. I found myself dreading such a loss. I now felt as though these were my people yet I barely knew them.

Tam made new weapons. Matthew made me a leather hauberk to go under my mail. My men at arms planned new defences and,

The Bloody Border

each day, two riders rode to Otterburn and back. I had already spoken with my farmers and they knew what was expected.

What I did not expect was the visit from Sir Eustace of Rothbury. A week after my return, when I could move a little more freely and the new homes were started, he and six riders appeared. I recognised Godfrey of Etal. Sir Eustace's face was as black as thunder.

I smiled, "Welcome to my castle, Sir Eustace."

He jabbed a finger at me, "Listen to me you arrogant young cockerel! I am here to ask you what you have done!"

I was taken aback at the vehemence of his words. This was my castle and my manor! I squared up to him, "And I will ask you to speak civilly to me or I shall be forced to use my sword."

"You would threaten me?"

"You are a baron as am I and I will be treated with respect or know the reason why. What will it be? Do you moderate your tone? Leave? Or do we draw swords! Any are acceptable to me!" His men's hands were edging towards their swords and I saw my men at arms drawing close. "Make your decision quickly or this will become a bloodbath and I would hate to have to explain to the Bishop why I had to slay you!"

He was outnumbered. He waved a hand to his men, "Sheathe your swords. Sir William and I will retire inside his keep so that we may speak in private."

I smiled, "If I invite you in."

I saw the anger on his face but he saw the futility of his position, "I beg leave, Sir William, to enter your keep."

"Of course. Matthew, fetch us some wine. John, see to his lordship's horses. Roger Two Swords, entertain our guests, would you?" I said nothing until we were in my hall. I gestured to a chair. They were still the crudely made ones. We had had no time for better. I saw the look of distaste on Sir Eustace's face.

When we were alone with our squires, he became angry once more, "What possessed you to attack the Scots?"

"There were captives who needed rescuing."

"You could have negotiated!"

"And they would have been moved. As I recall neither you nor Sir Ranulf showed much interest in helping me when the captives were taken. I sent messages, I wrote you letters telling you of the attacks. You did nothing." His silence told me that I had been deliberately ignored. This was not an oversight. "I will say this, Sir Eustace, I am a knight who has been brought up to be both chivalrous and loyal. If you had sent to me for aid then I would have come. I will not make the mistake of relying on you again. I will deal with the Scots, with bandits and with my enemies, my way,"

"You risk making this border run with blood! There has been enough fighting. We should speak with the Scots. We could have bought back the captives!"

"Paying bandits and thieves encourages them! That is appeasement and it rarely works."

"And what of the Bishop?"

"I told the Bishop what I intended. It is sad that a young knight and an old one are the only two who will stand up to this brigandage and banditry!"

He downed his wine, "You go too far, Sir William."

"When we were in my bailey, I gave you the opportunity for satisfaction. I do so again."

"I am not afraid of you! I have won tourneys."

"I think, Sir Eustace, that you are afraid. If you were not then our blades would be clashing already. I have wasted enough time on you. I would like you to leave my castle. I believe the Scots will seek vengeance. I intend to be ready for them."

He stood, "You are a fool!"

"Probably but I am a fool who still has his honour. Can you say the same?"

He and his squire hurried out of my keep. Sir Eustace was in such a hurry that he almost tripped. It would have been unfortunate had he fallen. It would have added to the indignity he felt. Sir Eustace and his men galloped out of my castle. We were now enemies. I had one friend left, Sir James. I had made another enemy but part of me wondered what was his real reason for not coming to my aid. Sir Ranulf had had the excuse that he and his wife were ill. It still did not excuse him for he could have sent his men but it was an excuse. Sir Eustace had not even offered one.

Garth and Roger wandered over to me. Roger said, "That was interesting, lord." I cocked my head to one side. "A year since the Earl of Fife paid a visit to Rothbury. He went hunting with Sir Eustace. It may be innocent, lord. The sergeant at arms did not try to hide the fact. He was trying to impress us with the powerful friends Sir Eustace has."

That set me to thinking. I invited Alan of Bellingham and Brother Paul to dine with me. I needed to talk. We first discussed the plight of the women and children. Brother Paul was worried about the young girls. "Newminster Abbey has healers who might be able to minister to them."

Alan of Bellingham shook his head, "The solution to the problems of the girls does not lie with men who know nothing about women. We have good women here, Anne, Alice, Dick's mother, Mary, they will know the right words. We can make their house a house of women until they choose to live with a man. I think Sir William has had the right idea. Give them sanctuary and give them purpose."

Brother Paul was a monk and a clever man but he knew little about women. "I expect you are right. Your father, Sir Thomas, solved the problem of the women who chose not to stay in Durham by taking them back to Stockton."

"Now my next matter is more delicate. Sir Eustace did not come to our aid when we asked for his help. Now I have learned that he entertained the Earl of Fife last year. What is your opinion?"

Alan of Bellingham leaned back in his chair. "Lord, if I tell you that before you came the only knight to visit us and offer help was Sir James then you know my opinion of Sir Eustace."

"That is honest. Brother Paul?"

"I know nothing about him but like you, Sir William, I know that the Earl of Fife seeks to be the Earl of Northumberland. If he is a friend to Sir Eustace then I do not trust him either."

"Keep this news to yourselves and listen for any other information which might help us. As soon as the accommodation for our guests is finished then I intend to begin to add stone to our walls. We and Sir James are on our own!"

We were spurred on by the thought that we were alone. Our patrols found no sign of the enemy and we worked during the increasingly long days. By the end of April, our new sheep had arrived and the women were weaving. Gradually they showed

The Bloody Border

that they were happier. It was not a quick process. They were referred to, collectively, as the Yalesham widows. The women from Byrness were included in the group. Their captivity and the hurts they had endured bonded them. The boys who had come to us were keen to help protect their mothers and we trained them to sling stones. There was little training needed. Boys loved to throw stones.

I also received letters from the Bishop, my father and my mother. I read mother's first. It was chatty and asked how Matthew and John were faring. The letter made me smile. My father's letter was more serious. He told me he was still looking for archers but King Henry's mission in Gascony meant there were few to be had in England. He asked me if I wished him to come. I did not honestly know. Could I embroil him in this bloody war? Would he be damaged by it? He had lost all once before and I would not be the cause of losing it a second time. I decided to write a letter which would make him less anxious.

The Bishop's letter was more comforting and yet disturbing at the same time. He supported my action and he approved of my decisions but he warned me of enemies both in England and in Scotland. The King's absence in Gascony and the illness of Sir Ranulf and the Sherriff had encouraged those who saw Northumberland as Scottish. Was Sir Eustace a traitor? If he was then his visit was even more sinister. Was he spying out my defences?

I tossed and turned that night but, when I woke, I knew what we must do. I had the horses hitched to the two wagons and, leaving just four archers at my castle, I took the rest to Otterburn. "Sir James, I intend to take some of the stones from the Roman fort to build a stone gatehouse at my castle. If you wish some too…"

He laughed and patted the walls of his tower. "This tower is made from the stones of the fort. Yours is a good idea."

I waved my men off and then took Sir James to one side. I told him of the encounter with Sir Eustace and the information my men had gathered. "I had heard rumours but I took them to be malicious gossip from those who were envious of Sir Eustace. I will keep a good watch. You should know that I intend to ride to the New Castle to plead with my nephew. I have no child and I would like this manor to be kept in the family otherwise my life would be wasted."

I headed down the road. I did not think that he was right but I could understand his feelings. The walls which faced the Scottish border I would leave. We might need them for defence again. Sir James and the farmers had already demolished some of the walls. We laboured all morning and loaded the stone into the wagons. It was good, well-cut stone. I had a stone keep and I intended to make the gatehouse of stone. As we rode back, I explained to Roger and Wilfred what I planned to do. "In addition, we will make the bridges across our ditches so that they can be raised. It will, in effect, make a double gate. Our ditches can also be deepened. I want to make it hard for an enemy to get close to our walls." When the wagons had been loaded, I had examined the Roman ditches. Although eroded over time and over-grown with vegetation you could still see the shape. Ours were better than they had been but they could be improved even more.

Alice had given birth in April and David of Amble now had a son. Rafe's sons had cleared land. The spring lambs on Cedric's farm meant that the women of Elsdon now had more work. They were happy working together. The captives had endured much together and it had bonded them. Had they been men I would have said that they were shield brothers. We did not take our goods to Morpeth market. Alan of Bellingham wanted to take them to the market at the New Castle where they would fetch a higher price. We were waiting until we had a wagonful.

It took until May to build the stone abutments for the gatehouse. The top was still made of wood but there was now a stone lintel over the gate. We had been lucky to find the lintel. John had gone wandering off to find stones to use for slingshot and he found a piece of stone sticking out of the ditch. When we excavated it, we found a perfectly preserved lintel. We had wood above it for now but the lintel meant we could add stone to the upper course of the wall. I joined my men to build. The only ones who did not toil were my patrols. They still rode to Otterburn each day.

The close proximity of my builders and the women meant that liaisons began to develop. It was the younger men and those women who had been barely wed when they had been taken.

Mary, mother of Dick, would never take another man. She had confided as much in me. She was older than the others anyway but she now lived for her son. He had been her youngest and was all that was left to her. She acted almost like a mother superior to the Yalesham widows. She kept the relationships under her watchful eye. I told my men that the women were to be treated well. I did not mind any marrying but it would be done properly under the watchful eye of Brother Paul.

We became almost isolated. It was the folk of Otterburn we knew for no other came near. It was almost as though we had leprosy or the plague. We no longer needed Morpeth market. We had our own grain and animals. The spring had been a bountiful one and many of our animals had birthed. Our small flock and herd had done better than most. They had had the advantage of the walls of Elsdon during the winter. It was Phillip the Priest, David of Amble and Rafe's sons who needed help and I gave each of them animals. It meant my herd and flock did not increase but I did not mind. My people prospered. I had been in the manor less than a year and yet we had achieved much already.

We had not heard from the Bishop for a month or so. I fretted a little about that and so Brother Paul rode to Durham. John and Matthew went with him. I made do with Dick as a servant. Mary was keen for the boys who had been captives to be kept busy and so they acted as servants to my warriors. It pleased all for the boys enjoyed the company of warriors. Rafe's daughters had duties at the farm now that their brothers had departed and so the young females worked in their place. My keep was cleaner and tidier. It was a comfortable life. The wound in my back had healed. It no longer caused me pain at night. Tam had repaired the hauberk so that it was even stronger than it had been. That and Matthew's new hide gambeson would keep me safer in battle. Of course, we knew not when war would come. Each day could bring the sound of alarm. Each day brought us closer to another confrontation with the Scottish clan who were our neighbours.

When Brother Paul returned, he brought with him the news that the Bishop of Durham was in London. That explained why he had not written to me of late. There appeared to be nothing sinister in the visit. Even better was the fact that John had been able to buy some metal for Tam. I had given him coin and the son of the smith knew how to buy metal. As summer began Elsdon was a happy place.

Chapter 11

It was the middle of June when we spied the column of men riding from the south. We had had so few visitors that their arrival stopped work in the castle and drew all eyes to the gate. It was the husband of my sister, Sir Robert, and he led twenty men into my castle. He dismounted and I embraced him. "This is a joyous meeting, Sir Robert." I looked up, "Where is Richard?"

He smiled, "You mean, Sir Richard. Your father knighted him." He handed his reins to a young warrior, "This is Edward, Sir Ralph's son." He looked up towards the keep. "You have been busy! This looks stronger now than when I was castellan here."

"What brings you here? Do not get me wrong, I am more than happy for you to visit but I know that you would not just abandon Isabelle. She is well?"

"She is and it was at her behest and your father's that I came here. I will become a father again in less than six months and Thomas has shown me that is a busy time."

I led him up the path to the bridge into my castle. "And my father?"

His face fell a little. "He would have come, in fact, we planned for him to be with us but he is hurt." My heart sank. My father was a rock. He could not die. Robert saw my face, "He fell from his horse while out hunting. He broke his leg. It was well set by your father's doctor, Erasmus of Ghent. He will recover but he is no longer a young man. He will limp. He is like an angry bear. Your mother is at her wit's end. Sir Thomas has ever been active and now this forced idleness does not sit well. Henry

Samuel and he play chess. That is the only diversion which calms him. Your nephew has grown."

We passed through my gate, "I took stone from the Roman fort north of here. The men my father sent were put to good use. We rescued the captives and did not lose a man."

Sir Robert waved a hand towards the lower bailey where the men he had brought were unsaddling their mounts. "Your father has secured six archers and four men at arms for you."

"That is good but I am not sure that I can afford them."

"They are paid for a year. At the end of that time, if you cannot afford them, then they are happy to return to Stockton. Your father plans for the future." He lowered his voice, "The King has a marriage which is close to being arranged. Eleanor of Provence will be his bride. It strengthens the King's position in Gascony. Your father is certain that the King will try to retake his lost lands and that the King will call upon the knights and men of Cleveland to fight. The wedding will not be for a year or two. The maid is but eleven years old. The King plans for the future."

I was relieved, "Then all is well. How long can you stay?"

"Not above a month." We had entered my keep and I saw the memories flooding back, Sir Robert's face looked pained. He turned to look at me. "You have made it homely. She would have liked that." He took off his cloak and handed it to his squire. "Take this, Edward and then go to see to my horse."

I knew he wanted to speak, "Matthew, take John and fetch us wine, bread and cheese, then leave us alone. Ask Mistress Anne to prepare us food and we will need your chamber emptying for Sir Robert and his squire. You shall share my chamber."

"Aye lord."

We sat. One of the tasks John had completed was to smooth the roughly hewn furniture which had so offended Sir Eustace. My guests no longer risked splinters in the buttocks!

"I came, William, to exorcise my demons. I have lost sleep thinking about how I abandoned these good people. When you were appointed it happened so suddenly that I had little time to dwell on it. My wife has been woken by my nightmares. The news of the attacks by the Scots, the loss of Walther of Coxold all made me unwell. It was Isabelle suggested I come with the men. She is right. Already I feel better for I can see the changes you have wrought. You are no longer the callow youth I first met. I see steel in your eyes and confidence oozes from you. I will have to speak to Rafe and the other farmers. They need to know why I left them."

I nodded. Matthew and John returned with the refreshments. "We will go and move our gear, lord. Mistress Anne says there is a deer ready to be butchered. Garth Red Arrow hunted it three weeks since. It is ripe for eating."

"Thank you." I poured the wine and, after sipping it to make certain that they had brought my best wine, I cut a hunk of oat bread and cheese. "Know you, Robert, that the farmers did not blame you. Rafe told me that had his wife been the one killed then he would be dead for he would have gone to the land of the Scots and tried to kill all of them!"

"He is a strong one. I know that but I have to look them in their eyes and tell them myself." He smiled as he quaffed half of the beaker of wine, "You do not mind my presence?"

I laughed, "I am delighted! It will be good company. I am just saying that you need not do this."

"And Sir James?"

"He is ready to…" I shrugged, "I know not what he is ready to do but I know that he is weary. He asked his nephew to take over the manor. He refused."

"Sad. As I recall Sir James has a small manor on the south bank of the Tyne. I am guessing that he would like to retire there. This is a bleak place for one who has lost his family." I knew he was talking about himself.

I told him all that had happened and he gave me the news from the valley. "My brother seeks a manor but I have told him to be patient. He is young. I think he sees your success and envies you."

"Success?"

"You have done, in less than a year, that which we could not do. You have kept your land safe. More, it has prospered. I have never seen the fells with so many grazing animals."

"Perhaps you are right. I just try to make decisions the way my father would." I told him of my encounter with Sir Eustace and my fears.

The Bloody Border

He laughed, "You are your father's son. Only the son of Sir Thomas would challenge an older knight! I knew not Sir Eustace. He came after I had left. Sir Ranulf I knew."

"It is now just Sir James and myself who guard this bloody border and it is, indeed, a perilous task. The men you bring are a godsend. The Scots have been quiet for these last months. They will seek vengeance."

The small feast was a fine one. The men at arms and archers ate in the warrior hall and Alan of Bellingham and Brother Paul joined me and Sir Robert in my keep. It was as though we had been in a closed room and suddenly, we had let in light. Our world had been the handful of miles to the Scottish border and now we heard news from far and wide.

The next day, while the new men became acquainted and continued to improve my walls, we went with Sir Robert and his men. We rode first to Otterburn, where we met Sir James. Afterwards, Sir Robert said he was shocked at the changes time had wrought. For his part, Sir James was delighted to see my brother in law. As we drank wine he said, "I fear the Bishop of Durham is ignoring my pleas, Sir William. My nephew has gone south. He has been promised a manor close to Stratford. His wife does not like it in the north There is little likelihood of a replacement for me. This will be where I will end my days. It is a shame. I have a small manor I have barely seen. I thought to end my days learning how to fish. It seems God and the King have determined otherwise,"

When we left the old man both Sir Robert and I were in a reflective mood. We stopped at the Roman fort and the sight of the place where Walther of Coxold had died did nothing to improve it. The next day Sir Robert asked permission to visit with the farmers. He asked to do it alone. I was more than happy for him to do so for I had yet to properly greet my new archers and men at arms.

The men at arms were all foreigners. By that, I mean that they had served abroad rather than in England. They had all been on crusade in the Baltic. They had served Jarl Berger. He had been my father's friend. The four of them just sought employment. Kurt the Swabian, Jean of Landvielle, Eric the Dane, Gilles the Frank were all grizzled veterans. Their arms and armour showed that they had been fighting for their whole lives. These were men who knew how to fight. I was pleased to have them but I worried that I would not be able to afford them and they would leave me when the money ran out,

The archers had come to my father because he had let it be known in York and Lincoln that he sought archers. Dewey of Abergele was from Wales. Ged Strongbow and Adam Green Arrow were father and son. Jack son of Jack, Alf Broad Shoulders and Tim son of Tom had served in the garrison at Lincoln. The difference between these men and the ones who were already here was experience. The ten men had served in wars from the Baltic to Wales. They would be good additions to my men and now meant I could afford to leave a couple behind when I went on patrol.

Sir Robert spent three days travelling my manor and spending time with those he had known. His face, when he returned, showed that it had been worthwhile. The ghosts of the past had been laid to rest. I had not hunted for some time and so the first day after Sir Robert's visit with my farmers, we took our squires and my page to go hunting. I took Garth Red Arrow with me for he was not only my best archer he was also the one who knew my forests better than any. The day we rode was an overcast day. It was the first day of July when we left my castle to ride north and east. Garth had hunted to the north and west. Thus far we had not ventured into these woods save to look for signs of bandits. We had bows with us. Matthew was more confident with a bow than a spear and his broad shoulders meant he could pull a war bow.

When we found sign of deer we dismounted and tethered our horses. Four of us had bows and John had his sling and a short spear. We followed the tracks as they first climbed up the game trail and then descended towards the water. We knew they were fresh tracks from the dung. Garth had brought us so that the smell of the deer came towards us. The five of us were all silent. Had we had more men then we might have been heard. We tracked them for what seemed like miles and then I spied, not far below us, a flash of red. It was a deer. Garth had already seen them and he nocked an arrow. He would only release if we missed. The day was a day for lords and their squires to hunt.

The trees were pine. There were needles on the ground and so we stepped carefully. Our squires flanked us and Garth and John followed. I saw that it was a small herd. The male had fine antlers. We would not hunt him. We would come again after the rut when there were damaged and injured stags. Our hunt then would make the herd stronger. I saw the hind I would hit. She was favouring one leg and she had no fawns about her. Timing was all. I saw the stag raise his head and sniff the air. I drew back on my arrow. Even as I released the stag took off with the herd behind. I heard three other arrows as they flew towards other targets. Edward's arrow had hit a young deer in the rump. It was not a killing blow. Then a red-fletched arrow hurtled through the air and struck it in the neck.

Matthew had sent an arrow at my hind and it died quickly. We had to follow Sir Robert's kill. We found it six hundred paces from us. It was dead. We slung the deer over our sumpters and headed back. We were all in good humour. Three deer would feed the castle for a week or more. The hides could be tanned and used. The hooves could be used to make glue. Bones could be carved. Nothing would be wasted. If we had to then we could salt and preserve the meat. We had plenty and we would eat it fresh.

When we reached the castle, Garth quickly gutted the animals. The heart, liver and kidneys were put to one side and the rest fed to our dogs and hounds. We could have hunted with dogs. It would have been quicker but I preferred the challenge of man against animal. Garth organised the archers to skin and butcher the beasts while we went to wash and change. It had been a good day. You learned a great deal about men when they hunted with you. Edward was hasty while Matthew was steady. Sometimes you needed a squire or a knight who was hasty for it normally meant that they were fearless. I preferred one like Matthew, steady. We had arrived back in the late afternoon. The nights were almost non-existent. The overcast day had not produced rain but we would be denied a sunset.

While we waited for the food to be prepared, we took a stroll around my fighting platform. To the northeast, close to where we had hunted, I saw rain was falling. Sir Robert pointed to it, "We were fortunate. Rain would have spoiled the hunt."

The Bloody Border

"Indeed. God smiled upon us."

We walked around my walls until we faced north-west. I saw a thin column of smoke rising in the distance. Sir Robert said, "That will be Sir James' manor. I wonder what he is burning?"

"He has moorland there, perhaps he is burning that although it is normal to do so in August. There will still be nesting birds." I turned and pointed to the structure we were building close to the kitchens. "We are building a dovecot. We will have eggs and doves during the winter."

"You have thought of things here which will make this a good place to live. You should seek a wife."

"You were lucky, Sir Robert. You found my sister. I have seen none who would be suitable since we came here. I will wait."

"If I am a lesson to anyone it is to seize the moment. Do not tarry. Be as Edward here, be hasty. This is not the time to put off something which may never come."

It was my afternoon patrol who brought us the dire news. Harold Hart and Ralph of Raby galloped in even as the smell of cooking venison wafted towards us, "My lord, Otterburn is under attack. The houses are on fire and the tower is surrounded."

I wasted not a moment. "You and Ralph stay here. Matthew, have the men armed and ready to ride. Let us pray that we are not too late."

Sir Robert turned as he hurried to change into his hauberk, "At least you have twelve more men this time."

"Aye, it is almost as though you were sent here for just such a purpose." I looked to John, "You stay here too but first warn Alan of Bellingham, Brother Paul, Rafe and the rest of the villagers."

By the time we reached my horse, the men were all ready. Harold had told the men my news. My original men all knew old Sir James and his men. This would be personal. I mounted Eagle. Matthew handed me my spear. "Do I need the standard, lord?"

"No, Matthew, today you fight." I wasted no time and spurred my courser through the gates. We still had about three hours of good daylight left. I wondered if the plan had been to take Otterburn and then attack us in the early hours. From now on we would need night sentries and not just rely on the dogs and hounds. We did not need scouts out. When we crested Monk Ridge, we would see the tower. It would be laid out below us. It took less than an hour to reach the ridge for we rode hard. Even as we reached the top, I saw the kindling around the base of the tower begin to burn. I saw that there had to be almost eighty men attacking it. The smoke from the burning houses drifted north and west. That was the smoke we had seen. There were bodies littering the riverside. Sir James and his men had defended themselves.

"Garth, take the archers to the west of the river. Use the river for defence. Harass them. The rest of you we fight in a line the width of the road! For King Henry, England and for James!" I lowered my visor and hefted my spear. I spurred Eagle.

We were six hundred paces from them and it was all downhill. Sir Robert and I were in the centre and we were flanked by four of Sir Robert's men. I knew that Roger Two Swords and my men would take offence at that. I was his lord and he wanted our men protecting me. The Scots saw and heard us when we were three hundred paces from them. None were mounted. The fire was licking the walls of the tower and smoke poured across towards the river. It had helped to hide us. When we were spied the Scots ran for their horses. The ground flattened out when we were two hundred paces away and I spurred Eagle again. Sir Robert kept pace with me and we lowered our spears together. I heard cries from my left. My archers were killing the enemy.

The smoke would make it harder for us. A figure loomed up out of the smoke. I instinctively rammed my spear and it caught him in the shoulder. Blood spurted and I twisted the spear to free it. A Scot lunged at me from my right. Sir Robert's spear punched forward and tore through the man's cheek. A sudden gust of wind flurried the smoke away and I saw that the Scots were trying to organise a shield wall. As Garth and my archers were sending arrows into their unprotected right sides it was difficult for them. My spear flashed forward above the shields of the nearest two warriors. It struck one in the chest but the other used his sword to hack off the head of the spear. One of Sir Robert's sergeants fell from his horse as an axe-wielding Scot hacked at him. Drawing my sword, I made my horse rear. The warrior whose sword had taken my spearhead had his skull caved in by my horse's hooves.

The shambles of a shield wall had bought enough time for some of the Scots to mount. I recognised Sir Duncan and as the knight close by him was wearing the same livery I took that to be his father, Sir Malcolm. There were ten mounted men in total. I pointed my sword at Sir Duncan and shouted, "I promised you death the next time you were in England. Today is the day you die."

I spurred Eagle. This was now a mêlée. There was no longer any order to it. We had broken their wall but the battle now ebbed and flowed around us. If we had not had the support of our archers then things might have gone ill but Garth and my archers were less than forty paces from the Scots. They picked their targets. I saw a red-fletched arrow knock Sir Malcolm's squire from his mount. Roger Two Swords had the freedom to ride through Sir Robert's men. He used neither a shield nor a spear. Instead, he laid about him with his two swords. The Scots had never seen anything like it.

I rode at Sir Duncan aware that Sir Robert and his squire were on my right and Matthew on my left. This would be Matthew's first serious battle and I prayed it would not be his last. Sir Duncan did not have a spear. As he turned his horse to come at me, I worked out how I would end this. I held my shield horizontally across my cantle and my sword behind me. I intended to let him have the first blow. It was a calculated risk. When I had fought him before he had not struck me as a strong warrior. He was a clever one. Perhaps he had learned his fighting in tourneys. I had told him I would kill him and he would put all of his effort into the first blow. That suited me. As we neared each other, he swung his sword from behind him in a long sweep intended to take my head. He saw an unguarded shoulder. I flicked up my shield and his blade made my arm shiver. I quickly stood in my stirrups and brought my sword down towards his head. He could not react quickly enough and my blade hit his helmet. I dented it. His arming cap and coif had taken some of the force from the blow but I had driven the helmet lower down so that it was now over his eyes. I punched him with the side of my shield. I broke his nose. I pulled back my arm and lunged towards his open mouth. He was disorientated and he did not move.

I heard his father scream, "No!" My sword ignored him and the young knight, dying from a mortal blow, fell backwards from his saddle. His father came at me. Sir Robert, Edward and Matthew were fighting three men at arms. I would fight the old lord. He had an axe. His open helmet was a mask of hatred, "You will die, you English bastard! I will gut you like a fish!" He spurred his destrier at me. He was swinging his axe as he came. I spurred Eagle and my horse raced beyond the swinging axe. He struck fresh air and I wheeled Eagle to come behind him He had unbalanced himself and his axe was on the same side as his shield. I hacked into his side. He had good mail and it held but I bent links and hurt him. He swung his axe instinctively at the blow but I had passed him and I turned Eagle. I rode at his right. He would not be able to use his shield for protection. He pulled his arm back to swing at me. As he swung I aimed my sword at his axe and hacked down. I drove the axe down and watched it gouge a hole in his chaussee. He wounded himself with his own axe. A piece of wood was chipped from the axe.

"Surrender or you will suffer the same fate as your son."

"We outnumber you!"

At that moment four arrows flew and three of his men, rushing to his aid, fell. "But for how long?" His leg was bleeding and I had hurt his back. I swung backhanded at him. He tried to block it again with his axe and this time my blade hacked it in two. He was weaponless. I pricked his cheek with my sword, "I ask again, will you surrender or shall I send you to meet your son?"

Many of his men seeing that I had my sword close to his face, decided that the battle was over and they turned to run. Sir Robert and the rest of my men continued to fight. Matthew slew Sir Duncan's squire.

"These men will continue to die until you surrender. They are brave men and deserve a leader with courage."

"You are the devil incarnate! I yield."

"Louder so that men may hear you."

"I yield!". Those that had not fled threw down their weapons.

I turned and shouted, "Garth, have our men douse the flames!"

The Bloody Border

I turned to look at the battlefield. Four of Sir Robert's men had died. They had all been in the fore. Matthew had escaped injury as had most of my men. I saw a couple of the newer warriors nursing wounds but all stood and looked to be whole. The same could not be said for the tower of Otterburn and its occupants. It looked like they had used water to douse the flames while we had been fighting and when Garth and my men began to use the river water then the flames started to die.

"Matthew, watch our prisoners. Sir Robert, I thank you."

He shook his head, "The victory belongs to you and your men."

I dismounted and handed my reins to Matthew. "Let us go and see how Sir James fares."

Even as we approached the tower, I saw the door open and the last men at arms of the old knight carrying his body from the tower. I shook my head, "He should have enjoyed a quiet life on the Tyne fishing." Brother Abelard was with him. The priest had his arm in a sling and a bandage on his head. "What happened, Brother Abelard?"

"They came just after dawn. It was Sir James' habit to walk to the river and back before dawn. It was he who spied them. I was with him for we liked to pray facing east and the rising sun. It was his warning that saved those who now emerge from the tower. We saw them and he slew four while his people ran into the tower. Six of his men managed to join us and the eight of us fought." I cocked my head to one side. "Aye, lord, I fought. I could not stand by and watch my old friend die alone. His men were slain and then he was struck a mortal blow. I barely managed to get him inside the tower before the Scots were upon us. We barred the gate."

I nodded, "You had no time to send for help."

"No, lord. We barely managed to get inside the tower. At first Sir Malcolm and Sir Duncan tried to persuade Sir James to surrender. They said that people would be treated well. We both knew that to be a lie but Sir James kept them talking. It cost him his life for I could not tend to him properly. It was almost noon by the time they gave up and resumed their attack. Sir James died in the middle of the afternoon. He made me promise to hold out. He knew that you would come. He said you were the hope of the north." He shook his head, "How did he know that you would reach us?"

"He was an old warrior. He knew I would spy the smoke and wonder. He also knew that I sent a patrol here each day." I walked over to his body, "I promise you, old friend, that I will watch over your people until we have a new lord appointed by the Bishop of Durham."

It was too dark to return to our home. The buildings were too full of smoke for us to use. We camped out before the tower. We put the captured Scots to collect the bodies. The Scottish dead would be burned and we would have the folk of Otterburn buried in the churchyard. Brother Abelard tended to the wounded. He was not gentle with Sir Malcolm.

The next morning, we buried our dead before we burned the Scots. Once more I was angry. Sir Duncan and his father should have attacked me. There would have been more honour in that. I spoke with Sir Robert. "I would have you take Sir Malcolm and his men back to my castle. I will escort the remaining squire to the border and ensure that none of them remain on the soil of England."

"I will do so."

We walked to the prisoners. "Sir Malcolm, choose a man to ride for your ransom."

"You took all the coin we had when you captured my son!"

I nodded, "Then we shall ride back to your manor and take your goods as recompense. I am certain the captives we recovered would appreciate a more comfortable life."

He shook his head, "You are a fool! They are peasants! Their husbands were villeins! Why do you worry about them?"

I was becoming angry again. "Sir Robert, we will ride and take all that there is to take from Sir Malcolm's hall."

"Wait! My cousin the Earl of Fife may pay my ransom."

"Then choose your man to take the message."

He waved over, not a squire but a scarred veteran. "Angus, ride to the Mormaer of Fife and tell him my predicament." He suddenly seemed to find his position amusing. "Aye, go to my cousin and the wrath of God will descend upon Sir William."

"Wait, Angus. Tell the Earl that he sends coin to the value of two hundred pounds in silver. If warriors come then I will hang

Sir Malcolm from my tower. This family is treacherous! Do you understand?"

"Aye lord." He turned to Sir Malcolm, "Dinna worry, my lord, we will fetch the man's silver and then we will raise an army and wipe them off the face of the earth!"

"I admire your courage, Angus, but leave now without saying another word or it will be the worse for both of you."

When he had gone, Sir Robert led the prisoners down the road. With my archers before us, we rode to the border. We passed a dozen men who had succumbed to their wounds on their flight back to their homes. There was no sign of armed men and I led my warriors back to Otterburn. We would stay for a couple of days and repair the damage.

Chapter 12

In the end, we stayed for three days. Brother Abelard took charge. Thanks to Sir James the damage to the manor had not been critical. The men who farmed there still lived and, thanks to his staunch defence, the Scots had not raided the farms which lay close by. We had been lucky but I would need to send a message to the Bishop. This was not over.

When we reached my castle, I was greeted by Sir Robert, Brother Paul and Alan of Bellingham. All were keen to know what were my plans. I know that they looked at me and saw someone who was too young for such a weight upon his shoulders. They were wrong for the death of my brother in York had helped me to grow up far quicker than most young men. Martin Longsword was a reminder of that day in York. It had changed us both. I had watched my father and when I had followed his banner I had learned. I suppose I was like him after Arsuf. I had to trust my own judgement and I did.

"We have guests for a while, Brother Paul. While Alan of Bellingham sees to their spiritual needs you will have to ensure that they do not eat as they would in their own castle. We have hard times ahead."

Brother Paul smiled, "And you, lord, how are your spiritual needs? You are now the last bastion between the heartland of the north and any bandits and brigands who choose to raid us."

I nodded. The priest had a good point. "I pray that the Bishop will do something about that. Until the ransom is paid, we have a hostage. I told the Scots that if they attempted any sort of military action, I would hang their lord and I meant it." I saw the shock on the faces of Alan and Brother Paul. I turned to Sir Robert, "Sir Robert, I thank you for your help in this matter. You have lost men and I cannot recompense you for them."

"They died as warriors, Sir William. Redmarshal is a safe manor. They are less necessary there."

"I would have you leave and report all to the Bishop."

"He may still be in London."

"Then speak to the Dean. We need a lord in Otterburn. I know that Sir James had the foresight to try to plan for his succession but it did not happen that way."

"Aye, William, I will and your father? Do you wish his aid yet?"

"My father has been ill and if I send to him each time I am under attack then I might as well build a chamber for him here in my castle. No, I will find a way to deal with this threat. What I will do is ride myself to Morpeth. Sir Ranulf may find this new threat a reason to stir himself."

Despite the fact that we had just returned I had my two-man patrols restarted immediately. The men who rode forth now knew the size of their task. They also knew the land better. Garth Red Arrow suggested that they should use more circumspect routes around Otterburn in case there were watchers. They had known when my men would arrive. Sir James' early morning ritual had foiled their plans. We could not rely on such luck again. Sir Robert and his men left and my castle felt emptier. It had been good to have a brother in arms with me.

Alan of Bellingham had much to occupy him, even without the recent attack. August was almost upon us. The next few months would be his busiest. With the additional mouths to feed the Reeve of Elsdon would work from dawn to dusk and often beyond. Brother Paul waited until I had spoken with my Reeve before he approached. Sir Robert and his men were barely five miles down the road when we returned to the life of a border fort. "Sir Malcolm's wound was a bad one. He will not walk properly again." It was not a critical statement.

"You know it was inflicted by himself?" He nodded. "Some might call that divine intervention."

"God is a forgiving God. Sir Malcolm's sins will be weighed." He made the sign of the cross. "I had to stitch it and he will not be able to be moved for a week at the very least."

"I doubt that the ransom or attackers will be here before then. He has sent to the Earl of Fife and the journey to Fife will take more than ten days. And the others?"

"Minor wounds."

"Good then, Sir Malcolm apart, I will have them work on our defences. We need another hall building in the upper bailey." I could see the look of disapproval on the priest's face. "Brother Paul, when I rescued the captives, reprisals were inevitable. These men we captured are little better than brigands. I have already shown them generosity by allowing them to live. We begin the work on the morrow. Alan of Bellingham has too much work already. I will supervise this building."

I sought out Tam the Smith. We had brought back captured and damaged weapons from the battle. "Tam, we will need weapons. Do you know how to make caltrops?"

"Aye, my lord."

"Then make a couple of hundred. If we are attacked, we will seed the outside of the walls with them. Make spear and arrowheads. We have a period of grace."

He nodded, "You are doing the right thing, lord. When we heard what happened, Mary and the others you rescued sang your praises. They endured much at the hands of the Baron's clan. They are happy that you are their lord. They have confidence in you."

I hoped it was not misplaced faith.

We now had more men who could work. The ones who had been injured apart I would have all the rest helping us to build the new hall. It was after noon when I gathered them in my upper bailey. "Tomorrow we build a new hall. I intend to use the Scots to labour for us. We will gather stones from the beck. I will attach the new hall to the keep and it will go as far as the stable. The three buildings will be joined and will be easier to defend. If we are attacked then this will be the last refuge for our people. For that reason, I want as much stone in it as we can manage. We will use wattle and daub where we have to. I intend to have the Scottish prisoners dig a ditch all the way around the two

The Bloody Border

buildings. We will defend the outer wall and if that falls retreat and defend the upper bailey. If those walls fall then we have the keep. I hope that by then we will have bled an attacker dry!"

One of the new men, Kurt the Swabian asked, "Are you so sure that they will come again? If they attack here it is tantamount to an invasion of England. Will King Henry countenance such an act?"

"The King is an ocean away and is distracted by negotiations for a bride and alliances. He may well be angry and react but unless we prepare then all he will find will be the burnt-out remains of Elsdon. What you may not know is that there is bad blood between my father and the Earl of Fife. Sir Malcolm must have known that when he sent to him for ransom. The Earl of Fife claims the land upon which we live." I waved a hand, "We build. Tomorrow we hew trees and collect stones. Roger Two Swords I need you and four men to help me to supervise the Scots. They can dig the ditch and the holes for the foundations."

As I expected, when I gathered the prisoners together the next day, they were not happy about the work they would have to do. Roger had chosen my biggest warriors, Ralph of Raby and Harold of Hart amongst them as guards. I nodded as the Scots complained. "You are here because you lost. You are brigands and bandits. This is your choice: work and live or refuse and I hang you. It is that simple. If I am to feed you then you will earn your bread. Roger fetch me a rope." Roger went to the keep. I put my hands on my hips. "The shovels are there and the line you are to dig is marked. Either pick up a shovel or stand by the keep so that we may hang you." When Roger returned with the rope they stood and went to the shovels. They worked.

After two days we had made enough progress for me to ride to Morpeth. It coincided with Alan of Bellingham's trip to sell the woven wool my women had made. Although we had wanted to sell it at the New Castle, we could not afford to leave Elsdon for too long. Matthew, John and I escorted him. John drove the wagon. He had grown a great deal since he had left his father's smithy. Matthew, too, now had to shave each day and his already broad chest showed that he would be a warrior who would be as big as Sir Peter. I smiled, he would need more armour than most men. I was aware that I had filled out too. Mary and the women

The Bloody Border

cooked hearty meals. They cooked plain and wholesome fare and I benefitted.

Morpeth was even more prosperous than it had been. I saw that Sir Ranulf was making his wooden walls and hall into stone ones. Was this a sign of prosperity or was it a sign that, like me, he feared war? While John and Alan of Bellingham visited the market, I went to the castle with Matthew. It soon became clear that the new castle was one for comfort and not for war. Sir Ranulf had not heard of the death of Sir James. There was no reason why he should. I had the prisoners and none had fled to his manor.

His face was worried when I told him. "Does the King know?"

"I told the Bishop and the King is still in Gascony."

"I liked old Sir James. He was a friend of my father's."

That friendship had not helped Sir James. "I think that the Scots are not yet done with us." I knew not if I should trust Sir Ranulf and so I was circumspect. "I have heard rumours of conspiracies, Sir Ranulf. There are men, it seems, who conspire with the Scots."

Surprisingly he nodded, "I have heard such rumours." He flashed me an angry look. "You cannot think me a conspirator!"

"Lord, I am young and have been in this county for less than a year. The only lord I knew well enough to trust completely lies dead. All I do know is that the only ones who have bled for this land are from the manors of Elsdon and Otterburn."

"I was ill." He must have realised how pathetic his excuse sounded. "Now I am well. If you need my help again then send a man to me. I will come. I swear, Sir William, that I am a loyal baron!"

I was relieved, "I thank you, lord, and when the Bishop appoints another lord, I will tell you."

"And I will visit with the Sherriff. He needs to know of the dangers, too."

With a wagon full of all that we could not produce ourselves we set off home. I was not as perceptive as my father. I could not always detect deception but I thought that Sir Ranulf had been honest with me. He might err on the indolent side and like his comfort more than his duty but I did not see him as a traitor. Sir Eustace, on the other hand, was a dissembler!

By the time we reached the last day of July, there had still been no word from Scotland. Had they abandoned Lord Malcolm? We now had a hall which linked the stables to my keep. We left both empty. Firstly, the wattle and daub would need to dry out and secondly, we would not need them until we were attacked. I was pleased with it. We had gathered enough stones to give a wall which rose, above the ground, the length of a man's leg. It was a double wall and filled with river pebbles and sand. Above it rose the wattle and daub. The roof was covered in the turf we had dug to make the ditch. The ditch was just six feet deep. It was only intended to slow an attacker down and make it hard for them to use a ram. In the bottom were caltrops. The inconvenience was minor. We had a single bridge to gain entry to the keep and hall. In times of danger, we could seed the ditch with stakes and spikes. They would be added to the caltrops already there.

The completion of the hall coincided with the news that Stephen Bodkin Blade and Margaret of Yeavering were to be wed. She was one of the Yalesham widows. She and Stephen were of an age and seemed well suited. The wedding seemed to have been sent by God for it was a joyous time. The widows and my men were, symbolically, joined. I gave the couple a dowry of two pounds and a piece of land between Harry Sourface's farm and Rafe's son. It was big enough for a house and enough land to grow vegetables and raise fowl. Margaret had a small son and daughter. The couple was happy with the gift. The wedding celebrations were joyous. I watched the Scots, along with Matthew, John, Roger and Garth. For the rest, it was like May Day. We had good ale brewed and there was dancing. Alan of Bellingham and Brother Paul looked, for all the world, like a couple of fathers whose children had wed.

We allowed the captives to watch from the upper bailey. Sir Malcolm had been carried from the keep by two of his men. He looked, sourly, at the dancing and shook his head, "Make the most of this for when my cousin pays my ransom, we will build an army to make this a wasteland." It was an empty, idle threat.

The Bloody Border

In the two battles and the raid, we had slain his best warriors. If there was a threat then it came from Fife.

"Your cousin does not think much of you, my lord. It has been three weeks and more since we took you and there has been no messenger." If the knight wished to use his tongue like a sword then I would answer him.

I saw doubt flicker across his face then he shook his head, "It matters not how long it takes just so that I am returned to my manor."

I went close to him. "You have lost a son and you have lost men. Have you not learned your lesson? You cannot defeat us. My men are better armed, mailed and trained than the rabble you lead." I saw a couple of his men bridle at the insult. "Oh, they are brave enough but at the end of the day, it is skill which wins battles and not raw courage. King William the Lion discovered that."

My words silenced them for they knew it to be true.

Three days into August my patrol galloped in to bring word that Scots were coming. "It is the Earl of Fife, lord. I recognise his banner."

"Have they come for war?"

Idraf shook his head, "If they have then they are ill-prepared. They have just twenty men and a wagon. They are all mounted."

"Do they have spare horses?"

He shook his head, "No, lord, why, is that important?"

"They must have spies who have observed us and know that Sir Malcolm cannot ride. We will need to have men watching the woods close by." I berated myself. It was an oversight. It might not hurt us but it was a lesson learned.

I sent for Roger Two Swords, "Have the prisoners brought to the lower bailey. Ask Garth to man the walls with his archers. There should be no tricks but this will ensure that there are none."

The Earl of Fife had become older and a little fatter since the last time I had seen him. Sir Ranulf of Morpeth had told me that the Earl was now a close confederate of the Scottish King. Some, however, saw him as a rival for the throne. If he could wrest Northumberland from the hated English then it would ease his passage to the crown.

I was mailed as were my squire and my men. We outnumbered the Earl and his guards. I saw his eyes flicker to the walls and my archers. I did not think he had anything planned. My preparations guaranteed that he would not attempt anything.

He dismounted and slipped his coif from his head. He looked over to Sir Malcolm who was supported by two of his men. "I hope my cousin has been treated well."

"He has been treated better than the captives you hold in Fife, my lord."

He scowled at me, "The wound has been treated?"

"Aye, and it is healed. Ironic eh, the wound was caused by the knight's own axe. Perhaps God guided it."

I could see that he was becoming angry for I had an answer to all that he said. "The ransom is in the wagon."

"Roger Two Swords."

"Aye lord. Come on lads."

The Earl looked down at me. I think he thought being on the back of a horse made him superior. It did not. "You should not have raided my cousin's hall."

"And he should not have razed Yalesham to the ground. This tit-for-tat will not end well for you, my lord. King Henry made it clear that there should be no further raids. I was there at Norham when your King said so. My father is surety for that peace. You do not want my father to head north, do you, my lord?"

He came closer to me. His face was infused and reddened. He did not like to be reminded of the defeat, "Sir James is no more. Perhaps we have had enough of this tit-for-tat. Perhaps we wish it ended. Your King is in Gascony and cares not about the fate of a bachelor knight and my King, well, let us say that he and I have an understanding. It may be that tit for tat is not enough. If you have a canker then the best thing to do is to cut it out!"

"You threaten me?"

"Let us call it a friendly warning. This land is harsh and unforgiving. I am certain that your father can find a better manor in the rich valley of the Tees. Forget Elsdon. Forget its people. Enjoy your life. I paid the full ransom. Use it well."

"And I shall!"

The Bloody Border

We watched the wagon, now filled with Sir Malcolm and his men as they passed through my gatehouse. The baron shook his fist at me. It was an impotent gesture.

"Alan of Bellingham. Take twenty pounds from the ransom and divide it amongst my men. Take another ten and give it to the Yalesham widows."

"That is generous, lord, they will not expect it."

"Then they should for they have all suffered. All helped in this victory. Bury the rest in the cellar. We will save it for time of need."

The next day I had my men scour the woods which lay close to my land. We found signs of intruders. We had been watched. It was one of my new archers, Adam Green Arrow, who came up with the solution. "Lord, I have seen plentiful signs of rabbits in these woods. Let your archers come each day to hunt them. It will be good practise for us and will let us watch for the enemy. If we simply patrol then they will know where we ride. They must know of our patrol to Otterburn each day."

He was right. We began the change immediately. I also went with six men at arms to Otterburn. They had recovered from the attack. The damaged buildings had been repaired.

I spoke with Brother Abelard, "Is there aught you need?"

"You mean apart from a lord of the manor, lord? It may be that we need grain when winter comes. The harvest will be a good one but there are tares and weeds which should not be there. We were building when we should have been weeding."

"You need not fear. I will not see you go hungry."

"And a new lord? Elsdon had to wait years for you. I fear that the people would drift south if there was no lord to protect them. Byrness and Yalesham still lie empty."

"That I cannot answer. It is a few weeks since I sent the message. Who knows?"

The end of August was when we began to harvest our first crops. It was a time for vigilance. With my archers scouring the woods my men at arms and I rode the roads. We went as far north as Otterburn, northeast to Rothbury and south-west to Bellingham. The ride to Rothbury was to warn Sir Eustace that we were being vigilant. That was the direction from which I feared danger.

The Bloody Border

It was at this time that Tam found he would be a father. I found out from John. It was not a surprise that the son of a smith and a blacksmith should get on. John, when he had time, often helped at the forge. In truth, John was now more of a squire than a page. With just the three of us, there was little need to wait at table. The three of us got on well. We had changed the sleeping accommodation so that I had my own chamber and the other two shared a chamber. We had a third one in case I had guests. When Sir Robert had been with us then the three squires had huddled together in the smallest room. We had also built a pair of garderobes. We built them on the fighting platform. In winter it was cold but if we had added one to our sleeping chamber then that would have made the sleeping chamber cold. I knew that if I married then I would need a kitchen closer to my keep but my new arrangements suited me. The heating stone by the fire kept our food warm. Anne was a clever woman.

It was at the start of September when we saw riders from the south. I hoped it was news from the Bishop but when my sentries reported that it was mailed men and a number of them at that then I had the garrison stand to. The direction of their approach did not suggest danger but it could always be a trick. I stood on my gatehouse peering south. It was Matthew who identified them, "It is my brother, Mark. That is the Earl! I do not recognise the knight next to him. His face is hidden by his coif."

I cared not. It was my father and I had not seen him for such a long time that my heart soared. "Stand down! Roger, ask Mistress Mary to prepare the new hall for guests." I turned to Garth, "Have we game?"

"We have rabbits aplenty, lord, and Alan Whitestreak took a fox yesterday. We have meat for a stew I think and there is still some venison from our hunt."

"Good."

I descended to the lower bailey. I saw that the other knight was Sir Richard. I was slightly disappointed. I had hoped that the Bishop had sent a new lord of the manor. My father dismounted next to me and handed his reins to Henry Samuel. My nephew had grown too!

My father embraced me, "Son, I am sorry that I was not able to come sooner."

I held him tightly and said, "Sir Robert told me about your illness. You are well now?"

"Aye, the leeches cured me." I knew that he did not mean it. He was making light of it. That was always my father's way. He could be dying and he would joke.

As I stepped back, I saw that he was greyer and leaner. He was not totally over it. "And you, young Sam, you have grown."

He grinned, "It is Henry now, Sir William! Soon I will be a squire and then a knight. I shall be Sir Henry then."

I tousled his head, "To me, nephew, you will always be Sam." I turned and spread my arms, "Come, gentlemen, we have accommodation newly built for you and we shall feast this night."

I walked with my father and Sir Richard. I turned to Sir Richard, "And I nearly forgot, congratulations, Sir Richard. Now, all that you need is a manor."

"I have one already!"

"Then I am doubly pleased. Where is it?"

He pointed north, "Otterburn. I am the new lord of Otterburn!"

The Bishop had, indeed, answered my prayers but was it another poisoned chalice? I turned to look at the men who followed us. Only four wore my father's livery. The rest wore the livery of Sir Richard. He had sixteen men with him. It was not enough but it was more than I had had when I had come, little more than a year ago.

Chapter 13

We had double cause for celebration. My father had brought some of the wine from La Flèche and we both ate and drank well. My mother had also sent clothes she had had made for me by her ladies as well as the food I enjoyed. I missed my mother. Once we had got over the pleasantries about the family, both of my sisters were with child again, we moved on to more serious matters. Sir Richard was keen to know what sort of problems he faced.

"There is a blood feud with the clan who live across the border. It was begun by their raid but I fear it will not end until they are destroyed." I told them of the visit by the Earl of Fife and his words to me.

My father shook his head, "I should have ended this the last time."

"Impossible, father. That would have necessitated riding through Scotland."

My father smiled, "We had just defeated the largest army they had. It was the right thing to do. The King had given me command and I should have used the power he gave me." He shook his head sadly, "I do not think he will give me such power again. I am afraid that we are pawns used by the King to his own ends."

Sir Richard said, "I do not understand. How are we used?"

"To me, the burning of Otterburn is enough evidence to allow the King to invade Scotland and to punish them. When King William was captured it was not just the treaty which was draconian, England almost bankrupted Scotland. The King's sister is married to Alexander. That fact means he needs a better reason to invade." He looked at me, "However, William, I am concerned. Your news about Sir Eustace is disturbing. Perhaps we will ride there in a few days' time. Let Sir Richard settle into his manor and then the three of us will introduce his new neighbour. Perhaps this old warhorse can annoy him enough to make him indiscreet."

The next day my men at arms escorted Sir Richard to his new home. I understood his need to be presented alone as the new lord of the manor. Brother Abelard would be happy and my men would be able to help my friend to settle in. My archers hunted and scouted in the woods and I walked with my father, our squires and our pages around my castle. He approved of all of the improvements but, as we stood on the fighting platform above the gates and viewed the lower bailey, he shook his head, "You are thinking of this as a castle such as Stockton."

"Not really but I like many of the features of Stockton castle."

"We are luckier there, my son. The Warlord built a castle as part of the town. The town wall makes ours a stronger castle. We have a bigger river. Your strength lies in the hill on which stands your keep and your two baileys. Use them."

"How?"

"You need to protect what you have. You have your smithy and your wool hall there already. What about your cattle? Your pigs? Your sheep?"

"They graze on the fells."

"And there they can be raided. You have good pasture by the river. You have cut down trees already. Pull the stumps and grass will grow. Build cow byres and pig pens inside the lower bailey. Put the animals out in the day and at night they will be secure. You have dogs here, good dogs. Use this space. Your warrior hall in the lower bailey is unnecessary. Build another one close to your keep. You have begun well. Take it to the extreme." He saw my worried look. "You have ransom. Use it! Buy stone!"

"Then I am here forever?"

"That is your choice. You can return to Stockton any time you wish although I have a feeling that you would not wish to leave these people until they had a strong lord and weaker enemies."

The Bloody Border

He knew me well, "You are right and we will begin when my men return."

We then rode the manor. My father knew only the main roads. I took him along greenways and hunter's trails. I showed him where we had found enemies. In short, I showed him a complete picture of my land.

That evening, as we dined, he put his palms together almost as though he was praying. Then he leaned back. "The four farms and the house in the village are not a problem. David of Amble can reach your castle walls when he hears danger. They can be in your castle walls as soon as an attack is detected. It is Cedric the Sheepman, Rafe's sons and Phillip the Priest who are at risk. You have to impress upon Cedric that if they are attacked, he makes his way here and leaves his sheep."

"He will be loath to do that. The sheep are his life."

"Then you must reassure him that you will make good his losses."

"That would be expensive!"

"Not if you take them from those who robbed you."

"You mean raid across the border?"

"The fact that you have not yet done so shows that you have honour but this is not about honour. Despite what kings might think or wish, this type of raiding has existed since before the Romans. While you are lord of the manor then you must be better at it than the Scots!"

"But what about the King? The Bishop?"

He laughed, "I defied King John and rid myself of an evil Bishop. Let me worry about that!" My father's confidence terrified me.

Three days later Sir Richard returned with my men at arms. He had ridden to the border and my men had shown him wherein the danger lay. My father gave him the same speech he had given to me. "And tomorrow we give a different message to the Scots. If you are right, William, then whatever we say on the morrow will be sent directly to the Scots. They wish to play a game? Let us show them that we are better at it!"

We did not take my archers. I left them hunting and scouring the woods. They had found tracks, two days since, and Garth Red Arrow was keen to hunt down the scouts. We rode with

The Bloody Border

banners and with polished helms. As my father said to me, we were making a statement. He was not only an earl but the leading earl of the north. Sir Eustace would have to defer to him. My father was the cleverest lord I knew. I watched him as we rode towards Rothbury, He was looking at every inch of the road as a potential battlefield. When he stopped us, which he frequently did, I said nothing but I knew he was assessing its potential for ambush. He knew my archers and how to use them well. He said nothing as we rode but I knew I would have a commentary when we returned home.

We halted two hundred paces from the castle. "A good position and a well-made castle."

Sir Richard asked, "Is that why we stopped, lord?"

"Partly but mainly to allow Sir Eustace to begin to panic and wonder why the Earl Marshal of the Northern Marches is paying him a visit. He will have quarters prepared and a feast. When we tell him that we cannot stay he will be put out. A small victory but a victory nonetheless."

We rode into the lower bailey. Sir Eustace, his wife and some knights awaited us, "Earl Thomas, this is an honour. Had we known we …"

My father gave him no chance to take charge of the conversation, "I have little time for the proprieties. We need to speak." He bowed, "Good day, my lady, I am sorry to have arrived unannounced. Next time I will write so that you can prepare properly." He smiled at her and then turned to Sir Eustace, "And now Sir Eustace, we need to have words!" His tone implied censure and I was glad that my coif hid my mouth. The illusion would have been ruined had they seen my grin. He strode towards the hall like a ship under full sail. Sir Eustace was shorter and struggled to keep up with him. When we reached the Great Hall, he stopped and waited. I was in awe of my father. I could see that he had forgotten more about strategy than I would ever know.

Sit Eustace said, "Wine for our guests. I pray you, Earl Marshal, please sit."

Richard and I flanked my father. He had told us to do so on the way to the castle. He sipped the wine. We did too. It was acceptable but my father wrinkled his nose and pushed the goblet away as though it was not good enough. He was playing a part. "Sir Eustace, there are many reasons for my presence. The first is to introduce the new Lord of Otterburn, Sir Richard."

Sir Eustace beamed, "If there is anything I can do, Sir Richard..."

My father went on to the offensive, "Then that would be a first! When my son sent to you for help to recover captives he was ignored. Is this the sort of support Sir Richard can expect?"

"No, no, Earl I..."

"Sir James of Otterburn died and his people could have followed him yet you squatted like some toad behind your walls while my son saved them! It is not good enough."

"I am sorry, my lord. I promise it will not happen again."

"You hold your manor not as my son does, through Durham but through the crown. It would be difficult for you, Sir Eustace, if I were to recommend to the King that he appoints a different lord."

The silky words slipped out so easily that Sir Eustace appeared not to notice them. When he did his face was a picture, "Earl! I beg of you! I will make amends."

My father leaned forward, "Baron, I have also heard that there is a conspiracy in the north to take Northumberland and give it to the Earl of Fife. What do you know about that!" The word '*you*' was emphasised.

The colour flooded from Sir Eustace's face. "You think I am a traitor?" My father said nothing. "It is a lie! Who is spreading this foul calumny?"

"If it was just one source, I would ignore it, Sir Eustace but, since I have been north of the Tyne, I have had many reports of the conspiracy. You can see how your recent inaction makes you look guilty. You may be innocent. For your sake and that of your family, I hope so but know that I will be gathering knights and barons. We will be riding north to make this border safe. If that means executing traitors as well as bandits then so be it." Silence fell in the hall. My father stood and smiled, "As I said, this is a brief visit although I shall be at Elsdon, Otterburn and Morpeth for at least a week. Feel free to speak to me if you hear any information about the conspiracy. I am certain that, if you are innocent, you will understand the need to find out the guilty parties… for all our sakes."

We left a stunned knight and his co-conspirators shocked to the very core by my father's words. We said nothing until we were at the col which led to our valley. We stopped and my father looked down the Coquet Valley towards Rothbury. "He is guilty. Your instincts were good ones. Now the question is what will he do? He can abandon his masters or tell them what we plan. We will soon discover if that is the case. We will find out in the next day or so."

I looked around. Padraig the Wanderer was no longer with us. He smiled at me.

Realisation dawned, "You left a watcher."

"Of course. It is time we took the offensive. So far the action has all been initiated by our enemies. It is time for us to grasp the nettle! Let us see what they are about." He smiled, "That has given me an appetite!"

It was late the next day when Padraig the Wanderer rode in. He dismounted and bowed to my father, "Sir Eustace rode to Jedburgh and then headed north. I saw a wagon with his wife and family. They headed south and east. Sir Eustace was neither stopped nor hindered despite that he rode with ten mailed men. Once it was clear that he was heading north I returned. I did right, did I not, Earl?

My father grinned and flicked a coin to his man at arms. "Of course!" After Padraig had gone, he turned to us, "So now we know. There will be an attack. If we had more men on whom we could rely we could attack first. We will have to endure an attack and then counterattack. I will leave on the morrow. I will do as I promised and visit, first with Sir Ranulf, and then the Sherriff. This should be just enough rope to hang Sir Eustace and to finally quash the ambitions of the Earl of Fife." My father saw the looks on our faces and he smiled and, as we finished off a jug of good wine, he explained his plan. At the end of it, I was happy, although it was clear we were bait.

While my father spoke to my people before he left, and Matthew spoke with Mark, I took Henry Samuel to one side, "It is an education with your grandfather, is it not?"

The Bloody Border

He nodded, "I play chess each day with him. When he was ill it was three times a day. I can never defeat him, even when he gives me a start and he seems to know what men think before they know themselves."

I nodded, "Be as a sponge, Sam, soak it all in. I am still in awe of him. I have been here for a year and yet he seems to know exactly what ought to be done. I feel safer, somehow, knowing that he is in the world."

"The injury he suffered was severe. He had badness in it. Father Harold heard his last confession. Grandmother feared he would not survive but he did and, I know not how, he is stronger now than he was." I nodded. "Uncle, be careful here. You live in a dangerous place. I have spoken to John and I know how close you came to death."

"Yet each time I fight and survive it seems to make it easier for me to do so again." He smiled. "Give my love to your mother, my sisters and your grandmother. I will return to Stockton one day. My place is here. I know my duty."

Before he left my father spoke with me, "I hope to be back here within two or three months. It takes time to raise an army and, as I said, I have other lords to see. There is a conspiracy. How deep it goes we do not know." I nodded. "I will return. Do nothing until I do. Watch and be vigilant but do not cross the border. You and Sir Richard can stand a siege. There are now two knights who can stop the Scots. Both are precious to me." We hugged and I felt the warmth from him. He would not abandon me.

When he had gone, I could still feel my father's presence. We had the same blood but he had endured events which I had not. I had to believe that this time would make me stronger. The day he left we began to make the changes he had suggested. We built new halls, cow byres, pig and sheep pens. I added another warrior hall close to the keep. The warrior hall in the lower bailey would be used by my people. I made certain that I rode every other day to speak with Sir Richard. We both knew that we would have to endure a violent war and we could expect little help from anybody.

My archers found a pair of enemy scouts two days after my father left. Garth had been determined to do so. The two men

The Bloody Border

were good but mine were better. They were dragged behind horses into my castle. They had been beaten by my men. I saw bloodied knuckles.

"You two are spies. Who do you work for?" They spat an answer to me in Gaelic. It confirmed what we already knew. Fife was behind this. "You will become my prisoners. You may never be freed. Do you understand that?"

Suddenly one of them pulled a dagger from his boot and lunged at me. I had quick reactions and I punched my forearm to deflect the dagger in the air. Garth and Idraf's swords were even faster than the two men and the scouts had their heads taken.

"I am sorry, lord, I thought we had searched them."

I nodded, "Take their heads to the border and place them on spears. Their families will know that they are dead and the Scots will know that we know."

That evening I sat and thought in my keep. I stared into my fire and I planned. We had all worked hard and were weary but I had needed to speak with those upon whom I would depend in the coming months. The next day I invited those closest to me to dine. Alan of Bellingham, Brother Paul, Roger Two Swords and Garth Red Arrow came to my keep. When Matthew and John had brought the food from the kitchens, I invited them to dine with me too.

"My father has begun a stone on a journey. It will continue to roll no matter what we do. I believe it was the right decision but it puts us in great danger. Sir Richard, at Otterburn, will be in even greater peril. I will visit with him tomorrow. The fact that Sir Eustace has gone to his masters in Scotland tells me that the next attack may well be on two fronts. We now know that he is a traitor but, worse, the Scots know that my father will bring an army from the south if we are attacked. That may make them act sooner rather than later. Hitherto we regarded the road from Rothbury as safe. We can no longer do so. Phillip the Priest, David, Dick and Tom the Miller will all be in as much danger as Cedric the Sheepman. We must have the mill protected."

Garth put down his knife and picked up his beaker, "Lord, it is just two hundred paces from the gatehouse to the road and the mill. We are higher than the river. I believe we could send arrows to deter an enemy from investing the mill. Tomorrow I will test the range." He sipped his ale and smiled, "We will warn Tom. I would not wish him to think he was under attack."

"Good. I intend to have Tam cast a bell. We have enough scrap metal from the Scots and we can mount it in the keep. We will test it when it is finished. I am sorry that it will not be a bell for Brother Paul's church although, when peace does come here, we might move it from the keep."

Alan shook his head, "I am a devout Christian, lord, but I am not certain that this land will ever be peaceful."

"I have to believe that it will be." We finished the food and I said, "John, there is still some of the heady wine my father brought with him. Fetch it and a jug of water. We will enjoy its flavour and you can water your own." Although it was warm, we had a fire lit. It was cheery and the castle could be cold at night. We took our wine and stood around the fire. Like me, my men liked to watch the flames dancing around the logs. Seeing the wood-burning I said, "Alan, we have a need for timber to build the new buildings. Cut back the tree line. Even if we do not use the timber, we can store it behind our ramparts and it will add to the strength of the walls. It will increase the grazing for the animals."

He nodded. I wracked my brain for more ideas. Alan put his hand upon my shoulder. "Lord, your mind must be a maelstrom. You have done all that you can. The people of the manor and all of your men are behind you. You have deceived no one and everyone knows the danger we are in. Believe me, we are much stronger than we were little more than a year ago before you came. We have more farms, more farmers, more people and everyone, even the Yalesham widows, are better off. You worry but your decisions are good ones."

"Perhaps." I was not certain. Had I done enough? "Roger, I will need just two men and two archers tomorrow when I ride to Sir Richard. Garth, we will not relax our vigilance, send two men to the woods. As for the rest, they work under the supervision of the Reeve."

We rose early every day. These were still long days and the weather was clement and so we worked hard. We had now endured a winter and knew how harsh they were. As I walked my horse through the lower bailey to speak with Tam, the young

The Bloody Border

boys driving the sheep out to graze waved cheerily at me. They would watch the cattle and the sheep. The dogs we had would guard them too. The boys would not waste their time in idleness. They would collect stones from the river and practise with their slings. Sometimes they downed wood pigeons to enrich the pot. The alewives, cheesemakers and butter churners waved to me as I passed. I could hear the mumble of conversation in the weaving hall. There were neither scowls nor depressed faces. I was greeted by the warmth of smiles and I heard the cheer of laughter.

"Tam, I need a bell to be cast. Can you do it?"

"How big a bell, lord?"

"It needs to be heard by Phillip the Priest."

He looked relieved, "Then it will not need to be too big. I have never made one and Black Bob did not make one either but in the workshop was Old Harry. He had worked at Durham and helped to cast the bell there. I enjoyed hearing his tales. I know the technique. We would use river clay and we would make a mould. Aye, lord. I can do it. When do you need it?"

I laughed, "Yesterday!" He nodded and laughed too. "How is Anne?"

"She grows and is healthy. Mary and the Yalesham widows all watch over her. Margaret, who recently wed, is also with child. Mary will be midwife to both women."

"It is good. When danger comes, I will have all within my walls. You and the men of Elsdon will have to fight on my ramparts."

"We talk of that when we practise on Sunday afternoons. We are ready. Your men have trained us well. I have good arrows and we have fine yew bows. If these raiders come again, they will leave their bloody bodies here at the manor. We will not relinquish what we have. We work for the small comforts we have. They wish to steal from us!"

I rode north feeling much better about my manor.

Sir Richard had also begun to make improvements. I had hoped that Sir James would have done so but he saw what he expected to see. Sir Richard looked at the tower and the manor with new eyes. The young knight was stripped to the waist and toiling with his men. They were digging a ditch. I turned to my four men. "Strip off and help the men of Otterburn. Matthew, John, take our men's horses and water them."

Sir Richard came over to me. He wiped the sweat from his body and face with a cloth. He waved the cloth at the ditch. "This is a fast stream. I thought to divert a channel to make a moat. It cannot completely surround the tower and village. I would have to change nature for that but we can protect the side from which the Scots will come."

"A word of warning; we found scouts in the woods close to Elsdon. They may not attack the same way the next time."

"I know and that is why we are building a new wall on the other side. When we dig the ditch, we find many stones. We build a ditch and moat first then a wall."

"Do you ride to the border?"

"Every couple of days. We have seen no sign of intruders but they will be circumspect."

"I am clearing the woods to give a killing ground around my castle and I am having a bell cast to summon the villagers."

"That is a good idea. If I had a smith then I would have one too."

"I will ask Tam to cast a second. If he can make one then why not two?"

"Thank you, William."

"Of course, the real problem will not be the Scots. It will be the viper in our midst, Sir Eustace. He is clever and I think he will disguise his men. My father put fear in his heart. He will still work for the Scots but he will give himself some way out."

"What do you mean?"

"He will use his men but they will be disguised and he will be absent from the attack. He is a snake but his men are well armed and well trained. When first I came here, I was given some who worked with me. They are hard men and veterans. I do not underestimate them." I took him by the elbow and led him to one side, "Richard, if we are attacked, we stay within our keeps and we defend. Do not come to my aid and I will not come to yours."

"You fear they will try to draw us out of our castles."

"Aye. They will try tricks. They may try to use deception. You know my men and I know yours. I will ignore any request from one I do not know. We use our bells to tell the other of

The Bloody Border

danger but we just hunker down and ride out the storm. When the battle is fought and won then we see how the other fares. If you find us dead then you can exact vengeance."

"I will not need to do so for your father will visit them with the wrath of God and the border will be as a wasteland."

I turned, "Come men. We have aided Sir Richard enough. Let us ride to the border and see what stirs there."

I had with me; my squire and page, Jean of Landvielle and Alf Broad Shoulders as men at arms. Erik the Dane and Tim son of Tom were the archers. They strung their bows as we left Otterburn. The four were the newest men to join me and I wanted them to see the border. We passed the Roman fort and I saw the two older men at arms taking in the potential for defence. When we passed through Byrness I saw their faces harden. It was a visual reminder of the parlous nature of life on the border. People had lived and worked there and it was now inhabited by ghosts. John had good eyes. He rode just ahead of us. Since he had grown big enough to ride a palfrey he could see further. "Lord there are riders ahead, ten of them."

Riders coming south meant one thing, the Scots. "Erik, Tim, dismount. John, you will be horse holder. Jean, Alf and Matthew, we will test their resolve." I hefted my shield and drew my sword. The other three did the same. I saw that the men who came towards us were led by a mailed man at arms riding a palfrey. There were three other mailed men on sumpters and the other six had the hardy hill ponies.

I was talking to myself but I said, "I think these are more scouts and we have thwarted them."

"Lord?"

"We put two heads on the road yesterday. They are sending more scouts to discover our defences. They should have gone across country. We can stop them."

I saw their dilemma. They had four men at arms and I had but three. They outnumbered us but we were better mounted. Suddenly the mailed leader turned and shouted something. Six more men appeared. They were on foot. They would make a fight of it. I turned to my archers, "Erik and Tim, when they charge try to kill as many as you can."

"Aye lord."

"We stay together."

My two archers moved to the flanks to allow them a better sight of the Scots. The first arrow hit the mailed man's horse as the Scots closed with us. The second struck another in the shoulder. When they were one hundred paces from us two more arrows unhorsed two more men. The next arrows were sent just a heartbeat later and the mailed horseman was hit.

"Charge them!"

I spurred my palfrey and held my shield before me. The mailed horseman was retiring behind the men on foot. I swung my sword at the last remaining man with mail. He held his shield before him but my blow struck it so hard that he fell backwards over his horse. Even as we passed through them, I back swung at one on a pony. He jabbed his spear at me but it struck mail. My sword hacked into the side of his head.

The wounded man at arms on the horse shouted, "Back! Back!"

In the time it took for them to disengage three more men were hit by arrows and Jean and Alf slew another two. John shouted, "Lord, Matthew is hurt!"

I turned and saw that he had been speared in the leg. "Erik and Tim, remount and make certain the Scots return home. Alf and Jean, collect the three ponies and search the bodies." I dismounted and walked over to Matthew. The spear had missed his arteries but there was a great deal of blood. I tore a piece of material from one of the dead Scots and tied it above the wound. "John, take Matthew to Brother Abelard. We will follow."

My archers returned with the news that the Scots had returned home. We had gained three ponies, two poorly made hauberks, five swords and three spears. There were also eight daggers. John the Archer held out his two hands. They were filled with small denomination coins. "Considering they were so poorly armed and horsed they had much coin about them."

"Hired men, mercenaries. That tells us the problem. They are hiring any who can hurt us." I nodded, "You four share the coin. Leave the bodies here. It will remind them when they pass that I have the finest warriors protecting this land.

My encounter was a warning for Sir Richard. He nodded when I told him what had occurred, "I will now need to leave two men to watch the road at the fort."

"Use your archers. Two men can control the road. The Scots are easily deterred. I fear that they now avoid the roads and use hidden ways into our lands. This time of harvest is a crucial one. They will seek to weaken us by preventing us from harvesting or stealing that which we do harvest. Keep a good watch on your animals."

He smiled, "You forget, William, that I lived here. I have the cattle protected. Father Abelard has tended to your squire's wound. He will not be able to ride for a couple of weeks."

"I have John. He can take on Matthew's duties." I headed back to my castle knowing that hostilities had resumed.

Chapter 14

The metal we had recovered would make the second bell. Tam was enjoying a new challenge. Black Bob had limited his work. Here he was his own master and he thrived. Matthew could not ride, nor could he walk very far but he was a hard-working squire and he would not sit idly by. He became a sentry at the top of the keep. My tower had a clear line of sight to all the farms but Cedric's. He supervised the construction of the bell tower. While we toiled to make our home safe and secure, he watched. It was he spied the first raiders. It was four days later and he saw movement in the woods close by David of Amble's farm. David had the smallest of farms. He had a field of barley and one of oats. He had three sows and four cows. He had a flock of fifteen sheep. All were within sight of his farm. We now knew the pattern of life around the manor. The archers were to the north of David's farm. They were by Phillip the Priest's land. Matthew cupped his hands and shouted, "Intruders by David of Amble's land!" Had the bell been ready it would have alerted not only the castle but the farmers and the patrolling archers.

I heard, as did John. He was already racing for my horse as I shouted, "Roger Two Swords, mount four men and come with me. Intruders by David's farm." We now wore mail all day. The only time it was removed was when we prepared for bed. It was like a second skin. I mounted Eagle and, without waiting for my men at arms, John and I rode out of the castle and turned east.

David and Alice had none to work their farm. They were alone. With a young child, Alice stayed close to the farmhouse and that saved her. We heard David's dog barking and, as we headed up the track towards the farm, we saw David loosing arrows. He was not an archer trained but he knew how to send an arrow at a foe. There were four men and they had neither helmets nor shields. They were cattle thieves. David had a small herd. They were after it. The track rose and then fell. The cattle thieves lost sight of us as we dropped into a natural hollow but I headed off the road to cut them off. David had harvested his oats and it was just stubble with his three sows grazing. They scattered as John and I rode through them and then we emerged from the hollow. We were just forty paces from the four men. One had stopped to pull the arrow from his arm. The others had spread out and David's dog was racing towards them. The distraction of the dog had helped John and I to close to within thirty paces. They turned and saw us. The one with the arrow in his arm ran. David sent an arrow into the chest of another. The other two ran. I turned my sword so that I could hit one with the flat of my blade. I leaned out to strike the one on my right. I smacked him hard. He fell to the ground. The other ducked and kept running. John had no such compunction. This would be his first kill and he raised his short sword and brought it down to split open the head of the man he chased.

I turned and saw Roger and my men appear, "There is one left!" They galloped after the wounded man. Dismounting I handed my reins to John. "Well done, John." He was a little green. The dead man's brains oozed from his skull. I picked up the unconscious man and, after removing his dagger, draped him over the back of my horse. I led my horse to the house. Alice and her suckling babe emerged. The man David had hit with his arrow tried to rise and then fell back, dead. David nodded, "Thank you, lord. That might have gone ill for us had you not seen us in such dire straits."

"I think there may be more such attacks. Next time do not be so brave. Go into your house and bar the door."

"But my animals!"

"They will not move far. The fact that we take our animals indoors at night has made them change their approach. It shows how desperate they are. Attacking at night is one thing but daylight means that they have to risk being spotted. I will have my men patrol on foot too."

The Bloody Border

I turned as Roger and his men rode with a body slung on the back of one of the horses. "He fought, lord. I am sorry."

"No matter, I have a prisoner. Burn the bodies. At least their ashes will fertilise your soil, eh David?"

"Aye lord, this has been a lesson."

John and I returned to Elsdon with the prisoner. Brother Paul treated his wound and we bound his hands. When he awoke, I saw the amazement on his face. He thought that he was a dead man. When we questioned him, we discovered that he came from north of the Forth. The Earl of Fife had spread the word that there were many cattle and sheep to be had with little risk to the thieves. The man and his friends had come south. It soon became clear that there were large numbers of them. This was a clever plan. It cost the Earl nothing and no blame could be attributed to him. These were poor men with little themselves. Their lords were lazy and did not help the folk in their manors. They encouraged them to raid the English. It would weaken us. When I asked why they did not raid Rothbury, which was richer, I was told that the Earl had ordered them to leave it alone. I sent the prisoner to Morpeth with Alan of Bellingham and Wilfred of Sheffield. "Advise the baron to be merciful. We have learned much and the man is not a bad one."

As September came to a slow close, we found we were working as hard as the farmers. Our buildings were almost complete but my archers now not only patrolled the Otterburn road but also the woods. My men at arms patrolled the Rothbury road and also walked the farms of my manor. Cedric had his horn and he had his sons. If raiders came then he would be able to summon help. My worry was now our horses. The daily riding took its toll. We would need more mounts. I wrote a letter to my father. I asked him for remounts. I would not take charity. I would pay him. He had promised he would return but I did not expect him yet. I also wrote to the Bishop and informed him of recent events. As it was Tuesday, I was able to let Brother Paul ride to Durham. He enjoyed the company of his priests and the ride would allow him to spend a night in Durham and still be back for services on Sunday.

Tam finished the bell by the last day in September. He had cast one for Sir Richard. It awaited finishing. He had spent some time polishing his first bell. He had even engraved it. It took half a day to mount it in the bell tower atop my keep. It was a wooden tower but an archer could use it to send arrows in case of attack. I sent messages to my farmers on the day we tested it. I did not wish them to panic. I allowed Alan of Bellingham the honour of ringing the first chimes. It was clear and true. It had, because of its size, a higher pitch. That was no bad thing. I saw the pride on Tam's face as we descended from the keep.

"If I had continued to work for Black Bob then such work would be denied me."

"Then you do not regret my offer of work?"

"It was the best decision I made, Sir William. These are good people. My wife and the Yalesham widows are happy. Their children are occupied. You know that Brother Paul teaches them to read?"

I nodded, "I had heard he did."

"Where else would such children gain an education? They may never need it but it is good, lord, that they can. I cannot read and I envy them."

"Then join the classes, Tam. What stops you?"

He looked at me and I saw the light in his eyes, "Nothing, lord! I am a foolish man."

"If you cannot read, Tam, then how did you carve the bell?"

"I know not what I carved, lord. I copied the marks Brother Paul made. He told me what I wrote. It was Latin!"

He said it with such pride. He thought he was lucky but I knew that I had been the fortunate one.

As the weather changed, we worked even harder. Soon it would be time for the bone fire. We had fewer animals to slaughter for we had byres and we had winter fodder prepared. Cedric brought his animals from the high fells. The animals we did slaughter were the old and the sick. Nothing was wasted from them. Men went into my woods to fetch kindling. We had startled and killed four other men who had been found hiding in my woods but the collection of the kindling guaranteed that none would be in my woods over winter.

I stood at the top of my keep and I surveyed my land. A little more than a year ago I had come and found a manor which was run down. Now it bustled. Our walls, ramparts and ditches were strong. We had buildings in the inner and lower bailey. We had roads which were dry all year. We had a mill which now ground grain and cereal for the neighbouring manors. Even Morpeth sent cartloads of grain to be milled. The river was controlled and our bridge strengthened.

Alan smiled at me. "You have done much for this manor, lord. When I saw one so young riding towards our walls I feared for our future."

"No more than I, Alan. The people have pulled together but there will be harder times coming."

"The Earl of Fife." He nodded.

"The good news is that when he comes, he cannot use masses of knights. He will come thinking that we are what we were, a rundown manor with poor defences and inadequate numbers of men. He is in for a shock."

"Will your father come?"

"He promised to return but his return is not for some time. If he can he will but it is four days from Stockton to here and that is still a hard ride. We need to be able to withstand a siege of a month or so. Can we do that?"

"We have a well and we have the river. There are barrels of salted game and we are well provided with grain. If we do not lose the lower bailey then a month will not be a problem."

I nodded. That was all that I could hope for.

When Brother Paul had returned it was with the news that the Bishop had informed the King's officers of the border problems. I was unsure how long it would take the message to reach the King and I also worried that I might be censured. I knew I had done nothing wrong but my father had learned that kings did not act as ordinary men did. When he returned, he examined Matthew's leg. It had healed and coincided with the completion of the bell for Otterburn. We loaded the wagon and rode to Otterburn. We delivered the bell to Sir Richard and Tam helped to fit it.

Sir Richard had also encountered cattle thieves. He had not sent them to Morpeth, he had hanged them. He built a gibbet at the end of the village and the rotting bodies swung there. He showed me his new moat. It was fordable but men would not be able to use a ram. Men with ladders would be subject to arrows from the tower. He had also strengthened the base of the tower. The bell delighted him. "We will fit it as soon as we have built a tower for it. I will send coin to your smith. A skilled man deserves payment." He grinned at me, "We heard your bell!"

"Tam tells me that this one will sound different. He used the same mould but a different mix. When you sound it, I will tell you." I gave him the news from the Bishop and of our encounters with raiders. "I believe that they will come before Christmas. Last year we had such snow as to hamper movement. This autumn has had storms and rain but, generally, it has been benign."

"I think you are right. God will test us soon enough." I asked Richard to sound it the next day as a test. We were back in Elsdon by then and we heard it clearly. It was just three peals of the bell. If there was danger it would be continuous. It worked. We heard it clearly. I sent a rider back to Sir Richard with the good news.

And then the rains came. The farmers who had already harvested their crops were pleased but those, like Dick Jameson who had been waiting to collect their beans, were not. The beans would not suffer too much but it was simpler collecting them when they were dry. It made them easier to store. It was too wet to collect kindling and, instead, my villagers set to preparing their homes for winter. Inevitably wattle and daub became damaged. In summer it did not matter but a hole in winter could make a house feel like ice. Those who had slate rooves checked them while the ones with turf rooves repaired them.

After three days the first of the autumn rains stopped and the women hung washing out to dry. It was then we heard the sound I had been dreading. It was the bell of Otterburn. I sent a man at arms to the keep to sound ours. My men at arms and archers manned the walls and Alan of Bellingham went to the gates with John and Matthew to shepherd the villagers to their temporary quarters. Dick, Tom and Harry were the first to arrive. They had the fewest animals and lived the closest. David of Amble and Alice, along with their son and animals were next.

I was becoming anxious. If the Scots had timed their attacks to coincide then we could expect an imminent assault. Margaret, wife of Stephen, and her children helped Rafe and his family drive their animals towards us. Despite the fact that I had ordered him to come in to the castle I knew that Cedric the Sheepman would disobey me. It could not be helped. Rafe's son Rafe and his other son, Henry, brought their families and the last to arrive was Phillip the Priest and his wife. Once they were within my walls we went to the sluice and opened the leat from the mill and the mill pond began to empty into the ditch which ran around the lower bailey making it a moat. We would have to refill the pond when the threat was over but this was a small price to pay for security. Finally, we raised the bridge over the ditch. We were ready.

With archers in the half dozen wooden towers we had built around my palisade and in my keep, the men of my village dispersed themselves along the fighting platform. I walked with Roger Two Swords to allocate my men at arms. This was the first time we had done this and it did not go smoothly. In the end, there was no need for worry. We were not attacked.

As darkness fell, we sent the villagers and half my men to eat. I stood with Roger, Matthew and Garth at the top of my keep. Alan of Bellingham climbed the ladder to join us. "Was this a false alarm, my lord?"

"I am not certain, Alan. We heard Otterburn's bell and that means they were under attack. I suspect that the Earl of Fife thought to trick us. He hoped we would go to the aid of Otterburn. Then he could either attack Elsdon or ambush us along the road." I peered to the northeast. My fear was not the Scots but the men of Rothbury. "We leave one man in five to watch the walls. The rest eat and then sleep. Tonight, we have half of our garrison stand a watch. The villagers can rest. If we need them then we call them."

"What of Cedric the Sheepman, Sir William?"

"We have not heard his horn, Alan of Bellingham. He may not be under attack and even if he were it would be folly to go to his aid. Sir Richard and I have made our plans and we must be resolute. Alan, here, thinks we can hold out for a month or more. Let us show the Scots that Englishmen have backbones."

Roger and Garth went to send the men to eat and I wandered amongst my folks. They were all eating at long tables out in the open. We had emptied the two halls in the lower bailey of all furniture. We would be crowded. The men looked happy enough and, to the children, it was all a grand game. The children who lived outside the castle suddenly found new friends with whom they could play. The women looked nervous but the Yalesham widows who should have been the most apprehensive were laughing and joking. Mary, widow of Harry, patted the bench next to her, "Come, my lord, and sit here. Mistress Anne has made a fine stew. The rabbits are so tender that they fall from the bone."

"I have much to do. I merely came to see if all was well."

Mary of Yalesham banged the table, "Mistress Anne, food for his lordship. All is well, my lord. We are all safe inside your walls and we are all content. You have good warriors and they watch your walls."

Mistress Anne now had a slight bump and she looked radiant. She brought me a bowl of food, "Mary is right, my lord. All is prepared. We have a priest amongst us. There is more food than I have ever seen and besides, the Scots are only dangerous when they strike in the night. These walls will keep them hence."

Mary nodded resolutely, "Aye and this time the women of Yalesham will not go easily. If they breach the walls, which I doubt, then they will have to fight us too eh?"

The women all cheered and banged the table. "Very well then, I shall eat!"

I ate. I drank freshly brewed ale and I laughed. Mary and the others had the joy of life for they had been slaves and then freed. When I had finished and wiped my mouth with my napkin, I turned and said, "A fine meal! And now..."

Anne sat on the other side of me, "Master John says that you are a fine singer, lord?"

I shook my head, "John would not know a good voice and I..." I now regretted singing for my men when we had first arrived.

"Come, my lord, you have had your supper, now you shall sing for it."

I looked at the expectant faces. The whole of the lower bailey had become silent. Anne leaned in and whispered in my ear, "It will make those who are nervous forget their fears, my lord."

The Bloody Border

I nodded and stood. I saw John coming from the upper bailey. In his hands, he held my crowd. I would have words with my page! He handed me the crowd and gave me a sheepish grin. I checked the tuning. When there was silence and I was ready then I began. I sang the song I had sung when I had been knighted. It was a song of unfulfilled love and sadness. The children did not understand it but I saw some of the women wiping tears from their eyes.

John stood close by looking apprehensive. He said, "Lord, give them the one about Sir Hubert. It will make them laugh."

"I think I have made enough of a fool of myself for one night."

Mary put her rough hand on mine, "Lord, you have done no such thing. Look at their faces. You are held in higher esteem now than before and that is hard to do. If you can make them laugh now then all fear will fly from their hearts."

I nodded and I sang.

Hubert de Burgh is a fine fat man
He can count his numbers better than a miser can
He roars and struts when the enemy cheer
But when they are close he flees in fear
You know where he is for he cannot hide well

I only sang three verses. They did not know Sir Hubert but they knew the type of knight and they laughed. When I had finished, I stood, "And now I must go. It is time for Brother Paul to hear my confession. War is coming and your lord must be ready!"

My people cheered and it was the best war cry I had ever heard.

I arranged with Garth and Roger for one of us to be awake all night. I spoke to them before I retired, "They might come tonight and they might not. We need to be alert but make certain that our sentries do not move around. Remain still and let our eyes do the work. When we see them then the cry is 'stand to'. We ring the bell. We stop them from getting to the walls."

"That is why you are convinced that they will come at night."

I nodded, "It means they can get closer to the walls without our archers hurting them. They know of our strength. They will try to avoid our arrows."

I took the middle watch. It was the hardest one. You rose from sleep, watched and then had to try to get back to sleep. I told Matthew and John to sleep all night. When Roger woke me, I was dozing anyway. I seemed to be able to wake myself up whenever I needed to. I sluiced some water on my face as Roger woke the rest of the watch. I swallowed some ale and took a piece of dried venison upon which to chew. I donned my mail and slipped my coif over my head. Strapping on my sword I left the keep and headed across the upper bailey to the fighting platform. It was an overcast night with a hint of fog in the river bottom. It was the sort of night the Scots would choose to make their attack. Despite my warning to my men I would have to walk the fighting platform. My men needed to see that I was on duty and, more importantly, I needed to see what they could see. We had just twelve of us on duty. One was in the bell tower on the keep. Four were walking the fighting platform of the upper bailey and the rest had the harder task of patrolling the lower bailey. We had equal numbers of archers and men at arms. None spoke as I passed. They were too well trained for that. They nodded and then turned to peer into the dark and the murk.

The dogs had been let loose but they had smelled nothing and were sleeping, I saw them in the upper and lower baileys. So long as they were sleeping then we were safe. When they smelled strangers, they would growl. I estimated that it took me an hour to return to the upper bailey. I climbed the steps to the tower. Idraf was perched on the bell tower. On a clear night he would have had an uninterrupted view almost to David of Amble's farm but this night he would barely see one hundred paces from the walls. I looked up and waved and then I walked to each side peering into the dark. It was as I looked east along the Rothbury road and towards David of Amble's farm that I spied a movement. Of course, it could have been an animal. Deer were nocturnal creatures. I had given clear orders and I obeyed them. I attracted the attention of Idraf and pointed to the woods which lay to the east of Rothbury and then I descended to the keep.

I roused John and Matthew, "Go and wake my men, tell them to stand to."

Matthew was awake in an instant, "Do I wake the villagers, too, lord?"

I shook my head, "This may be a false alarm. Let them sleep. John, when the men are roused then go along the fighting platform and warn the men that their lord thought he spied danger from the east."

I grabbed my helmet and shield. I headed back to the fighting platform. It was Harold Hart who guarded that side of the platform. I leaned in to him and, pointing east, said, "I am certain I spied movement there. Watch for it."

"Aye lord."

I returned to the keep and climbed the steps once more. Already the three archers who would man the keep with Idraf were climbing the steps to take their positions. Idraf had left his perch and his bow was already strung. He nodded when I emerged. "You are right, lord. There are men making their way across David's land." The archers arrived and Idraf pointed to the east. They began to string their bows.

"I will leave you here. I will be needed on the fighting platform. I will send John to sound the bell."

Roger and Wilfred were waiting for me in the upper bailey. "You two take charge of the fighting platform and the lower bailey. Get the rest of the caltrops from Tam and scatter them beyond the ditch and close to the walls. You can wake the village men as you pass. I will sound the bell when the enemy commit to the attack. I would rather we man our walls silently. Send a child to me if you think the walls will fall. I will leave open the gates to the upper bailey."

"That is a risk, lord. If we are overrun then we might lose all."

"I trust my people. Once daylight comes then the enemy loses whatever advantage they have."

I hurried to the walls of the upper bailey. I passed Alan of Bellingham. "I will join those on the walls of the lower bailey, lord." I saw that he wore his Hospitaller surcoat. He smiled, "I never thought I would need this again." Patting his sword, he said, "I am glad I did not turn this into a ploughshare."

The Bloody Border

Matthew was already mailed and ready. I climbed the steps to the walls of the upper bailey. I had seven men at arms and just four archers to aid Matthew and myself. That was planned. There was no external gate close to the upper bailey and the hill was the steepest there. The ditches were seeded with stakes and caltrops. The one around the lower bailey was flooded now and the stakes would not be seen, even in daylight. The ditch around the upper bailey was dry and they would see them when the sun rose.

Placing my helmet and shield on the fighting platform I peered over. I could now see the shadows moving closer to the walls. They were using the cover of David of Amble's farm but soon they would be exposed and coming across the grazing which my animals used. They had two hundred paces to cover without anything behind which they could hide. The slope which rose before them was covered in animal droppings until they reached the bank which protected my ditch.

John arrived and I pointed to the keep. "Join Idraf and take your bow. When we send our first arrow then ring the bell. We will rouse our folk and warn Cedric and Sir Richard that we are under attack."

"Aye lord. The men of the village man the walls of the lower bailey and the women are waking." He smiled in the dark, "Mistress Mary woke them."

We were ready. I turned to Matthew. "They have been checked already but make certain that there are plenty of darts and spears on the fighting platform and then stand at the north wall in case they attack from more than one direction."

"Aye, lord."

That was my fear. An attack on one side of my castle could be contained but we would struggle to defeat an enemy who attacked from two or more sides. However, to attack from more than one side would involve an attack by many hundreds of men. They must have already committed many men to an attack on Otterburn. I hoped that Sir Richard could also hold out. This would be a defensive fight. We would be outnumbered. I had thirty-two trained men and then the men of the village. It was not a large number. When they closed with the walls then my women and boys would be able to fight. There were plenty of darts!

I picked up a dart. They were simply made. A point and a weighted lump of metal could just be hurled down. Thrown from the walls they were difficult to return and although they could not penetrate mail or helmets if they found flesh, they would cause a wound and a wounded man rarely fought well. I could now make out that the shadows were men. They were channelling towards the lower bailey. A few looked to be trying to ascend the slope. As the lower bailey bulged out towards David of Amble's farm, they would reach the flooded ditch there before they reached my wall. It would be Roger Two Swords and Alan of Bellingham who would give the command to release. Garth Red Arrow was at the southern end of the fighting platform of the upper bailey. He would command our archers.

I heard a cry from the south and then a shout, "Release!" The battle had begun.

My four archers in the keep had the greatest range for they had the advantage of height. Idraf and the others began to send their targeted arrows at the men who were struggling to climb our hill. John began to toll the bell. Leaving my men to watch I hurried to join Garth.

I saw that the attackers had thought us all asleep. There were four bodies lying close to the ditch. The first ones had died quickly. There were sixty or so men moving closer to the ditch. They had shields. These were not Scots. These were Sir Eustace's men. I recognised one, Peter of Wark. He had been one who had come to help me settle in. Garth saw him too. He took a bodkin arrow from his arrow bag and licked the flights. He nocked it and drew back. It would be a prodigious hit for Peter of Wark was more than a hundred and fifty paces from us in the dark. The arrow plunged down and struck him in the right shoulder. The force was so great that it knocked him over and, as he fell, another arrow was sent from my wall and he lay still.

The first of the attackers reached my ditch. Holding their shields above them they stepped into the water. It was dark and they had no idea of the steep slope beneath the black water. Some slipped while others lost their footing. As men stepped onto hidden stakes and caltrops they were wounded and they screamed. Their plan had been to catch us unawares. When they began to fall back any sense of elation disappeared. There were too few men in the attack to guarantee success. Cupping my hands, I shouted, "Man the west walls! Idraf, look to the north and west."

Garth looked at me, "We have beaten them off, lord. They have failed."

"And where were the Scots?" I pointed to the dozen or so bodies which littered the ground. Even in the dark, we could see that they were English warriors. The half-dressed clansmen who made up the bulk of Scottish raiders were absent. We had fought them enough times to recognise them. "Stay here. I will go and look."

I ran along the fighting platform and across the gatehouse leading from the lower to the upper bailey. I reached the west wall. Here there was more cover for Rafe's farm, the church and Harry Sourface's farm were there. The east side had open fields. I had barely reached it when I saw faces peering from behind buildings. I picked up a dart and, as I reached the palisade threw it towards the nearest man. He was thirty paces from the wall. He was struggling up the slope to the walls. He wore no helmet and the dart struck his skull. He tumbled down and knocked a companion down too. Idraf and the archers in the keep sent arrows at the Scots who were struggling to reach the rampart. I hurled another dart but the shield held above him protected the Scot I had tried to kill. Even so, he lost his footing and tumbled down. Garth had now joined me. His arm drew and released so quickly that I wondered how he managed to do so. And then the Scots pulled back. Thirteen bodies littered the slope of the mound. We had beaten them back but now we were surrounded. We were under siege.

Chapter 15

When dawn broke, we saw the Scots and the English traitors begin to demolish and destroy the farms and the buildings. Rafe's wife's clothes were taken from the farm ripped, torn and then waved at the walls. It was vindictive mischief. Matthew shook his head, he had brought me ale, "There is no need for that lord!"

"No, Matthew and it is foolish." He looked puzzled and I explained, "Had they left the buildings then they could have used them for cover. They would have had somewhere to sleep. This does not hurt us. The animals of Rafe and Harry are within our walls. Brother Paul brought all that was valuable from the church. We can rebuild the buildings. Let them sow the seeds of their own destruction and we will reap the benefit." I had half the men stood down to eat and I walked along my fighting platform, "Men, go to your families and eat. It is now daylight and we will have a warning of an attack. They thought to take animals from us."

Alan of Bellingham said, "Cedric the Sheepman has his flocks. He is in danger."

"I offered him sanctuary, did I not? What else could I have done?"

"I know, lord. I am merely pointing out that they can be fed from Cedric's flocks."

"I know. We will see what will happen. He may have already taken his flock and family to safety." I did not think that had happened but I had to appear positive.

Tam said, "Will there be help coming our way, lord?"

I shook my head. "If we are lucky then our bell may have been heard in Morpeth. Sound travels a long way in winter. We have visited the market and we may be missed. If Alan does not show up next week and they heard the bell then they may investigate but I doubt it. Our visits have been infrequent." My father could be due but something made me doubt a sudden end to the siege.

He nodded, "We suffered no losses lord and they did."

He was right. We had counted more than twenty bodies. There were others who had managed to crawl back to their lines with wounds. We had hurt them but not enough. Garth wanted to recover our arrows but I forbade it. There was too much danger. We had blank arrows and we had a forge. We could make arrows if we were running low.

By noon they had not attacked and Brother Paul forced me to eat. I found I was ravenous. I had forgotten my hunger. I had just finished my food and made water when I heard a shout from the gatehouse. I fastened my breeks and hurried to the walls. Roger Two Swords pointed to the woods beyond the farm of Rafe's son Henry. "They are hewing trees, lord."

"They are building a ram, good."

Roger said, "Good, my lord, how is that good?"

"It takes a couple of days to build a ram. When they have built it, we know where they have to attack, our gate. There the ditch is at its widest. They will have to build a bridge also. A ram means they will not be able to attack for three or four days. When they do attack, we will have oil and fire ready for them." We had laid in supplies of seal oil we had bought from the fishermen of Bamburgh from Morpeth market. It was intended to light our homes but it could also be used to burn a ram.

I knew that the longer the siege went on the more likely it was that we would be relieved. Had they brought a ram with them we would have been in trouble. They had gambled on catching us asleep. They had lost that gamble.

When it began to rain, in the afternoon, then we knew that God was on our side. The water would raise the level of the moat. It would make the ground slick and slippery. The enemy had destroyed their own shelters. The knights had a couple of tents but the men would be forced to live in hovels. They would become increasingly weaker as nature aided us.

I held a council of war with Rafe, Tam, Brother Paul, Alan of Bellingham, Garth and Roger. "They will come again tonight. They will try some mischief. If I was their leader, I would try to bridge the ditch. All that they need to do is to use some of the farm buildings. They are big enough."

Garth said, "If this rain continues then our bows will not be effective."

"I know. We use the boys with slings. They will be keen to hurt them."

"They will not be able to kill."

"I know but they can hurt. A broken hand cannot wield a sword. If they make them slip and fall in the ditches then they may be spiked by a stake. They may even have men who risk swimming the ditch and then climb the walls to put fear in our hearts. I want one in three of every man and boy on the walls this night. We will use the same system we did last night."

The wanton destruction of their farms had hardened the hearts of my villagers. If they caught a Scot it would not go well for them. As they were leaving Rafe said, "God sent you here, lord. If you had not come then my sons and I would lie dead and our wives would be Yalesham widows. We will not let you down. We may not be trained warriors but we are English warriors!"

I was heartened.

In the end, they did not come. We found the reason the next day. I was summoned at dawn. I had managed a couple of hours of sleep. Cedric's head and that of his second son, Will, were on the top of two spears. They had been put just on the other side of the ditch in the night. We could smell cooking mutton. Cedric had paid the price for his stubbornness. What concerned me was the fact that we had not heard Cedric's horn. How had they surprised him? He had been a wily old man. He was not like Old Will. I put the speculation from my mind as we listened to the sound of construction. Even more depressing was the thought that they were eating Elsdon sheep!

We had built two devices to pour boiling fat from my stone gatehouse. They were crude cauldrons which could be tipped on a fulcrum. Tam had made two metal gutters to take the fat beyond the wooden gate. The last thing we needed was to set fire to our own gate. Tam's forge was closer to the gate and we would use his fire to heat the fat. That was the safest way. We had the two cauldrons and a block and tackle to raise it to the fighting platform. We would keep the fat in the cauldrons at the forge. We would only need to light the fire once we saw the ram approach. It was almost half a mile from the wood where they were building it. In the time it took to trundle down we would be able to heat the oil and fat. The fire from the forge would keep it warm. My decision to cut back the trees had been vindicated. They would have further to push the ram.

They spent three days and nights building the ram. No help had been forthcoming. My father's men did not appear nor did Sir Ranulf. I had not expected any. If they came it would be after a week or more. It was not all bad. I smiled as I viewed the woods close to Henry son of Rafe's farm. The Scots and English attackers had cleared enough land for him to increase his grazing. Alan of Bellingham joined me. "They have cut more wood than they need to build a bridge and a ram, lord."

"I know." I pointed to some pavise they had built. They were using them as a screen. "Unless I miss my guess, they are also building a stone thrower."

"That will take longer to build"

"It will. I wonder now, about this conspiracy. Why has not Sir Ranulf sent men to investigate? Either he cannot or will not. I hope it is the former for I have made enough enemies already. Do you notice that they have stopped cooking mutton?"

Alan turned and said, "I had not but now that you mention it. There has been no smell of cooking."

"And that means they have none left to cook. Yet Cedric had a large flock. They did not display the heads of Cedric's other sons nor parade his family."

"You think that they escaped with the larger part of their flock, lord?"

"It is the only explanation which makes sense, Alan." He nodded. He was an old soldier and understood such things. "What I do know is that they will be hungry. The rain might have stopped but there is a cold east wind and Rafe told me, last night, that the wind from the east brings snow. I know it is early but this is winter and if snow comes then they will hurt."

"Aye lord, when I was a boy in Bellingham, we had the same; a cold east wind meant snow. It will not lie but it will make the ground even slicker and more slippery. That will aid us."

"It will indeed. We had better bring the pig fat and seal oil from the keep and put it in the cauldrons close to the forge. We can have the forge heat it slowly. As soon as we spy the ram trundling towards us, we will need to begin to heat them. I think that they have a day more and they will be ready."

The camps did not encircle us. There was one close to David of Amble's farm. A second was on the Rothbury road. The largest one used our church. The other buildings had been destroyed. A fourth was on the Otterburn road and a small one lay to the west of my castle. It was as I completed my daily walk around my fighting platform that I realised I needed a sally port on each side of the walls. If we had had one it would have been child's play to slip out and rid ourselves of the small camp.

It was the next day that we heard, not long after dawn, the sound of wood rolling over wood. They had built the ram in the woods and to get it to the road they needed wooden rollers. I ordered the fat and oil mixture to be heated. That was Tam's task. It was a simple process. The cauldrons were next to the forge and they just needed moving directly over the heat. The smith and Dick, son of Harry, would tend it. John would watch the ram and he would be the one I would send to have the cauldrons fetched to the tackle. I now kept just two archers at the top of my keep. Two more watched the walls of the upper bailey. The rest of my men were on the walls of the lower bailey. That was where they would attack. A ram meant they were going to take the gate. The pavise were moved closer and I saw the half-finished stone-thrower when the screens were removed. Had they planned properly they would have brought it ready to be assembled. Sir Richard and I had thwarted their plans. The pavise were set up close to the flooded ditch, the moat. Even though they were careful my archers managed to hit two of the men who had brought up the protective pavise. We saw crudely made ladders as they were carried and dropped behind the wooden pavise. They had learned their lesson and the ladder carriers were protected by shields. The ram lumbered slowly towards us. It was moving at the pace of an old man. Even when it reached the cobbles of the road it struggled for the stones were slippery still.

Alan of Bellingham knew sieges from the Holy Land. "It will take most of the day for it to reach us, lord."

"They mean to attack at dusk or night."

"Aye."

"How is it made, lord?" Matthew was naturally curious.

"It looks like they have used a single large log and cut six crude wheels. See how it moves unevenly. That will weaken it. They have not used hide for the roof. They have used wood. It will make the ram heavier. I would guess that it takes thirty men to move it. They have no shelter. It will take another thirty to protect them with shields."

"That helps us eh, lord?"

"Aye for it will divide their attacking force by at least a half." I turned, "Roger Two Swords, have the men fed. I will watch with the men of the village. This will be a long night for us."

After the first night, I had not bothered with my helmet and shield. I would not need them this night either. I leaned on the stone of the gatehouse. I had not seen either Sir Malcolm nor the Earl of Fife in the enemy camp. That did not mean they were not here just that they were remaining in shelter. I had not seen Sir Eustace but I had seen another eight of his men. Now he could not deny his involvement. He had cast the die and would have to live with the consequences. I lifted my head and looked south. Where was my father? He was Earl Marshal of the North. Why had he not come to my aid? He had left me and promised that he would return. What had stopped him? There would be a good reason. I tried to work out how long it was since he had left. So much had happened that I found it hard to put the events in order. Sir Richard had taken over the manor and it was only then that my father had gone. He had said he was going to make visits before reaching Stockton, I was doing my father a disservice. He had probably only been home for a week or so. He would need to organize if he was going to come north. He would have to summon his other knights. Perhaps I should have sent a rider when I heard Sir Richard's bell. Hindsight was always perfect. Each day was a lesson to me in how to be the lord of the manor.

Matthew was with me, "Go and see how long before the fat is hot enough."

"Aye lord."

Rafe and his sons came to join me. "I am sorry about your home, Rafe."

He shrugged, "We can rebuild. Poor Cedric cannot rebuild his life. Besides, lord, we have learned from you. We can live with my son Henry until we have built a new hall and we will build it like yours. Strong stone does not burn! If we add barns and byres around the side then we will be almost like a castle. We will be able to defend it."

His youngest son, John, pointed, "They are getting closer, lord."

Although they had made progress, they were still four hundred paces from the moat. Once they reached the moat, they would have to endure caltrops, stones and arrows! It was as I turned to face south that the first snowflake fell against my left cheek. While we had been talking the clouds had rolled in. The snow was beginning.

Matthew returned, "The fat is beginning to bubble. Tam says he will take it from the heat before it flames."

I nodded and, glancing to the south, saw that they were now just two hundred paces from the walls. The snow and clouds combined with the time of year meant that it would soon be dusk. "Fetch our men. Rafe, when my men arrive then have the villagers fed and get some rest. I will call them when we need them." What I was counting on was the fact that the enemy would be tired. They had half of their men pushing and pulling the ram. Others were still toiling with the stone thrower. I had not seen it yet but I knew that there had to be a bridge they were going to use. Until that arrived, they could not begin their attack.

My men began to filter down and take their places on my fighting platform. We had more men at arms than archers. I had the archers spread out. With two in the tower and two watching the upper bailey we were stretched thinly. We could have used Walther of Coxold.

"Garth, we use your archers judiciously. When they put their bridge across, they will have to expose themselves. Make the bridge an expensive one."

"Aye lord. I will move the archers to the gatehouse. I can judge their flight better. We could use the archers in the tower and upper bailey, lord."

I nodded, "Matthew, send three of the archers from the keep here. You and the other archer will be our sentries and guards for the keep."

He looked disappointed but he nodded, "Aye, lord."

The attackers stopped before they reached the moat. They had suffered from our archers before and knew that the moat was in range. What they did not know was how few archers we actually had. It was why I was allowing the men of the village to eat and rest as long as possible. They would be used when the enemy crossed the moat. It would increase our archers. I knew that they would cross. The question was, how many could we kill before they managed it? Men with shields and the men with the pavise formed a line before the moat. They were bringing the bridge up behind the shields. The Scots and the English had archers and crossbows. The crossbows could not release from behind their pavise. As soon as the pavise were moved the crossbowmen began to level their crossbows. In the time it took to level and aim ten arrows had flown from the walls and hit all eight of the men with crossbows. Not all were killed but a crossbow needed strength to load it. A wounded man could not do it. Their archers could release from behind the pavise but they were not as good as my men. Some fell short and the ones we saw were caught on the shields of my sergeants.

We had won the first round. Men with shields formed up and I saw the bridge being manhandled into position. The caltrops took their toll. When men holding the shields stepped on them and moved my archers took advantage. My archers were patient. They watched for a mistake and then they struck. The ones who had joined us from the tower raced up the ladder and quickly nocked their bows. They waited. The shields could only protect the enemy while the bridge was on the bank. As soon as it edged over the moat there was no protection for the men pushing it. The two men pushing at the side fell into the flooded ditch with arrows in their heads. The rest kept pushing and the bridge edged across but it cost them eight men to reach halfway. Once there the bridge floated and they were able to push it across to the other side.

"John, Tam, it is time for fire!"

"Aye lord."

"Men of Elsdon, stand to!" Men left their food and raced towards the ladders.

I donned my helmet. The arrows sent at us had been poorly flighted up to now but once they crossed the moat, they would be closer. It would be foolish to risk being struck by one. I left the visor up. The arrows were being sent into the air and were falling vertically. By the time the bridge reached our side of the moat twelve of those attacking us had been struck with arrows. Some were just wounded but none would be able to help in the attack. The enemy took their places at the ram. As I had expected they needed almost as many men with shields as they did to push it. I heard Tam and the strong men from the village as they hauled on the rope to raise the steaming cauldrons of heated fat and oil. I glanced over and saw that it was still bubbling. In a perfect world, we would have a fire on the fighting platform to continue heating it. We did not. The fighting platform was made of wood.

The walls had filled with the archers from my village. It doubled the number of bows and they began to release at the men pushing the ram. Behind the ram were men carrying ladders. They had slightly miscalculated. The men carrying the shields were perilously close to the edge of the bridge and when one or two fell into the water our archers suddenly had clear targets. The men pushing were brave. I saw men with arrows in their legs and they were still pushing.

Tam climbed the ladder. He had a large bar as did Rafe's son Rafe. They stood by one of the cauldrons and moved it towards the fulcrum and the gutters. John held two torches. I peered over the side. The ram was close to the gate. There were two obstacles before they could break into the lower bailey. We had the drawbridge and then the gate. They would have to break through two thick pieces of wood. All of our archers now had targets. The men with shields had been thinned out. The ones with ladders scurried across the bridge and some of those fell. Then I heard the crunch as the ram hit the gate.

"Now, Tam!"

The two levers lifted one end of the cauldron and the steaming liquid flowed down the metal gullies, away from our walls and on to the ram. The fat and oil landed halfway along the war machine. It splashed and spattered. Boiling fat dripped through the gaps in the roof. John hurled one torch as Rafe and Tam ran to the other cauldron. There was a whoosh of flame as the torch ignited the fat mixture. Men screamed as boiling droplets of fat came through the wooden roof to burn them. Then the roof caught fire. Flames rose so high that I thought we might be singed. Then the second cauldron began to pour its deadly mixture to the burning ram and bridge and, even before John had hurled his torch, the oil and fat had caught fire. Not only the ram burned, so did the bridge and the ladders the men had been carrying. It was too much and the survivors fled back to their side of the moat. They did not go unmolested. My archers slew many of them as did my slingers. Men were still trapped inside the ram and their screams told us of a horrible death. The attack was over. They might attack again and they might build a new ram. They might even concentrate on their stone-thrower but we had bought ourselves some days and that counted as a victory!

"Throw water on the gate!" Men began to wet the smouldering gate and drawbridge.

I watched as the fire consumed the ram. We saw men set alight by the fire throwing themselves into the flooded ditch. The bridge was soon destroyed by the intense fire and then, as the structure of the wood was destroyed, the whole blackened mass sank below the water into the flooded ditch. The water hissed as it consumed the war machine. I looked along my fighting platform. Men cheered as though it was over. I saw none dead and knew that we had been lucky. We had hurt them but the enemy still surrounded the castle and they outnumbered us. This was not the moment for a dour face. I took off my helmet and, raising my sword, shouted, "Elsdon and King Henry!"

It was the right shout for all cheered. As men celebrated, Alan of Bellingham joined me, "Well done, lord, you judged the moment well."

"You are right, Alan, but let us wait until dawn to see what follows eh?"

My men forced me to sleep and I managed a couple of hours. When I woke, the snow, which had fallen throughout the attack, had stopped. As I had thought the snow had not lain. It was already melting and puddling. It would muddy the ground again and make an attack by the enemy less likely. Men had managed sleep and food had been cooked. We still had plenty of food. I had yet to begin rationing. This victory deserved a well-fed populace. I walked my walls. The enemies were in their camps and well out of range of our arrows. They were cooking food. There were fewer men around each camp. When I reached my gate, I heard the sound of axes in the woods beyond Henry's farm. They were still building the stone thrower.

Roger Two Swords approached me, "Lord, my men and I have counted the enemies who surround us. They barely outnumber us. We have hurt them."

"What do you suggest?"

"We end this, lord. We lower the bridge and use our horses to drive them hence. Garth and his archers, not to mention the men of the village, can use their arrows to thin them out. We men at arms have done nothing. The men would like to do this."

I smiled, "As would I but we have almost won. Let us not throw all away just to make ourselves gain a little glory. We have lost not a man. Let us keep it that way but you are right in one respect. We should exercise the horses. Have the men fetch the horses to the lower bailey. We will ride them. Perhaps we can fool our enemies into thinking we do plan an attack."

It took time for the horses to be saddled. It was late morning by the time Roger led the horses from my stables in the upper bailey. The sound of neighing horses and the drumming of hooves on the bridge from my upper bailey had an instant effect upon those besieging us. They stopped work and I heard horns. I smiled for the ridiculous plan appeared to have worked. I stared out to the south. It was strange. They formed up and made a shield wall yet they faced south and not north. Whom did they face? It was my men who were exercising their horses and it was their hooves they heard. Why were they facing south? My archers and my villagers manned the walls. From the keep, I heard the bell toll! Had more enemies been sighted? It had that effect on the Scots and English too. Matthew was still in the keep and he ran through the gate and the lower bailey. Men and horses scattered. He stopped below the gate, "Lord, there are men approaching down the Rothbury road and from the south, from the direction of Bellingham!"

Had he said just the Rothbury road then I would have feared enemy reinforcements. However, the road from Bellingham was not in the enemy's hands. There were men coming to relieve us, "Roger Two Swords, mount!" I turned to Alan of Bellingham and Garth Red Arrow, "Defend the castle. We may be able to break the siege."

I climbed on to Eagle's back. Matthew handed me a spear and then mounted his own horse. He did so somewhat awkwardly. His leg was still to heal completely.

Alan of Bellingham shouted, "Brother Paul, David of Amble, Tam, let us lower the bridge and open the gate."

The bridge landed with a splash. The snow had puddled on the other side of the already flooded ditch. Tam lifted the bar on his own and, as he carried it away Alan and David pulled open the gates. One man had been burned to death close by the gate. I could still smell his burning flesh. I looked ahead and saw that our enemies were forming up to fight the two columns which were coming to our relief. I spurred Eagle and he trotted across the bridge and then splashed through the melting snow. The bodies had fallen on the caltrops and we picked our way through them. It would not do to ride too quickly until we were on the road. There were just over fifteen of us and many more enemies were before us but we were mounted and, as I led my men to the church, I knew that the ones we attacked would have to endure blades from before and behind.

"Form line!" Matthew and Roger flanked me as we cantered through the devastated houses of the village.

I heard Scottish voices cry out as they heard our hooves. The warriors heading from Bellingham were afoot! They knew the horses were behind them. Spears and shields turned to face us. We passed the heads of Cedric and his son. It hardened our hearts. The shields and spears of our foes were not locked. The men who wielded them wore no mail. They had fought at our

The Bloody Border

walls and had lost. Any confidence they had had was burned away with the ram. I saw no knights leading them yet they faced us. They had courage. I heard a couple of older men keening a lament. They were singing a death song. As the men of Bellingham charged into the ones further away from us, we hit the spears and shields of the ones facing us. Spears shattered on our shields and mail. We struck from a height. My punch was so hard that the man I hit had little chance to defend himself with his shield. My spear drove into his right shoulder and as it crunched against a bone, I twisted the head and pulled it out. He fell to the side. I jabbed at the neck of the spearman who was fighting Matthew. The head of my spear struck something vital and blood spurted. Then they began to flee. One or two men, resigned to death, stood their ground and tried to fight against us but it was in vain. They caused little hurt and they died anyway. Their deaths bought a little time for the ones who had fled up the road to Otterburn. Horsemen with spears make short work of unarmoured men on foot.

"Wheel!" The men of Bellingham had come to our aid and we were duty-bound to go to their aid. Even as we turned the resistance of those fighting the men of Bellingham ended. We carved a bloody line through those who also joined the flight north. When I saw Cedric's son, Cedric, I reined in.

"Well met, my lord!"

"You and the men of Bellingham made a timely appearance."

"My father and brother bought us the time, lord. They held the farm while we took the flocks to Bellingham. He did not sound the horn so that we could sneak away to safety. They were brave men and we will make these Scottish bastards pay!"

"Aye, we will."

"Sir Ranulf sent a rider a day since and asked us to march to help him relieve you."

Then Sir Ranulf led the others! I looked down at the men of Bellingham, "I thank the men of Bellingham. I am in your debt. When time allows, I will reward you."

An older man stepped forward. He carried a two-handed axe in his hand. It looked ancient enough to be Danish! "I am Erik the Crusader, we thank you, lord. We only ask that you will send your horsemen to watch our borders too." He waved a hand at the devastation of Elsdon, "This could have been us."

I nodded, "Help yourself to weapons, mail and coins. I will take my men and go to the aid of Sir Ranulf!"

We rode towards the Rothbury road. There had been fewer men on that side and Sir Ranulf needed no help. The enemy were either dead or prisoners by the time we reached him. He had mounted men with him and he reined in as we met. We raised our visors. He held out his arm, "I am sorry we are late, Sir William."

"I am just glad that you came."

"Sir Eustace is a traitor. When we heard your bell sound, I sent a rider to Rothbury. He was told there was no danger and that you were just testing your bell. The man I sent was suspicious and he rode towards your castle. When he saw your manor ringed by the fires of enemies, he returned to me. I sent for the men of Bellingham for I did not have enough of my own men. It took some days to gather our men. We had to attack from both sides at once. My men and I had to head north first for I had no other way of relieving the siege and attacking the traitors who were to the northeast of you. That meant fording the river west of Rothbury." He waved his arm around, "Although the castle of Rothbury remains in enemy hands, we have dispersed the men who held the road."

"Aye lord but Otterburn is besieged too. We need to go to their aid. The men who fled here will join them. Those reinforcements may swing the balance against Sir Richard."

I saw him frown. "And I have to return to Rothbury! They lied to my man and I cannot leave an enemy who can threaten my manor." He looked at the wrecked camps, "I tell you what, Sir William, let me ride to Rothbury. If they are reasonable men then they will surrender to me. If they do so I will come back here tomorrow and we can march to Otterburn."

I saw the sense in his words. He was thinking logically. This was not vacillation but delaying might cause the fall of Otterburn, "Sir Ranulf, you must do what you think right for your manor. We will ride before dawn and go to the aid of Otterburn."

"With less than thirty men?"

"I would go with just my squire and page if that was all I had left to me."

"You are a good knight. We will come as soon as we can. Do not throw your life away unnecessarily!"

"I have no intention of throwing anyone's life away, my lord." I whipped Eagle's head around and headed back to my castle. I had much to do.

Chapter 16

My people had already begun to go through the village. There was much to do and more to repair. Cedric and his son's heads were removed. There were no bodies but we would bury the heads in our churchyard. The enemies' bodies, both Scottish and English, were gathered and the half-finished stone-thrower was used to make a pyre. We burned them. Their ashes would be scattered over the land they had tried to take. That would be the only part of Elsdon they held. The women began to cook food. The men of Bellingham would stay the night and they deserved a good feast. The man who had led them was an old soldier. Erik the Crusader had served in the Holy Land. He and I got on well. "We have no lord in our village, lord, but the priest and I make certain that the lads practise with their bows on Sundays and Holy Days. We cannot compare with your men but they have good hearts. With the arms and mail we have taken from the field we will all be better warriors in future." He waved a hand at our defences, "We will make our village stronger too!"

My archers began to collect the spent arrows. Some were whole. Others had tips and flights which could be reused. The mail and weapons were taken into my castle and then the men of my manor, my men at arms and my archers gathered in the church and Brother Paul gave thanks to God for our salvation. While all of the men were gathered together, and we stood outside looking at the desolation that was Elsdon, I told them of my plan.

"Many of your homes are destroyed. It will take until after Christmas to rebuild them. Until then you will live in my castle.

Tomorrow, I take my men at arms and archers to the aid of Otterburn. We may be too late but we cannot leave the people of that manor to endure what happened to Yalesham. Sir Ranulf has said that he will aid us but even if he will not, we will still go."

Rafe said, "If you need us with you, lord, then we will come!"

The men all cheered. They were in good heart. They were my people. I smiled and held my hands up for silence, "You need to begin the sorry work of undoing the mischief caused by our foes. We will now have a harder winter. If we delay in healing the land then it may harm us all. Stay here, Rafe, and help rebuild Elsdon."

It felt like a pathetically small number I led from my castle. A chill wind blew from the east and snow flurries followed us as we headed to Otterburn. Garth had two archers ahead of us as scouts. We stopped twice when we spied men on the road. They were dead men. They had fled the field and succumbed to their wounds. This land was a harsh one and the men had paid for their folly with their lives.

John the archer and James rode back and held up their hands. We stopped. "Lord, the tower still stands. It is ringed by enemies. There looks to be almost as many as there were around Elsdon."

"Has the wall of Otterburn been breached?"

"Aye lord, but not the tower. They have a ram. We heard men preparing their attack. They were sharpening weapons."

That made sense. They would expect me to come but not yet. They would try to use the ram on the tower. Sir Richard had had to endure a longer siege than we. His outer wall had been destroyed. His archers were fewer in number and they would be running out of arrows. He would not know that we had been relieved. The reinforcements he had seen arriving would not look like broken men. We had to do that which looked and sounded the act of a mad man. We would need to attack. We would be attacking five times our number and none would expect that.

"Garth, take John and my archers. Cross the river and do that which we did when we came the last time. Harass the enemy. This time we wait until you attack and they commit to an assault on your position. The ground is muddier and the river in full spate. They should not be able to get close to you but take no risks. Fall back if you have to. We will try to destroy the ram and then retreat to the ridge and await Sir Ranulf. I do not doubt that he will arrive sometime but we cannot allow the ram to begin to breach the tower."

"Aye lord. Come, Master John, you are becoming a fair archer. No holding horses for you today!"

They headed across the river. We knew this road as well as any. We had patrolled as far as the border. We had charged down the road before. The slope would aid us. We tightened girths and mounted. We walked through the dark of early morning. The fallen snow was beginning to lie. This was the start of the winter blanket. Soon it would grip the land. This was the last throw of the dice for the Earl of Fife, Sir Eustace and Sir Malcolm.

"Matthew, when I give the command to charge then sound the horn. Men, I want you to cheer as though we are leading the whole of Cleveland. Our aim is simple. Kill the men by the ram and then destroy the ram. If we succeed then we retreat to the ridge and make them bleed when they try to attack us."

I looked to the east. A thin light could be seen. Dawn would be upon us soon enough. This time we knew where they lay. A straggly and thin stand of trees would hide us. We could see the shape of the tower rising above the trees but nothing of the attackers. We knew of the disposition of our foes from our scouts. We knew the lie of the land and we would have to trust to the skill of our horses. I knew it would take Garth some time to get into position. They would leave their horses well back from the river and then crawl, unseen, to the river bank. The winter rains and recent snows had made the river burst its banks. It was wider now than the last time we had come to the aid of Sir James. That could only aid us.

Dawn began to break and still, we had not heard the sounds of alarm. We heard, instead, the sound of swords being sharpened as men prepared to begin the assault. I sensed the nervousness from Matthew. He was desperate to speak but he had been ordered to be silent and he would obey his orders. Suddenly I heard what sounded like birds taking flight. I knew what it was. It was the sound of arrows plummeting from the sky. The cries and shouts from the besiegers confirmed it. Garth and his archers sent flight after flight across the river. When I heard them strike wood, I knew that the enemy had turned their shields to stop the arrow storm. I heard a Scottish voice shout something. I had to imagine what was happening for it was hidden behind a screen of trees. Whoever commanded would send his own archers and crossbows to the river. Their attention would be split between the river and the tower. I raised my spear and led my men towards the road. We walked towards the high point of the road. When I reached it, I waved my spear to the left and right. Matthew tucked in behind me and the rest spread out in two lines. The men besieging Otterburn were just two hundred paces below us. There were twenty men armed with bows, slings and crossbows moving towards the river. Then there was a line of men with spears forming up and supporting the archers. The rest were gathered around the ram. A debate was going on. Their attention was divided.

"Charge!" The horn sounded and I spurred Eagle. He leapt forward and we charged. The horn had confused the attackers. They were being attacked from two different directions. When the bell in Otterburn began to peel it added to the chaos. I saw men looking east, west and south. In that time, we had covered one hundred paces. It was only then that a Scottish voice began to give commands. As I lowered my spear, I saw the Earl of Fife, Sir Eustace and Sir Malcolm. They had mounted their horses. We had charged from the south and the sun was rising in the east. They saw shadows coming from the trees. The shadows masked our numbers. To the west, I saw the men sent to harass my archers falling back and Garth began to send his arrows towards the Earl and the leaders. One struck a knight who was next to the Earl of Fife. It was such a true arrow that I knew it to be from the bow of Garth Red Arrow. It plunged down and hit the knight who was not wearing his helmet. He fell from his horse. He was dead.

Then my attention was on the men before us for they had belatedly begun to form lines. I lowered my spear. Eagle's snapping jaws distracted the two men before me. Their spears hit my cantle. My spear rammed into the chest of one of them and Eagle bowled over the other. Suddenly the door from the tower burst open and Sir Richard led his beleaguered men from the tower. Those attacking might have resisted but the Earl turned his horse and led his knights north. He was heading for home. Sir Malcolm, who was just thirty paces from me hesitated and then, seeing me, turned and followed his cousin. I felt a spear hit my shield. I stuck my own spear into the arm of a spearman as Matthew used my banner to hit the man who had struck my shield. There were none between me and Sir Eustace. I saw him and his squire, along with Godfrey of Etal, turn their horses to head north. I was sorely tempted to follow them but Sir Richard needed my help.

I shouted, "Garth! Fetch our archers." I wheeled my horse and, standing in my stirrups, made him rear. His hooves clattered on the skulls of the two men standing next to me. As they tumbled to the ground, they banged into two more men and my spear took one in the arm. Falling and turning he tore the spear from my hand. I drew my sword. Spurring Eagle, I galloped over bodies already slain by my men, towards the ram around which the Scots were fighting. I leaned from the saddle to hack into the arm of one man. Roger Two Swords was using both of his weapons at once and he and I carved a path towards Sir Richard and his men. The sun was now shining, albeit dimly through grey clouds and the Scots and English began to flee. When arrows descended upon them the trickle turned to a flood as the attackers realised that their leaders had, in the main, deserted them.

There was an exception. A young knight, his squire and two men at arms suddenly launched themselves at us. They must have been mounting their horses. Perhaps they meant to flee. I know not whatever the reason they rode at us. I saw that the knight had a blue quartered rampant lion. Even as I turned my horse to face him, I wondered if he was related to the King. He had a lance and he came directly at me. I could leave the other four to my men who were already turning to come to my aid. The lance was the wrong weapon in such a battle. This was uneven ground. Bodies littered the earth and his horse had to pick his way towards me. He did not have enough room to get up to speed but, worst of all, his lance tip wavered from my head to my foot. He was too excited and could not control the end. I brought my shield across my body. If the tip of the lance came towards my head I would simply duck. It was more likely that if he hit at all it would be my shield he struck. He had an open sallet type helmet and I saw his eyes were fierce and angry. A knight fought cold. He had to be calm and detached. I had been taught by my father and he knew his business better than any. The Scot stood in his stirrups and punched at me with his lance. He aimed at my head but the weight of the lance dragged the end down and it struck my shield. I was already swinging my sword as I deflected the lance to my left with my shield. I aimed at his middle but, as he sat down my sword slid up and rammed across his throat. He had a coif there for protection but my blow was so hard that I broke his neck. I saw the life go from his young eyes. He slid from his saddle.

The cheer from behind me told me that the other three had been defeated and we had won. Lifting my visor, I turned. Sir Richard raised his visor and saluted me with his sword. We had both survived. I knew not how but we had.

"I am sorry it took so long to come to your aid. We were besieged until yesterday."

Sir Richard shook his head, "We did not expect you at all. We both agreed that we would hunker down until we were relieved. Did you lose many?"

"We lost Cedric and his son but it could have been worse. Sir Eustace joined the Scots."

"I know. He was here at this siege."

"Did you have many losses?"

He nodded, "A family perished. It would have been worse but for the sacrifice of two of Sir James' men. They were heroic and we will honour them."

"Sir Ranulf and the men of Bellingham came to my aid. He has gone to Rothbury. He said he will follow us here."

I looked at the tower. The ram had not reached the stone and the main damage appeared to be to the wall. We had suffered worse. Our village would need to be rebuilt. I had ideas about that already. It took until dark to clear the field and to burn the Scottish dead. Knights had perished and they had fine swords, mail, helmets and coins. Sir Richard did not have enough space in his hall for us to use and so we used the tents the Scottish had abandoned. We captured many horses for only the knights and squires had had time to mount. The other horses were sumpters

The Bloody Border

but they would make good draught horses. We also had mail and weapons. Knights had perished and they had fine swords, mail, helmets and coins. We divided the booty. Sir Richard had not laid in as many supplies and so we had poor rations. My men did not mind. Soon we would be back home and there we would enjoy the finest of food.

Sir Ranulf arrived in the middle of the next day. He looked at the detritus of battle. "Sir Eustace has much to answer for. I sent word to the Bishop and the Sherriff after Rothbury surrendered. The question is, what do we do now?"

"King Henry appointed my father Earl Marshal of the North. He said he would return. I am surprised he has not yet reached here. The three of us could cross the border and chastise the Scots but I think it would have more legitimacy if my father led us."

"A wise head on young shoulders."

Sir Richard nodded his assent, "Besides, we have much to do before winter sets in. Already icy blasts are knocking at our doors. This mischief could still cost us dear."

And so we returned to Elsdon and began to rebuild our homes. Everyone worked. Women, children, the old; all toiled to make walls and rooves to keep us warm in winter. This time we used stone for the houses. They would not be destroyed so easily and we built using the same techniques I had used in my castle. Byres and barns made enclosed yards which could be defended like castles. The walls linking the farms were also built of stone. We had only lost four farms, a mill and a house but the farms and the mill had been the most prosperous in the village. Everyone joined in with the building. Cedric's family moved into the castle while we undertook the labour. With everyone joining in we repaired the mill first. We needed bread. Then we repaired Tom's farm. After hard days of relentless effort, we had half of the buildings almost completed. We just had the roof of each house to finish. The snows slowed down our work. I still had had no word from my father and that worried me. It was not like him to let anyone down, least of all his son.

I had little time to dwell on such matters. Like everyone else, we laboured from dusk until dawn. Once we had repaired the leat and the moat dried out we were able to recover the ram and the bridge. They were cut up for firewood. The church had been damaged. Luckily it was the least damaged of all the buildings. When we repaired it, we added a bell tower made of stone. We moved the bell from the keep to the church. That way Brother Paul could ring the bell to summon the manor to church. I kept my word and after the battle, we took tools, weapons and food to the people of Bellingham. We would not forget them.

The snows returned and we worked while a blizzard raged around us. We found it hard to see any who was not within six feet of us. Then the skies cleared and we had a night so cold that the water which remained in my ditch froze enough for men to walk on. Winter had come and come with a vengeance!

We were just finishing the bell tower when Phillip the Priest, who was at the top of the tower helping Brother Paul and Alan of Bellingham, shouted, "Lord, I see men approaching along the Bellingham Road. They have mailed men with them and there are knights."

We were all nervous of mailed men but the south was the one direction enemies would not use. I sent Matthew up the tower and he shouted, "Lord, it is your father, it is the Earl of Cleveland. He has come!"

**Part Three
Thomas, Earl Marshal of the North**

Chapter 17

When I had left my son, I had thought I would just head to my home, collect my knights and return to him. Things did not turn out the way I had hoped. The journey south took longer than I had expected. The King had told all of my new title. Everyone wished me to help them in some way. The King thought the northern border was secure and peace had come. He was wrong. It soon emerged that it was bubbling with unrest. My son's fears about Sir Eustace were not only justified, but they also hinted at a greater plot. King John's rule had left many men dissatisfied. King Alexander was weak and some of the Norman barons thought they had a better chance of manipulating him than King Henry. Sir Ranulf and the Sherriff insisted upon entertaining me for some days and it was there I learned of the plots and plans of unsettled barons. A sinister picture began to emerge. I learned much. By the time I finally reached Durham I was concerned and anxious about my son. He was beleaguered!

The Bishop of Durham was particularly worried. I told him my news and his face and words told me that he had the same fears. "The Sherriff of Westmoreland has told me of bands of men wandering the western fells. Cattle and sheep have been stolen. Some of my lords have suffered too. This is not isolated, Earl Thomas. I see a plan in all of this. He has asked for your help. All know of your prowess and the quality of your men."

"Bishop Poore, my son and Sir Richard are now isolated and surrounded by enemies. I will gather my men and return there. When the border is secure, I will go to the aid of the Sherriff."

Those were my plans. They crumbled to dust. It took longer to reach Stockton than I had planned. As soon as I reached Stockton, I wrote letters to my knights and to the King. I sent outriders. The first part went well. I sent for my knights and their men. It would be a small force but a highly mobile one. Sir Peter, Sir William of Hartburn. Sir Geoffrey Fitzurse, Sir Robert of Redmarshal, Sir Gilles of Wulfestun, Sir Richard of East Harlsey and Sir Fótr of Norton were all veteran knights. Now that Sir Edward had been wounded, I even had a reliable knight I could leave to watch my land. With more than a hundred and twenty men at arms, not to mention a hundred archers, the force I led would be more than enough to calm the border close by Otterburn. It took more than a month to gather them. Sir Peter and Sir Richard lived far to the south. They could not simply leave their people with winter approaching. They had plans to make and men to organize. It all took time. I thought we had enough of that commodity which you cannot buy. I was wrong. Sir Robert was anxious about leaving Isabelle. The birth of my next grandchild was imminent. When they all arrived, I held a council of war. We pored over maps so that they would know the land. I told them of the suspicions we had and the potential conspirators. We were ready to ride. We had delayed but I did not think it would be a crucial delay.

Then the message came from the Constable of Carlisle. Carlisle was a royal castle. Its castellan, Sir Baldwin de Ferrers, answered to the King. It was his rider found me. The letter almost demanded that I ride west to help the Constable to curb the banditry and brigandage along the border. Like Sir Eustace, he had lords who had expressed a desire to be part of Scotland. The debatable lands north of Carlisle had always been a bone of contention. Now they threatened the very security of the whole frontier. The Earl of Chester added his pleas to the letter and his missive meant that I had no choice. If I went to the aid of my son when he was not being attacked, I would be accused of nepotism. When my men were mustered, we left Stockton.

The Bloody Border

Instead of heading north we headed west. We rode to the aid of Carlisle and not Elsdon.

The journey to Carlisle would normally take between three and four days. This journey took longer. The one who was the happiest was Henry Samuel. This was his first campaign. He had his helmet, shield, short sword and mail. He had his horse and he was as happy as a puppy with two tails! He did not shut up all the way to Barnard Castle. I had planned on staying but the night. However, the attitude of the baron and the news he conveyed made me stay an extra day. I learned of the problems of the high passes. Once this castle had been controlled by my family. King John had given it to a man with estates in both Scotland and England. I did not totally trust de Balliol.

"Is this the work of Scottish lords trying to retake our land?"

Baron de Balliol shook his head. "They are not Scottish rebels they are chancers who take advantage of the disorder in this northern land."

He suddenly realised what he had said. I was the Earl Marshal of the North! "I am sorry, Earl, I meant no disrespect. You have only been charged with the Northern Marches for a short time."

I knew he meant exactly what he had said. De Balliol had sympathies with Alexander yet he held his fiefdom through Henry. He would do as little as possible to control the lawlessness. I waved a hand and smiled, I could play this game too. "Do not worry, my lord, I am not sensitive. What is it that they do?"

"They live in the lands around Hobkirk. The lands there are inhospitable. No lord rules there. Rather than farm they head south, steal cattle and slaves and head north. They are hardy men and they can live in the bleak highlands. The captives are sold north of the Forth and the cattle either eaten or sold to Scottish lords. When we reach their homes there is no evidence of their wrongdoing. The Sherriff has captured many of them and tried them. There is no evidence to convict them. He has had to let them go each time."

That did not sound right to me. There were ways of using courts to try men. It seemed to me that the Sherriff and Balliol had colluded with the raiders. Already I had a plan to destroy these bandits. What angered me was that de Balliol and the

The Bloody Border

Sherriff could have done what I planned to do. I knew why de Balliol had not, he enjoyed the disorder but the Sherriff? I would need to speak with him. I spent a day speaking with the burghers of Barnard. They told me much that helped me formulate a plan.

The next morning before I left, I took de Balliol to one side, "My lord, you know me? My reputation, I mean." He nodded and I saw fear in his eyes. "Good. I am the King's man but, more than that, I am of the blood of the Warlord. In times past this castle was controlled by my family and there was peace in this land. Now it appears there is not. You see where I am going with this? Do not play games. Do not try to play one side off against the other. You either keep this land safe or…"

"Or?" I heard the terror in his voice.

"You make an enemy of me. If that is the case then there is no hole in which you could hide." I smiled and gently patted his back, "But you are a loyal subject of the King who will keep these high passes safe!"

My knights had been close enough to see that something was going on but they had not heard what transpired. I trusted all of my men and, as we left Barnard Castle, I told them what I had said and why.

Sir Geoffrey asked, as we headed west, "How will you stop them? They are clever."

"You think bandits are cleverer than us, Sir Geoffrey?" He shook his head. "Good. I am glad you agree. It is simple. We use patience. We have the finest archers in the land. They circle Hobkirk. When they see the raiders leave for a raid then they tell us. This is the time of year when they will raid. We catch them returning with their ill-gotten gains. We kill them or hang them"

Sir Geoffrey looked appalled, "There will be no trial?"

"If any survive then they will be tried. I am keen to reach my son and so I urge you all to think of the people who live here. We cut out the canker and the ordinary folk will prosper."

It was only Sir Geoffrey who was shocked. My other knights all agreed with me and I did not need to speak to my sergeants and archers to know that they would slay any bandit in a heartbeat. Padraig the Wanderer's wife had been a captive of such men. If he caught them then it would be all I could do to make him kill them quickly! These bandits and brigands had made a choice and they would have to live with the consequences.

Carlisle had been much improved since the time of the Warlord. It was a mighty fortress. My thoughts went to the Sherriff. Why had he not solved this problem and, more worryingly, why had he sent for me? Robert de Vieuxpont had been the Sherriff I had known and the new one was unknown to me, Sir Baldwin de Ferrers was a newly appointed Sherriff. He had been in position slightly longer than my son at Elsdon. I had fought on these bloody borders many times but I had never encountered him. Why not? When I met him, I found that I did not like him. He smiled too easily. He was oily. He tried to flatter me and I never liked that. He tried to excuse his inaction by saying he was only recently appointed. I thought of my son and what he had done in the short time he had been Lord of Elsdon. I did not believe him and when he said that he was a cousin of Eustace of Rothbury then I became even more suspicious. He obviously did not know of the information my son had sent to me. The conspiracy began to crystallize before my eyes.

I took him to one side, "I will deal with this problem and then do that which I said I would do. I will solve the problem of the Tweed border. You will provide me and my men with every man at arms and archer that you do not need to watch Carlisle's walls."

"If I can be of any assistance…"

"What I need you to do is feed my men and horses and guard these walls." I stared into his eyes and let him know my innermost thoughts. I did not trust him. I now saw that this was a ploy to get me as far away from my son and the border as possible. As soon as I left him, I sent for David of Wales. "Take every archer we have. I want you to ring Hobkirk. Take supplies for you may have to watch for some time. You will stay hidden and watch. When these bandits leave their lair to raid and raid they will, then you shadow them and send word to me. Do not stop them. We let them capture the cattle and then, when they return home, we slaughter them. The animals and the captives will be evidence enough. The Sherriff has allowed them to escape before now by using the law to help them. We will use the law to kill them!"

He grinned. This was his type of work. "Aye, lord! There will be little treasure but killing vermin is always a task we enjoy!"

I took my knights riding the next day. I wanted privacy. We rode west to the coast and the end of the old Roman Wall. I dismounted and gestured for them to join me. We stared over the remnants of the turf rampart which had marked the western end of the Roman Empire. "We have been duped. The Sherriff has drawn us here so that I cannot go to the aid of my son and your brother, Sir Robert."

"Then let us go to their aid, my lord!" Sir Robert did not want to lose his brother and Elsdon for a second time.

"As much as I wish to there is a problem here and if we leave now then it is the men of Cleveland who will be blamed for the loss of animals, land and captives. The King would blame me and the Sherriff's position would be strengthened. There is a conspiracy here. I plan to end the terror of these bandits and then head to Elsdon. We have to trust that my son and Sir Richard can hold out. This means we rely on our archers but they are the best of men. I have the Sherriff's archers and they will ride with us, as will their men at arms. When we leave for Elsdon we will leave this county safe from enemies. The Sherriff thinks he plays a game. I will show him that he is a novice at this sort of game. We deal with the bandits and then Elsdon and Otterburn. When the border is safe then we come back here and settle accounts with the Sherriff. I brought you here so that you know my mind. When we are in Carlisle, we play the fool. We appear stupid, indolent, whatever it takes to lull the Sherriff into a false sense of security. David of Wales will tell us when we leave. The raiders will not succeed. We will stop them and kill them; everyone! Until then, enjoy yourselves!"

Once back in the castle I spoke with Ridley the Giant. He would tell the sergeants what they needed to know. Then we waited. It was hard to appear indolent and it was not in my nature. In addition, the time spent in the castle made me dwell on my son and his perilous position. Was I making the correct decision? That there was brigandage on a huge scale was not in question. Speaking in the town of Carlisle with burghers and merchants I learned that the debatable lands were still a bone of contention and the raids were the Scottish way of applying pressure. They wanted the lands under their control. I had visited the land and found little in it to warrant such bloodshed. For the Scots, it seemed almost a matter of pride. Christmas was approaching and I knew that I was keeping my knights from their homes and families. It made it hard to chat easily with the Sherriff. I had to play a part I did not enjoy.

The Sherriff thought he had fooled me. When we dined, he kept telling me how the Scots were slippery. "They will have the cattle and the captives dispersed and sent north before we even know. This is a thankless task, Earl. I am glad you are here but I fear that you and your men will become a permanent feature here in the west." His words confirmed my suspicions. We had been dragged here to allow the Scots in the east to take Elsdon and Otterburn. Until David of Wales sent to me we were helpless.

The weather began to change. My leg had healed but I had a limp and it ached in the cold weather. It began to ache as we peered north and east towards the distant hills. We saw snow appear on the hilltops to the east of us and the wind grew colder each day. The rain and sleet made life uncomfortable. I felt for my archers living outside. Then the snow began to lie. A slight thaw turned it to water and the ground became muddy and slippery. Winter was growing closer. Would we catch these thieves before the ground became too frozen for us to move?

The Sherriff, annoyingly, continued to smile. He thought we were being duped. I allowed him his delusion. My men at arms kept watch on messengers the Sherriff might send for help and I waited, each day, for the rider from the east. Eventually, it was Cedric Warbow who rode in, "We have them, lord." He spoke quietly to me. "They are five miles north of Gilsland and heading north. They are going home. Dick has two men trailing them and he has taken the rest along their line of march. We found their camps as they had headed south. They do not follow the main roads. These are little more than hunter's trails."

"How many do we face?"

"There are sixty men. No knights amongst them but they have two men on horses. They have captured more than sixty head of cattle; a flock of sheep and they have twenty-two captives already."

"Go tell Ridley that we ride." Turning to Mark and Henry Samuel I said, "Tell the knights we have our prey. I wish them mounted."

"Aye lord." They ran off. Both were eager for action. They knew that Matthew and John had been fighting for my son and they had been inactive watchers. It did not sit well with them.

I went to the Sherriff, "Have your archers mounted and fetch your horse. We have found the enemy."

His face fell briefly and then he rubbed his hands together, "Most excellent news, Earl. We leave in the morning?"

I shook my head, "We leave now." I watched his every move. When he went to his chamber to don his mail, I saw a servant slip out. Mark had returned to me. "Follow him and take Cedric with you. The Sherriff's man does not leave the castle."

By the time we reached the stables my men at arms and knights were mounted. I did not see Cedric Warbow. The Sherriff only had fifteen mounted archers. He saw my look of disapproval and gave me a nervous look, "We have few mounted archers, my lord."

"Which might explain why you have failed to stop these incursions." Just then Mark and Cedric appeared. Cedric nodded. The messenger had been taken. The Sherriff thought he had sent word to his confederates. His messenger was not going anywhere. "No matter, we end the threat this day and then I shall put in place measures to make this border secure."

We left as snow began to fall and to lie. Had the Sherriff been leading the chase we would have walked our horses. I knew we had but fifteen miles to travel and we galloped. We found Rob and Michael, my archers, twelve miles from Carlisle. They were north of Gilsland. I saw that the raiders had visited Gilsland. My archers had tended the wounds of the men who had fought to stop their cattle and families being taken. They looked accusingly at the Sherriff, "My lord! We pay taxes! Where is our protection? These bandits grow bold! Last year they did not raid this far south. Where next? Lancaster?"

The Sherriff rose in his saddle, "How dare you speak to me like that! I am Sherriff."

I turned to him and snapped, "For the present! This man is right. You have not done your duty and if you say that they cannot speak like that to you then I will have you bound and tried for dereliction of duty!" He was silent. I looked down at the man whose head was encased in a bandage, "Fear not, the raids will end now."

Michael pointed north, "They are not far ahead in that direction, lord. Their path is clear to see. They are heading north."

He was right. The large number of cattle and sheep they had taken left a clear trail of hoof marks and dung. The muddy track cut a dark line through the increasingly white landscape. The black muddy line wound its way north. The land rose and fell. This was not a Roman road. It followed the contours of the land. When we began to pass steaming piles of dung then I knew we were close to the warband. I had to trust that David of Wales was ahead of them. When we launched our attack, he would stop the flight of any who might try to evade us. We reached a rise and looked down at the shallow valley below us. The mass of animals, captives and bandits lay just a mile away. They appeared to be watering the animals. The Sherriff had been silent since Gilsland. I said to him, "What is it that we see? A river?"

Already the bandits had seen us and they began to press on. They had goads and they began to beat both animals and captives. The three riders mounted their horses. I saw light glinting from helmets.

The Sherriff said, sulkily, "I know not!"

I looked at one of his archers, "You! What is it called?"

"Caud Beck, lord. It can be jumped but at this time of year it is muddy."

"Good. Take your archers and ride to the west. Get ahead of them and then begin to send your arrows and kill the bandits!"

"Aye lord." He seemed eager to do my bidding. "Come on, you heard the Earl, let us ride!"

The Sherriff said, "We must capture them and put them on trial."

"I believe you tried that before and it failed. Let us try something a little more Draconian. Hitherto the blood spilt on this border has been English. Let us even it up! Form line! For King Henry and England!"

We began to canter towards the animals and captives. Those riding on virgin snow made the fastest progress. Those of us riding in the centre along the black and muddy line of mud and dung struggled. We were seen and the bandits knew the game was up. They did what they had done before. They left the animals and ran. It soon became obvious that the bandits had left the animals and captives to their own devices. The captives and animals waited just north of Caud Beck. The bandits were heading for Hobkirk. It was more than thirty miles away but they must have thought that they could evade us. They did not know of my ambush. We reached the captives and I shouted, "We will return for you. You are safe now!" I noticed the hateful stares cast in the direction of the Sherriff. Once we cleared the animals and captives the going became easier. The Scots, even though they were on foot, knew the land and they were like mountain goats.

Henry Samuel, riding to my left, pointed west, "Look, Earl!"

I saw that the Carlisle archers had dismounted and their arrows were falling amongst the raiders. It drove them east. The ones ahead disappeared over a low ridge. Our horses were tiring now. When we crested the rise I saw, ahead, a thin line of men and their horses. It was David of Wales. The archers of Carlisle were adequate bowmen. Mine were the best. They were hitting everything that they aimed at. The three riders leading the warband waved their men towards the east and tried to lead the survivors away from the two bands of archers and my horsemen.

"Charge!"

We wheeled and began to hunt them down. The Carlisle archers mounted their horses for they could not release without hitting us. David of Wales and his men continued to weed out the bandits. Ridley and my men at arms were ahead of us. I saw their swords as they struck heads and backs which had no mail to deflect the blow. The white snow became pocked marked with red. My men were so efficient that I had a clean blade. None I had passed were alive. Soon there were just three Scots who remained and they rode horses. "Ridley, follow them!"

"Aye, lord." He led my men at arms after the three horsemen.

The Bloody Border

I reined in and turned. "Where is the Sherriff?" I could not see him. The last sight I had of him was when we had crested the rise and seen the bandits being attacked by my archers.

Mark pointed to the northwest, "There, lord, with his squire!"

"Sir Fótr, Sir Gilles, after him. I want him as a prisoner."

"Aye lord."

"The rest of you, back to the captives."

As we rode, I looked to the sky. The afternoon had but a couple of hours of daylight left. "Sir Geoffrey, we will have to leave these animals and captives at Gilsland. Ride ahead and warn them of our return."

"Aye lord."

It was dark before we reached Gilsland. The captives were exhausted. The archer who commanded the bowmen of Carlisle was Richard of Brampton. "Richard of Brampton, I charge you with returning the animals and captives to their homes. They have suffered. When you return to Carlisle there will be a new order. The Sherriff, if he is not already dead, will be tried for treason."

"We did not enjoy watching people suffer, lord."

"I know. That will change. We will head back to Carlisle."

"Thank you, Earl, you have brought hope to the lands of the west."

As we headed down the Roman road to Carlisle I wondered if this delay would hurt my son. The conspiracy was clear. It would take two or three days, perhaps more, to get to Elsdon. His castle could have fallen. I had wanted to destroy the nest of vipers that was Hobkirk. That would have to wait. Ridley the Giant caught up with us when we were less than two miles from the castle. There were three horses that they led.

"They died?"

"They were piss poor warriors, lord but they resisted." He pointed to the three hauberks draped over the saddles. "All were sergeants at arms. One had the remnants of a surcoat. It was the livery of Fife, lord."

That was the last piece of the puzzle. The horses were exhausted and we were weary. Before they were stabled, I said, "We ride at dawn for Elsdon. Give the horses grain."

The stable master said, "I will have to ask the Sherriff for his permission, lord."

"The Sherriff is no more. I will appoint a new castellan until I can inform the King of the disorder and unrest in his northern marches."

"Yes, lord."

Sir Geoffrey had ordered food for us. We washed and then ate. I wondered why Sir Fótr and Sir Gilles had not returned. "Sir Geoffrey I would have you stay here as constable until we can have a new Sherriff."

He nodded, "You will arrest the Sherriff?"

"If we can capture him. He is a slippery man."

We had just finished when the doors of the Great Hall burst open and Sir Fótr and Sir Gilles hauled the Sherriff in. They threw him to the ground. Sir Fótr pointed an accusing finger at the former Sherriff, "He has no honour. He sent his squire to slow us down! He was a brave youth and he died."

"Sir Richard of East Harlsey, tomorrow you and your men at arms will escort the former Sherriff to Durham. Tell the Bishop all. This creature will stand trial. For the rest of us, we ride to do what we planned. We go to the aid of my son and Sir Richard of Otterburn and I pray to God that we are not too late."

Chapter 18

The late return of my knights and the arduous day we had endured meant we left late and travelled more slowly than I would have liked. As we left Carlisle and headed along the road which ran south of the wall the snow began to fall harder. My leg ached and I pulled my cloak more tightly about myself. Henry Samuel, who had been silent all morning while we had prepared, asked, "Lord, you and your knights fought the Scots before and defeated them. Are we destined to fight them for the rest of our lives?"

"When we fought last time, it was us against knights. We fought French knights and we fought Scottish knights. This is different. This is more insidious. There are traitors involved."

"Lord, what is insidious?"

I smiled at Mark. He still had a long way to go to become a knight. "It means less obvious. This is an attempt to retake England piece by piece. The men who fight were men at arms, some may even be former knights but they seek to make this land inhospitable. It is already a harsh and unforgiving land. If your family is taken captive and your animals were stolen then you might leave. If people leave then the lords who live here will have to leave also."

Henry Samuel nodded, "You said a conspiracy, lord?"

"Aye, Sam, the Sherriff and Sir Eustace have joined forces with the Earl of Fife. Until King Alexander exercises his power they will continue to conspire. The King does not know that his throne is at risk. The county of Northumberland is a rich prize. If the Earl of Fife could get his hands on that then he might be able to grasp the crown and wrest it from Alexander's head."

We rode in silence until we came to the small road which crossed the wall and headed north to the tiny village of Cawburn. The raiders had attacked the village. As we passed through some of the captives the archers had rescued waved at us. I saw men hewing wood to make a palisade. They would fight harder the next time the Scots came south. We were riding the borderlands. The border was not marked anywhere. There was no sign indicating which country we trod. There were no manors in this bleak and empty land. There were no lords with armed men to protect them.

Sir Robert nudged his horse next to mine. Just as I was worried about my son, so he was fearful for the fate of his brother. "Do you think we will be in time, lord?"

"I honestly do not know. We were tricked and manipulated and I was led west. That had to be for a purpose. If we had had time, I would have beaten an answer from the Sherriff but that would have taken too long. Time is something we do not have. If we are too late and find devastated manors then rest assured the Scots will suffer. The King has made me Earl Marshal of the Northern March. If he does not like the way I do things then he should dismiss me. Until that time I do things the way I have always done them; my way!"

Sir Fótr had joined us, "And how far do we ride this day, my lord? The horses are already weary."

I looked at Sir Robert, "You know this land as well as I do. Where can we find shelter for the night? This weather will do none of us any good if we have to sleep outside."

"There are no manors lord. Bellingham is large and has a small church. If the Scots have not taken it then that would be the place to which I would head but there is no castle there and if the Scots chose, they could easily take it and cut off your son from the south."

The Palatinate was too far south. The Bishop of Durham needed another manor and castle at Bellingham. I urged on my men. The further north we travelled the bleaker were the prospects for Sir William and Sir Richard!

The snow had stopped as we approached Bellingham. The night was clear and I could see the breath forming before me. Torches appeared in the dark and armed men stood before us, "Identify yourselves! I am Erik the Crusader."

I saw by the light of the torch that he was mailed and held a Danish war axe. "And I am the King's man, Thomas, Earl of Cleveland. My men and I seek shelter."

He stepped forward and grinned, "And right glad we are to see you, my lord! Your son will be even happier!"

"Then he lives?"

"Aye lord and no thanks to the Scots and that traitor Sir Eustace of Rothbury. Come we will find shelter for you and your knights. I fear the fare will not be what you are used to but it is honestly produced."

"I care not, Erik the Crusader. Already you have warmed my heart with your news and filled me with joy. We thought we had come too late."

Erik accommodated me, Mark and Henry Samuel. My knights and squires also shared accommodation with the villagers while my men and archers slept in the church and in barns. We were all sheltered from the icy night.

I heard from Erik the Crusader of the battle of Elsdon. I grew angry as he told me. The sinister plot had almost succeeded. Erik's account of the battle of Otterburn was second hand but I knew that Sir Robert would be relieved to know that his brother had survived.

"How is it that your village survived, Erik? I do not wish harm upon you but it seems to me that your village would be easier to take than Elsdon or Otterburn."

"You are right, lord. It has surprised us too. When we headed north to relieve your son, we captured a Scot. He was badly wounded. In return for absolution of his sins from our priest, he told us that this was a blood feud. Sir Malcolm is of the Clan Eliot and they are related to the Duncan clan. The Earl of Fife and Sir Malcolm are cousins. You have incurred the wrath of the Earl of Fife and he seeks to hurt you and your family. It is personal, lord."

I nodded, "Thank you for that information."

The Bloody Border

"I am sorry, lord, but that is the way it works. The Clan Armstrong live across the border from us and they are totally different from the Eliot clan. They are relatively peaceful by comparison. These feuds are passed down from father to son. So long as your son is here then they will try to kill him."

"You think I should take him to safety?"

"I know your reputation, lord, and that will not happen. No, I am just telling you the reality of life on the border. There are murders here which go unpunished. Cattle and animals are stolen. It is a way of life."

"And yet you came back from the crusades to live amongst it?"

"Aye lord," he laughed, "I served my God and now I serve my land. My family have lived here since the time of the Danes." He patted his axe. "This was carried by one of my forebears. I am of Viking blood and we know how to fight for what we have. Many of the villagers can also claim Viking blood."

"Then I understand. I served in Sweden. I am pleased that my son has you for a neighbour."

As we spoke, I learned that the Clan Eliot also lived in Hobkirk. The connection suddenly made sense. I would destroy that nest of vipers next.

The next morning, we rode the ten miles to Elsdon. I saw that it was like an ant's nest as men swarmed over the tower of the church. My son was making his manor stronger. I saw new walls and new buildings. I had been expecting a devastated manor. I saw that in the short time since the battles he and his people had worked hard. The buildings were not finished but they had achieved a miracle.

He ran to greet me. Even though it was freezing, he and his men were working without furs. "Father, you came!"

I dismounted, albeit slowly. The cold and the ride had stiffened my leg. I embraced him and said, in his ear, "Aye son but I am sorry that it took so long."

He stepped back, "Yes father, we expected you more than a month since. But I can hear in your voice that the delay was not of your choosing. Come, we will try to find accommodation for all of you."

I shook my head, "Not all of us will stay here. Sir Robert is anxious to visit with his brother. I will send him and Sir Peter, along with half of my men there. It will share the load and we are not here to feast. We are here to right the wrongs that was done to our manors."

I had left Sir Geoffrey and his men at Carlisle. Sir Richard and his men had gone to Durham. With Sir Peter and Sir Robert at Otterburn, there were just Sir William of Hartburn, Sir Gilles and Sir Fótr to be accommodated. I shared my son's chamber and the other three knights had the squires' room. The squires and pages hunkered down in the Great Hall. My son had good people. The women of the manor made a great fuss of us. We were fed better than I might have expected. While we ate, I told my son of our campaign. I saw his face as we told him of the depredations of the raiders and the perfidy of the Sherriff. It became darker and angrier.

"You are right, father, this is a conspiracy. Do you think the King knew of this? Was that why he appointed me here and you as Earl Marshal?"

"Perhaps but, if he did, then it was almost a miscalculation." I looked at my son with fresh eyes. He had managed to do, with a handful of men, that which lords with mightier armies had failed to do. He had withstood a siege and defeated an enemy set upon vengeance. "What is it that you wish me to do?"

I saw the surprise on his face. "You are Earl Marshal and I am just a humble knight."

"And I am your father as well as the Earl. What would make your life easier and safer?"

"From what you say I will never be safe so long as I am lord of Elsdon but I would not relinquish the title. I owe it to these people. They are good people, father, and they deserve my protection, our protection. You ask what would make my life easier? Destroy the Clan Eliot and end the life of the Earl of Fife."

"The former we can do. The latter?" I shook my head, "That may take a war for he is close to the King and he lives beyond my reach. We will rest here for a few days. I have no doubt that the news of my arrival will have reached our enemies. Let them worry about our intentions. I will send my scouts across the border. You say they have a tower?"

"Aye, and, since my raid, it may well be manned."

"You have preserved your animals and denied them to the enemy. We have denied Hobkirk the animals they stole. They will have to tighten their belts. I will send a message to Sir Ranulf. I would have him and his men ride with us too. None expect us to go to war in the middle of winter. Ridley and I fought in the Baltic. Snow does not stop the Swedes and it will not stop us!"

I would have gone the next day to make war but our horses had ridden hard. They needed rest. I knew that we strained my son's resources but I planned on making good by taking from the land of Sir Malcolm. We had endured Scottish raids. The Scots would now feel our iron fist. I would not take captives. We were not slavers but I would take every animal between the border and Hobkirk. You could not prosecute a blood feud if you could not feed your men! The Scots would starve.

I noticed a real difference between my men and those of my son. Mine were like me. They were well worn. All were married. Our scars told the story of our lives. We almost creaked when we moved. Of course, when the battle came then my veterans would fight as hard, if not harder than William's young bloods. It was as they ate and drank you saw the difference. Some had lost teeth either through war or ill-use. Anne and the women who cooked for us quickly realised this and my older warriors found the meat they were given was so tender that it needed little chewing. They were given the less crusty bread. They drank as though the ale was the last that they would consume. Like me, their joints ached. I wondered how many more campaigns would see Padraig, Ridley, David of Wales, Dick One Arrow and the rest following my banner. I would watch them in this campaign. They had served me well and I owed it to them to let them enjoy the twilight of their years in comfort. Edward had been a lesson for us. Since he had been injured and lost the use of his left arm, he seemed to have gained something. He smiled more. He might have put on weight but he looked to have more energy. His farms were the most fertile in the valley. I would like my men to enjoy the same life.

The Bloody Border

I rode with my son to see Sir Richard. The three knights needed to know my plans. If I was able, I planned on sending my knights and married men home for Christmas. To do so meant ending the threat of the Eliot clan. I had written to both the Bishop and the King. The King's letter would not reach him until the Spring. Sir Geoffrey would have to be away from my daughter until a replacement could be found. It could not be helped. Sir Robert, Sir Peter and Sir Richard had already scouted out the border and the tower. As my son had surmised, they had learned from his attack. There was now a ditch, and the tower was permanently manned. My son had learned too. He knew that fire could be the most effective means of destroying a tower. We would use fire to destroy it. We decided on an attack in two days' time. The freezing weather had actually helped us. The ground was as hard as rock. If there was a thaw then we might have difficulties but, at this time of year, thaws were rare.

Sir Ranulf and his thirty men arrived. Twenty were either men at arms or crossbowmen. The other ten were farmers who had horses. Morpeth had rich farmers. The quality of their arms was second to none. I was not sure of the quality of the men wielding the expensive weapons. My son thought that Black Bob would have made a fortune from his farmers. We left six men to guard the castle at Elsdon. They would also help the men of the village to continue to rebuild their homes. Although they each had a roof there was much to be done to the interiors. We rode first to Otterburn where the rest of the men awaited us. There we loaded our wagons. We were taking two. They would be strong points beneath which we could shelter and they carried that which we needed for the short siege we had planned. I hoped that they would not expect us until the spring and that, unlike my son, they would have failed to lay in adequate supplies.

If we had wanted to have complete surprise then we would have ridden at night. I chose to arrive in daylight for I wanted none of the rats to escape. I sent our archers on a long ride to the north, east and west of the hall and tower. They would stop an escape. I planned on setting up a perimeter during the day and attacking at dawn the next day. The fact that they would be expecting it would be offset by the fact that they would keep watch all night too. My son had told of his sleepless nights while he had waited for a Scottish attack. For lesser men that would have a debilitating effect. We rode beneath our banners. I wanted them to know who came for them. This was another reason for a daylight attack. I had no doubt that watchers along the route had warned them of our imminent arrival. They would send riders for help. Those messengers would perish at the hands of our archers. As we neared the tower, and as snow began to fall again, I saw men hurrying to the top of the tower and manning the fighting platform of the hall. My son pointed out another recently added feature. They had added a wall to connect the tower with the hall. That was lined with men. The Scots were using crossbows and hunting bows. They would wonder where were our vaunted archers. When arrows fell onto their backs, they would discover the answer.

We dismounted and tethered our horses. Each knight had been allocated a section of the perimeter to watch. Men went to the woods to hack down smaller trees. We would build a barricade. We would have our own fort. There would be women and children in the hall. We had brought with us, Brother Abelard. He was a brave man and he volunteered to walk close to them and deliver a message. We had none of our archers but I had Sir Ranulf's crossbowmen watch for treachery.

"I am here to speak for the Earl of Cleveland."

A voice from the tower shouted, "Speak priest and be quick. We are watching for tricks."

"No tricks. You are surrounded but the Earl Marshal is aware that you have women and children with you. He guarantees them a safe passage."

There was a loud laugh, "They need no such guarantee for your attack will fail and help will come from the Earl of Fife."

It was as I had suspected. They had sent for help as soon as we were spotted.

Brother Abelard persevered, "No matter how well-intentioned we are we cannot guarantee that innocents will not suffer."

"We have heard enough, priest. Move beyond the range of our crossbows or you shall die where you stand."

Brother Abelard returned to us. I smiled at him and put my hand on his shoulder, "You tried and, when we attack, we will be mindful of those without weapons."

The Bloody Border

"I was in Otterburn, lord. Good intentions are often not enough, I will pray that the Good Lord watches over them."

While half of the men watched the other half toiled. We built a low palisade of stakes to stop a nighttime attack and then we built shelters. With fires lit from the branches, we had taken from the hewn timbers, we cooked the food we had brought and we waited. It was dark when David of Wales and some of our archers began to arrive. They had done their job and, moving in, they had sealed the circle. I had no doubt that the men at the top of the tower had seen them. They would now know that their message had not got through. I was with my son and we were the ones closest to the tower. When we attacked, we would have the hardest task. After we had eaten, we set half of our men to watching and the other half to sleeping. We had no intention of spending a long time at the siege. A little loss of sleep would not hurt any of us and neither William nor myself wished to risk a nighttime sortie.

At dawn, we fuelled our fires to cook our food. We would also need the fires for a secondary purpose. If my plan succeeded then we would fire the tower. We brought forth the pavise we had made and carried in the wagons. We erected them within bow range. The crossbows were the only weapon which could reach our pavise. The bolts sent from the top of the tower thudded into them as they were marched forward. Men at arms then escorted archers and crossbowmen to them. When they were all in position, I had Matthew sound the horn and from around the perimeter bolts and arrows were sent towards the defenders. They were not sent blindly. They were aimed at those with crossbows and arrows. There was no arrow storm. My men aimed. When one crossbow and its operator tumbled from the top of the tower there was a huge cheer. It heartened my men. We knew that others had been struck but that tumbling warrior was a clear sign that we were winning. We cleared the top of the tower. Arrows came from all around and while they could protect men on one side most were hit by arrows in the back. When the returning arrows diminished and then died it was time for the next phase of our attack. Knights led our men at arms to carry kindling towards the base of the tower. We did not worry about the hall. If the tower was destroyed then the hall would fall. We used teams of men. Three men ran together. The knight carried the kindling and he was protected by two men at arms with shields. It made sense for it was the knights who were the best protected. We had the best hauberks and helmets. They forbade me from taking part. They persuaded me by pointing out, quite rightly, that my wound would slow me up and I would be putting two men at arms in jeopardy.

    We lost two men while we completed that. They were both from Sir Ranulf's contingent. They had not fought together. When my son advanced, he was with Roger Two Swords and Wilfred of Sheffield. They moved as one. They even had to endure spears hurled from the top of the tower but they still placed their faggot at the base of the tower. When it became obvious what they were doing, the defenders tried to clear it. The door opened and two men tried to use spears to disperse the faggots. One was struck in the hand by an arrow and the other in the foot. They did not try to repeat it. By the time the sun was setting we had almost enough oil-soaked faggots around the base to attempt a fire. David of Wales had shown the other archers how to make fire arrows. We had had time and they had made resin-covered bag arrows. They had to be prepared in advance. The advantage was that they were guaranteed to burn and unlike the cage type fire arrows would not be doused when they struck wood. Every archer had three such arrows. Teams of eight moved behind the pavise. We had a burning torch to ignite them. The first arrows flew true and struck the oil-soaked kindling. The faggots smoked and then erupted in flame. The defenders tried to use water but Sir Ranulf's crossbowmen discouraged them. We sent another four arrows at the kindling to encourage the fire and then saved the others. We had a hall to attack and that was made of wood.

    Darkness fell but we hardly noticed for the flames leapt up the walls of the building. It was made of stone but the door was not. The flames began to burn the door and the intense heat began to crack the mortar. We heard shouts from within. Water hissed as they hurled water to try to slow down the flames. There were arrow slits in the walls and when we saw smoke emerge, we knew that the fire had spread to the floor of the tower. The tower was made of stone but the interior was wooden. Floorboards would burn. Once it ignited the stairs or ladders within then the ones in the upper floors were doomed. They could climb to the top and then all hope would be gone. I saw ropes cascading from the top. No-one attempted a descent. That would be foolish until there was no other choice. Smoke began to pour from the top. The falling snow did little to slow down the voracious flames. The first man who attempted to climb down was struck by an arrow. It delayed the others but when we saw flames licking the top then we knew the end was nigh. They cascaded down the ropes. Some made it but most did not. Some were struck by arrows while others could not hold on and they fell to the ground. Then there was just the crackle of the fire as the flames consumed the tower. The wood which had been used to build the framework burned. A huge part of the upper tower suddenly crashed to the ground. It fell on a section of the newly built wall. Men died. The tower took a night to die. When dawn broke half had fallen and the other stood like a jagged stump.

I nodded. The first part had succeeded. The second part would be harder. We would have to use men to clear the newly built wall and the outbuildings so that we could burn the hall down. I hoped they would send the women and children out before it came to that. Such a decision was out of my hands.

We ate and we prepared. I had the horn sounded and we stood to. We would attack from all sides. We estimated that more than twenty men had already died. That number again must have been wounded. I gambled that we outnumbered the survivors. We made a shield wall. I was flanked by my son and Ridley the Giant. Our squires and pages would not attack. They would wait to come to our aid only if we fell. Behind us, our archers formed up. This time there would be an arrow storm. All around the beleaguered hall and newly built walls our men were forming up.

I said, over my back, "Now Matthew!" My son's squire blew and the horn sounded three times and we began to march. We stepped on to our right legs and held out shields before us. The arrow storm worked but, even so, I still felt the bolts as they thudded into our shields. Had I been using the crossbow I would have aimed at the legs. Luckily for us, the Scots did not.

We had spears for the wall they had built was the height of a man. When we had been watching, during the night, we had seen that the wall was not well mortared. In fact, it looked to have been laid in a hurry. We marched in time. Stones, as well as bolts, cracked into our helmets and shields. I heard a grunt as one of our men was felled. One of those from the second rank took his place. I knew that I was one of the lucky ones. I had a helmet with a visor. A stone could not harm me and it would take an incredibly lucky bolt to penetrate the eye holes. I saw the shields and the faces of the men behind them. They were not a continuous line. As we neared it, I saw a warrior raise his axe as he prepared to smite me. We were too close for bolts to hurt us and I raised my shield as I thrust upwards with my spear. Although the axe hit my shield and shivered my arm, my spear slid under the arm which held the axe and I pushed hard to drive the long spearhead into his body. He began to tumble and I stepped closer to the wall to allow his body to fall behind me. Putting my back to the wall I rammed my spear into the snow-covered earth and dropped my shield. I cupped my hands. Harold Hart was a big man. He ran at me and, placing his foot in my cupped hands, I thrust him upwards. He soared above the wall and I heard him land with a thud. All along the wall others were doing the same. Leaving the ones who had jumped to clear the fighting platform, I led the rest of my men to the door of the hall. We had the option of fire but the defenders saw that they had lost. The gates opened and a mass of humanity flooded out. My men had been told what to do. We stood back. The women and children were allowed to flee unharmed. The warriors were slain. It was too easy; they came out piecemeal. Behind me, I heard the sounds of battle on the fighting platform as my men swept it clear. I pointed my sword and Ridley the Giant led my men into the hall. There would be Scots who were hiding. We would find them and slay them. I had not seen Sir Eustace nor the Earl of Fife. We had caught sight of Sir Malcolm but that had been the day the siege started and he had been in the tower.

   By dawn, there were none left alive inside save for an old man. He had been the last and he stood facing my men while holding an old axe in two hands. Ridley would not hurt him. He walked up to him and tore the axe from his hand. "You are a brave one, old man, but we have killed enough."

   I said, "Where is Sir Malcolm?"

"His lordship burned in the tower, you English bastard."

I nodded, "Give the man warm clothes. We take what remains and then we burn the hall." I pointed to the man. "Tell your clan that they may rebuild here but if they ever raid Otterburn or Elsdon then I will salt the land! Now go!"

It was morning before we had gathered all their animals and emptied the hall. We found their treasure buried in the cellar. There was a chest with two hundred pounds in silver. We took it and then fired the hall. Their horses had all been in the stable and we returned to Otterburn with horses and wagons which were laden with booty. The first part of my task was done. The next would take a little more time.

Chapter 19

Sir Ranulf left us at Otterburn. I had spoken to him and he understood my mind. He would not become lax and he would aid the two young border knights. I sent my knights and most of my men home. I kept a handful of the single men. The rest would get to return home to their families. Christmas was almost upon us and they were eager to return home now that the danger had passed. I chose to stay in Elsdon. My wife would not be happy but she would understand. Our son would not be alone.

After our knights had left and we had rearranged the sleeping arrangements, we dined. My son said as we sipped wine we had fetched from Sir Malcolm's hall. "You need not do this, you know. I am content here alone."

"I do it not only for you but for myself. We had to do what we did. I regret nothing but it is an act of war." I saw William about to speak, "I know that the Scots began this and their raid on Yalesham as well as the attacks on Otterburn and Elsdon were acts of war as well as banditry. The difference is that we succeeded. We defeated their knights. We damaged their ability to attack us. However, the Earl of Fife was not amongst the dead. He will be bitter. As soon as he can he will seek an audience with the King of Scotland and demand action. If action is forthcoming then I need to be here. I can do as I did this time. I can order Sir Ranulf to join us. More, I can order the knights of the New Castle and the rest of the County to follow my banner and defend this border. Personally, I do not think that the King of Scotland will stir himself. He seems a little indolent or perhaps he plays a game." I saw William nod in understanding. "And of course, it saves me two journeys in deepest winter. I promised the people of Gilsland and of Carlisle that I would rid them of the threat of Hobkirk and I will do so."

We enjoyed a joyous if somewhat frugal Christmas. There were many young children in the castle and village. Their happiness made up for the fact that the special foods the women had prepared for the feast had been consumed by the Scottish and English attackers. I had Sam and William and I was content. The wine we had taken was good and I just enjoyed being with my son and grandson.

The rest of December and January passed. Had I wanted to I could not have left. Elsdon, like Bellingham, Otterburn and the rest of the north was cut off by snow which fell for a fortnight. If my son had not laid in enough salted food for a longer siege then things might have gone ill. We finished the fresh food we had brought when we had razed the Scottish manor by the third week in January. When we could not get out, I played chess with William and Sam. It was training for war. My son showed how much he had grown for he took men to visit Otterburn and Bellingham. It was hard going but it had to be done. The few miles took three times as long as it should have done. He did it to reassure himself that they survived. He even went to Rothbury. Still, without a lord, the people were suffering but they survived too.

In the depths of winter, we had a wedding to celebrate. Robin Greenleg married one of Rafe's daughters, Eleanor. This was a close community and there were many unmarried women. It gave us a cause to celebrate as January drew to a chilly end. Until the thaw, they would have to live in Rafe's new farmhouse. I gave them five silver pounds as a dowry. It was part of my share of the booty from Sir Malcolm. I had money enough. I remembered when I had been a newly married husband. Five pounds would have seemed like a king's ransom.

When February came it brought a thaw. The weather did not feel any warmer for the wind blew from the icy hills to the west of us but gradually the snow started to disappear. It made the rivers rise. The leat had been repaired and we were able to manage the flooding which ensued as water flowed over ground which was still frozen below the surface. Mounds of ice remained in the places where we had made paths. We needed the thaw. The animals were running out of feed. William's farmers did not want to slaughter the animals they had husbanded but they would if the alternative was animals starving to death. The grass in the pastures would be their salvation but only when the snow went and the floodwater followed.

This was not my manor and Henry Samuel watched my son as he went about the business of the lord of the manor. Sam was learning how to run a manor. If he became a knight it would be his work too. My manor was too big for such lessons and I had people who took the burden from my shoulders. We were standing on the gatehouse watching William, his farmers and his men diverting the floodwater into the ditch around the castle. Even while we watched we saw the waters start to recede and muddy grass appear.

"I did not think, before I came here and saw my uncle, that this was the work of a knight."

"And it is rare to see a lord toil as my son does. I did the same but it was not digging a channel for water. A knight who is worth anything is not afraid to get his hands dirty. See, Sam, how his farmers smile. Listen to their banter. William is one of them. They will fight for him harder than had he stood where we stand and watch others toil. Loyalty cannot be bought. It has to be earned. His men marrying the locals will bond the whole manor." I looked at his thoughtful face. Since becoming my page, he had changed physically. He had had to work harder. He had grown an appetite and he was taller and broader. More than that he was more confident now. "And you, Henry Samuel, would you still be a knight?"

He grinned and was, once again, the little boy I had first taken north. "Of course, grandfather! This is the greatest education I could have. Father Harold is a good teacher but this is a better classroom and preparation for knighthood. I know I have a long and arduous journey but I am content. I will manage it."

Word reached us from Durham once the road south was opened. The Sherriff of Westmoreland had been tried by a jury of his peers. Sir Richard of East Harlsey had been one of them. He was sentenced to death and awaited confirmation from the King. More, in absentia, Sir Eustace of Rothbury was also sentenced to death. We now had to await the return of the King from Gascony.

With the roads open and travel possible I summoned my knights. I wished to destroy Hobkirk before they could raid the lands around Carlisle. I asked for them to reach Elsdon by the last day of March. The Scots had not sought vengeance, yet. I had been in the north long enough. The winter had done my aching joints little good. My son was hardy. I ached from wounds and scars on every part of my body. Was my son content? One evening as we sat before a roaring fire and sipped the last of the captured wine, I asked him of his future. "You know that you can have another manor in the Tees Valley whenever you choose, William?"

"Aye, father, and one day I will write to you and ask for one but I cannot leave here yet. I have plans."

"Plans?"

"The Roman fort still has good stone. We now have more wagons and horses. When Hobkirk is no longer a threat, I would rob the stone which is at the fort. We need a stone wall. I know what we did to Sir Malcolm's hall. I would not have that happen here. I will make stronger walls for my people and I will build towers on my gates."

"Elsdon is a small manor, William. You cannot justify a garrison the size of Stockton's."

"Nor would I wish to. I have good men in the manor. They all have sons. I would make them warriors. They will be like the men of Bellingham. They will not go off to war as your men do. They will guard these walls. They will have helmets and armour. When all of that is done then I will ask for another manor."

"And a family? You have no bride and you are not getting any younger. I have grandsons but I would have more. Remember William, I was the only one to survive from the blood of the Warlord. You owe it to him to be married and carry on the line."

His face fell, "I know father and that is something I cannot control. I know that I must marry a lady." He shook his head, "I know not why for there are many here who would make good wives."

"I know, but you also know that a lady needs skills which the women like the Yalesham widows do not have. She has to play hostess to men like the King. Would they be happy to do so? I agree with you that they would make good wives but not for the lord of the manor. It is a fact of life."

He retired that night looking as though he bore the weight of the world upon his shoulders. He had learned much already but he still had a long journey ahead of him.

Henry Samuel and Mark had much to do also. Our horses had spent the winter in stables. They needed to be groomed and refreshed with new grass and daily exercise. They had mail to clean and to repair. My son was lucky. Tam was one of the best weaponsmiths I had ever known. We had him fit an aventail to Mark's helmet. My grandson was still growing and would have to wait until he was fully grown to have his first real helmet. I did not think that he would be in danger when we rode to Hobkirk.

In theory, we could have taken just the men of the three manors. Hobkirk had no real castle and we had already slain their best warriors. Others from the clan would have found their way there but I did not anticipate either a siege or a long battle. It would be a hard-fought fight and that was why I wanted my men of arms. Ridley the Giant and Padraig the Wanderer had few campaigns left in them. This one would suit them. The men my son had found raiding his cattle would be the ones we would face. The Scottish clans had threads which bound them to other clans. Men would come from even more inhospitable places further north. We would have men to fight but they would be unlikely to be mailed.

Sir Fótr and Sir Gilles were the first to arrive and they brought news. The Earl of Chester had appointed his own man as Sherriff of Westmoreland. I had not heard of Alexander Bachucton but I assumed that the Earl knew his business. I had written to him and told him of the treachery of the one now incarcerated in Durham. The Earl would have chosen carefully. Sir Geoffrey had been able to spend Christmas with my daughter, Rebekah. He now had another son, Geoffrey. Isabelle had given birth to a daughter, Isabelle. I was pleased. We also heard the news that the King had announced his wedding and it would take place the next year. As a senior earl, I would be expected to attend. That would necessitate a long journey to London with my wife.

The Bloody Border

Gradually the castle filled up as my knights and their men at arms arrived. I saw that none had brought their war horses. All rode palfreys. My knights knew that this would not be a noble war fought against mailed knights. It would be a scouring of vermin. When you hunted rats then you went prepared. When David of Wales arrived, I had him send Mordaf and Gruffyd to scout out Hobkirk. They were not only good archers they also had the ability to hide in plain sight. They returned after three days by which time all my men had arrived at Elsdon. I had one hundred men at arms, knights and archers. Sir Ranulf had another thirty he would bring.

Mordaf now had white hairs amongst the black yet he was still bright-eyed and keen. "They are gathering men, lord. There appears to be a lord leading them. We watched the village and saw one who wore spurs. He seemed to be giving orders. Men were arriving from the north all day."

Gruffyd nodded his assent, "If you want my opinion, lord, this was a mustering of mercenaries. I saw some wearing the remnants of surcoats. Others had helmets and shields. One or two came on sumpters or ponies."

"Numbers?"

"More than a hundred, lord. There are two warrior halls and we could not count those within."

"And the defences?"

"They look to have built a wooden tower and it is attached to one of the halls. My guess is that it is there to give warning."

Mordaf was an astute man and he said, "And they have had a hard winter. The villagers we saw had a lean and hungry look. We saw few cattle and sheep. They are desperate to raid, lord. They need English beef and mutton!"

"You have done well." I held a council of war with my knights. "I want this place destroyed. We will disperse the people but I will not risk our men in an assault while they are behind their walls. We would win but I would not risk the losses. I will send David of Wales and our archers to watch. We will head for Bellingham and bring the main body from the south and east. Sir Ranulf, you will advance from Otterburn with Sir Richard. My intention is to catch this warband in the open when they head to raid the lands south of the wall. It is now the time when the lambs and calves have been born. They will leave within a week. Had they all arrived already then we might have been too late. David and his men leave tonight and we leave in the morning. We wait out of sight. I have studied the maps. There is a road they will take south. We can intercept them. We will head through Falstone and follow the Tyne valley. Wolflee Hill will give us somewhere we can use to ambush them."

Sir Robert asked, "How do you know of such a place? I was lord here and I did not know of it."

"When we stayed in Bellingham, I spoke with Erik the Crusader. He is like a walking map. He knows the land well. He knew of Hobkirk and Hawick. He told me of this hill. It is an ancient feature and his Viking ancestors had fought there. The saga was passed down. A good lord of the manor talks to his folk. They have knowledge which is not written down!" He smiled and nodded. "It is far enough from Hobkirk that they will find it hard to flee back to their nest. David of Wales and his archers can trail them too."

"And we are within the law, lord?"

I smiled at Sir Ranulf, "If they are armed men heading south from Hobkirk then the only place that they can be heading to is England. We do not let them raid this time. I will bear the responsibility. I am happy about the position."

I briefed David and he and his men left shortly before dark. They would camp on the road. I wanted their movements hidden. Before we left, the next day, I impressed upon Sir Ranulf the need to go steadily and to stay hidden. "David will send a rider to you and when he reaches you then you attack Hobkirk." After speaking to my son, I was more confident about Sir Richard than Sir Ranulf. Sir Ranulf still needed to be coached! I then chose the horse I would take. Like my men, I would not risk Eagle. I chose one of the palfreys we had taken from Sir Malcolm's stables. She was a good horse and could bear both my weight and that of my mail.

The valley of the North Tyne had fewer homes than anywhere else I had visited. It was a lawless land. It had been ravaged so often that the ones who lived there were little better than hermits. They eked out a living in the forests. They hunted and they fished. There were few tilled fields. The further north we went the more we heard the Scottish language. We did not bother them. They were obviously not the ones who raided. When we halted and camped it was in fields and clearings in the woods.

The hill was all that Erik had said. If it had not been in such an isolated place then I would have expected a castle. It dominated the road and the river. The river was no longer the Tyne. It was a burn and needed no bridge. I knew not its name for we were now in Scotland. Camping in the lee of the hill and hidden from the road from the north I set men on the top to watch. We waited.

We had but a day to wait. It was Ged Strongbow who brought us the news. "They are heading this way, lord. They move like ants with little order but David of Wales thinks they will reach the road and the hill by this evening. He thinks they would camp here. He has sent word to Sir Ranulf and Sir Richard."

That made sense. We had found evidence of others who had camped here. I had the men mount. I sent half of the men and knights across the burn. They hid in the forested land there. I took my own men down to block the road and had my son with the rest of the men on the hill. They would be the ones who charged and used their horses. My men and I would be the bait. There would be just fifteen of us but I hoped that my banner would draw them to us. Ridley and Padraig flanked me. I had with me the most experienced men from Stockton. They were also, like me, the oldest. This would be our last battle.

The valley was on a north-west to south-east alignment. The dusk would come earlier. I heard the Scots before I saw them. They were noisy. This was their land and they had no scouts out. They came as a warband with the horses followed by the sumpters, then the ponies and, finally, the mass of men who were on foot. I said, without turning my head, "Mark and Sam, your task is to watch my back. You take no chances at all!"

"Aye, lord."

I heard Henry Samuel draw his short sword. I hoped he would not need it.

I had chosen a place to wait which was hidden behind a bend in the road. My son and his men were just out of sight in the slope of Wolflee Hill. As the leading rider, a knight, turned and saw me he drew his sword and shouted. We were closer to them than they would have liked. I saw the men at the fore looking around. My two bands of men were well hidden. They were back from the road. As soon as the enemy reacted, they would charge and my archers would rain death upon the men at the back of the warband. I saw a hurried conference. Then the knight pointed his sword at me and yelled something, I guessed it was 'Charge!' They hurtled towards us. They roared war cries!

"Wait until I give the command."

"Aye, lord!"

We had mail, good horses and better weapons. They were a mob. Then my men launched their flank attack. Horns sounded as my son led one half of my men and Sir Robert the other. They fell upon the flanks and rear of the column. The trap was sprung.

"Now!" Even as I spurred my horse, I saw the realisation that they had been trapped dawn on the leaders. The knight at the front tried to rein in but the ones close by kept coming. I lunged with my spear at the horseman on the sumpter. He was lower than I was and he only had a sword. My spear ripped into his shoulder and knocked him to the ground. Ridley the Giant's axe took a head. Then we were among the few horsemen that they had while up ahead there was the crash and clatter as my horsemen hit the sides of the column. I rammed my spear into the face of one Scot as another hit my shield with his spear. One wild Scot ran, on foot towards me, swinging his axe. He hit my horse's head, splitting it in two. I knew what was coming and I kicked my feet from my stirrups while hurling the spear at the axeman. I was lucky. It hit his right shoulder. Then my dying horse fell and I hit the ground on my left side. My shield bore the brunt of the fall but I was winded. It was my leg which failed me. When I had been younger, I would have leapt to my feet. Now I had to draw my sword and use it as a crutch to help me rise up. Four of the men on ponies saw their chance and they charged me.

I heard a shout and Mark and Henry Samuel forced their horses over my dead mount towards the four of them. Mark held the standard in his left hand as well as the reins. In his right, he held his sword. He did not hesitate. He might have been a poor rider but his lord was in danger and he rammed the standard into the face of one of the men while swashing at the other with his sword. Whatever shortcomings he had as a rider were more than compensated for by his strength. The standard knocked one rider from his pony while the swinging sword made the other swerve. Henry Samuel rode fearlessly at the other. He had been taught well and he protected himself with his small shield. The Scot thought he had a boy to face and he thrust his short spear at my grandson. The buckler deflected the spearhead while Henry Samuel's sword hacked into the arm of the mercenary. It was not a powerful blow but the edge was keen and it not only broke skin, but it also struck bone.

The last of the four came directly for me. The charge of my squire and page had given me the chance to rise. I held my shield and put my weight behind it. The bandit's spear hit my shield and I thrust up with my sword, along the side of the pony. I forced the tip up into his ribs and his chest. His blood spurted and then the pony was beyond me. Ridley and my men at arms reached my side. They formed a half-circle around the three of us. It did not matter. The battle was over. The raiders lay dead. A handful had escaped justice. William had slain the knight and I was given his palfrey. I clambered up on his back and surveyed the battle site. My men went among the wounded and ended their pain. Mark and Henry Samuel stayed close to me as did Ridley and Padraig. My life had come close to being lost and they took no chances.

When all was done and we had taken that which we needed we rode towards Hobkirk. We saw the flames, in the dark, as we neared it. Sir Ranulf and Sir Richard had taken it without loss. The women and children had been sent away. They would find relatives but none would live in Hobkirk until it was rebuilt. That might take a generation.

That night we camped by the burning village. Its fire kept us warm and we feasted on the slaughtered animals.

I spoke to my page and squire, "Mark, Henry Samuel, today you came of age. You saved the life of your lord."

Ridley nodded, "Aye, lads. We must be getting too old that two lads, one who does not shave, did what we have done for many a year. My lord, I think this is God's way of telling us to hang up our swords. You almost died."

"But I did not. Yet you are right. My oldest warriors, you have risked enough. When we return to Stockton then you shall join

Henry Youngblood and garrison my castle or you may farm if that is your choice."

"And you, lord?"

I saw my knight's faces turn to me. I shook my head, "I am a border knight. These last months have shown me that I still have work to do. We return home and I will await the punishment for our actions."

"Punishment, father? Surely you mean reward!"

I laughed, "You will learn that doing your duty does not always guarantee reward. I have been away from Stockton for long enough. Whatever the punishment is I will take it. Your Yalesham widows have shown me what happens when a knight neglects his duty. I will go home and tell Sam's mother that his father would have been proud of him today as I am proud. The blood of the Warlord still flows in the veins of its warriors."

Epilogue.

Summer came and still I had not been censured. The King's wedding was to be in Canterbury at the cathedral there. My son had also been invited. As we were travelling with my wife and her ladies, we allowed a month for the journey. We would take it easy. I wrote to the Sherriff to ask him to accommodate us at York. William had left all of his men at Elsdon. They now knew their task as well as any knight. The border would be safe.

My wife did not ride and we had a wagon in which she could travel. It was functional rather than elegant but Margaret was a hardy woman. She and her two ladies had shelter from the sun and cushions to ease the bumps. We stayed at East Harlsey for our first night away from Stockton. After York, we would travel south and head to Lincoln. William had left his castle in safe hands and the border was in the safe care of Sir Richard. The bloody border was less dangerous for we had scoured it of our enemies.

It was when we entered York that I noticed that men wearing the Scottish livery of the royal family were also in York. My wife saw nothing amiss but my son became alert. "Is this some sort of ambush, father? Are there assassins here?"

I laughed, "If it is then it is poorly conceived. Wearing livery is a poor disguise and besides, Sir Ralph is a friend and we have allies here. It will be a coincidence."

As it turned out we were both wrong. It was neither an ambush nor a coincidence. Sir Ralph greeted us at the tower, "My lord, the King and Queen of Scotland are here. They are also on their way to the King's wedding. When I told them that you were coming, they asked to wait for your visit. They were due to leave three days' since. It must be important that they have delayed their journey to speak with you."

I nodded. This was the censure I had been expecting. I would endure whatever I had to for I had been in the right. Margaret asked, "Will there be trouble?"

I laughed, "If you mean will there be swords drawn then no. The trouble will be of a different nature."

Sir Ralph said, "I have arranged for a small dinner. The King and Queen were anxious to speak with you privately and I thought that doing so over food might make the occasion a little easier. I will let Queen Joan arrange the table. She is the sister of King Henry."

I patted his back, "You were always a good squire."

As we were taken to our chamber William said, "I will shoulder my share of the blame."

Shaking my head I said, "You do not have to. I was the one given charge of the north and it is my responsibility."

We had brought our finest clothes for the wedding. We wore them for the King and Queen of Scotland. Sir Ralph had been true to his word. We were the only ones in the small hall he used when he and his family dined. This was not the Great Hall. This was intimate. When we entered, I saw that King Alexander and Queen Joan were there with one of Queen Joan's ladies in waiting, although she appeared to be a little young, no more than fifteen years of age.

The Queen smiled at me and came to embrace me, "I see you still wear the blue ring I gave you."

"Aye, your Highness. It is a reminder of a great lady who honoured me. May I present my wife, Lady Margaret, and my son, I believe you know."

The King smiled, "We have all heard of this young knight. I pray you sit. We have waited for your arrival for we would have conference with you. When your squires and pages have served us then we will speak."

Sir Ralph had provided servants to bring in the trays of food and drink. They were placed on large tables on either side of the fire. When they had gone the King's steward closed the door and stood before it. He signalled to Mathew, Mark, Sam and John to begin to serve us. The four of them were so nervous that I was sure they would spill something. Queen Joan quickly addressed the situation, "Fear not, young gentlemen. When I was a princess, I often had food spilt upon me by boys who are now my brother's advisers."

It put them at their ease. We ate in silence, at first. I was waiting for the punishment which I was certain was due to me. When King Alexander spoke, I knew that I had misjudged the man. "Sir Thomas, many men think me a weak king. I have been called indolent. That is not so. I am a king surrounded by those who would take my throne. You know the Earl of Fife and you know that he is the most powerful ruler in Scotland. He commands more warriors than I and he has far more coin. What he does not have is an ounce of royal blood. I allow him to stay close to me for I do not trust the man. He thinks he has me duped." He looked at his wife. "We have yet to be blessed with children and, until we have, then my crown is under threat. I have to put on a face and play a part. You bloodied the Earl's nose and, more importantly, removed those robbers and thieves who give Scotland such a bad name. For that we are grateful"

The Queen saw my face and she put her hand on mine, "You thought we sought to punish you." I nodded. She shook her head, "The Earl of Fife tried to get my husband to use the excuse of your reprisals to invade England."

The King nodded, "Fortunately, amongst those who were displaced was Lady Eliot. She was the grandmother of Sir Duncan and the mother of Sir Malcolm. She died a month after she fled but, when she confessed, she spoke of her shame at the attacks on Yalesham, Byrness, Otterburn and Elsdon. Thus it was that we knew you had cause for your attack."

"Thank you, Highness. I tried to act with honour, as did my son."

The King gave me a wry smile, "Then I hope that you will continue to do so. We would not have the Warlord of the North reborn!"

I smiled and sipped my wine. It suddenly tasted much better. I decided to be honest and frank. "I have to tell you, King Alexander, that we slew one who wore royal livery. He was a young knight and he fought us recklessly. If he was a relative of yours then I am sorry."

The King looked sad and his wife put her hand on his. "That is a death to be laid at the door of Fife and not Elsdon, Earl. Young Robert had some vague claim to the throne. The Earl of Fife used him as a pawn. He suborned him and planted ideas of the crown in his young mind. Nothing I could do or say had an effect. We do not blame you or your son."

I was relieved. I was glad that I had brought it up or else it might have eaten me from within. I had felt guilty about his death since the battle.

The Queen looked nervously at her husband then at her lady in waiting. The young woman had not said a word. Queen Joan smiled, "How rude of me. I forgot to introduce the King's ward, Lady Mary Kerk." The young woman bobbed her head. The Queen continued, "Now I shall embarrass Mary by speaking about her." She sighed, "When I married the King it was something I often endured. I sat and was spoken about by others."

The King patted her hand, "My love, let me." She nodded. "Lady Mary's father was killed by the Earl of Fife. It was in combat but the fight was not the choice of Lord Kerk. The Earl desired the lands of the Kerk family. He managed, through manipulation of the court, to succeed in stealing most of them. The one manor he could not take was in the west. I believe they are called the debatable lands of the Esk. Church law rules there. Lady Mary is still the rightful owner of a small manor, Creca. It is north of Annan. It is not rich but it provides the Lady Mary with an income." I saw the young girl blushing. I wondered where this was headed.

The Queen shook her head, "You are going a long way around this business to get to the point, my love. Sir William, you are a bachelor knight. Lady Mary needs to be wed and it cannot be to a Scottish lord. The reasons are manifold. You have shown yourself to be a noble and honourable knight. Even your enemies speak highly of you. Your father is the most powerful man in the north and we trust him too. The lady needs a knight to protect her. What say you to a marriage with Lady Mary?"

My wife's jaw dropped open. William looked up at the young noblewoman as though she had suddenly materialised before his eyes. He did not answer immediately. He wiped his mouth with a napkin and folded his hands before him. He smiled, "I know not what to say save that I would speak with the young lady privately first."

I was proud of my son. Any other answer could have been misconstrued. If he rejected her out of hand it would have been an insult. If he said yes then it would have suggested a shallowness. The King nodded, "Of course."

My son stood. He walked over to her and bowed, "My lady, I believe the river is lovely at this time of day. What say we wander there and talk? My nephew, Henry Samuel, can come with us to afford you security. I would not have your honour impugned."

She smiled and spoke for the first time. She had a soft and lilting voice, "Yes, my lord. That would be most agreeable."

My grandson tried to hide his grin as he followed them out. My wife waited until the door had closed and then said, "I was in a similar position until Sir Thomas came to my aid. My prospective husband was old enough to be my father."

The Queen nodded, "And mine is twelve years my senior but we are happy are we not my love?"

"We are." He looked over to me, "There is a dowry. Lord Kerk's lands were lost but not his treasure. That was kept at Jedburgh Abbey. Your son will be a rich man."

I shook my head, "Your Highness, my wife had no dowry and yet I think I am the richest man in the world. My son is his own man. He will make his own decision and I will support him. A dowry will not influence him at all. You should know this."

Queen Joan said, "Nothing that happens this night will change our opinion of you Sir Thomas and your son. If he says no, then we will be disappointed. She is a lovely girl and is left alone by the callous actions of the Earl of Fife. We just seek happiness for her. She cannot marry a Scot. Her husband would have to navigate a path through lords who sought the land and the dowry. Your son can have no claim to the lands now stolen by Fife. That is why he is a perfect choice. If he will have her and she, him."

"That is understood."

The couple was away so long that we had finished eating and were enjoying a sweet dessert wine by the time they re-entered. Lady Mary rested her hand on William's arm as they walked in.

My son spoke for both of them, "King Alexander, we have spoken. This is hasty. We both agree on that." He smiled, "There are many other things we agree upon and that is good. You may call me old-fashioned but I would ask permission to court Lady Mary. We have a long journey through England. We need to get to know each other. I promise you this, by the time we reach Canterbury Cathedral then the two of us." I smiled for he emphasised the word 'two', "will have made a decision and we will explain it to you and my father."

The Queen smiled and, standing, kissed first Lady Mary and then my son, "We could not have expected a better answer and our choice has been vindicated. I look forward now to a journey I was dreading!"

When I had been told of the presence of the King and Queen, I had expected a totally different outcome. What would King Henry make of all this? The Queen was right. We would have an interesting ride.

Glossary

Buskins-boots
Chevauchée- a raid by mounted men
Courts baron-a court which dealt with the tenant's rights and duties, changes of occupancy, and disputes between tenants.
Crowd- crwth or rote. A Celtic musical instrument similar to a lyre
Fusil - A lozenge shape on a shield
Garth- a garth was a church-owned farm. Not to be confused with the name Garth
Groat- An English coin worth four silver pennies
Hovel- a makeshift shelter used by warriors on campaign- similar to a '*bivvy*' tent
Marlyon- Merlin (hunting bird)
Mêlée- a medieval fight between knights
Pursuivant – the rank below a herald
Reeve- An official who ran a manor for a lord
Rote- An English version of a lyre (also called a crowd or crwth)
Vair- a heraldic term
Wessington- Washington (Durham)
Wulfestun- Wolviston (Durham)

Historical Notes

The clan Eliot did exist but I have fictionalized their activities. There were many border lords who raided both sides of the border. The most famous examples are Hotspur and Douglas as well as the Armstrong clan. The route from Bellingham to Hobkirk is now under Kielder Water. I used the map of 1868 to chart the progress of the Earl and his men. The Earl of Fife was the leader of the most important clan in Scotland but his activities have also been fictionalized. He is an amalgam of many other characters. King Henry did go to Gascony and spent some time away from England. He arranged a marriage to the 11-year-old Eleanor of Provence and he built up alliances against the French. As far as I know, he did not appoint an Earl Marshal of the North!

Books used in the research:

- The Crusades-David Nicholle
- Norman Stone Castles- Gravett
- English Castles 1200-1300 -Gravett
- The Normans- David Nicolle
- Norman Knight AD 950-1204- Christopher Gravett
- The Norman Conquest of the North- William A Kappelle
- The Knight in History- Francis Gies
- The Norman Achievement- Richard F Cassady
- Knights- Constance Brittain Bouchard
- Knight Templar 1120-1312 -Helen Nicholson
- Feudal England: Historical Studies on the Eleventh and Twelfth Centuries- J. H. Round
- English Medieval Knight 1200-1300
- The Scandinavian Baltic Crusades 1100-1500 Lindholm and Nicolle
- The Scottish and Welsh Wars 1250-1400- Rothero
- Chronicles of the age of chivalry ed Hallam

The Bloody Border

- Lewes and Evesham- 1264-65- Richard Brooks
- Ordnance Survey Kelso and Coldstream Landranger map #74
- The Tower of London-Lapper and Parnell
- Knight Hospitaller 1100-1306 Nicolle and Hook
- Old Series Ordnance Survey map 1864-1869 Alnwick and Morpeth
- Old Series Ordnance Survey map 1868-1869 Cheviot Hills and Kielder Water

The Bloody Border

Other books by Griff Hosker

If you enjoyed reading this book, then why not read another one by the author?

Ancient History

The Sword of Cartimandua Series
(Germania and Britannia 50 A.D. – 128 A.D.)
Ulpius Felix- Roman Warrior (prequel)
The Sword of Cartimandua
The Horse Warriors
Invasion Caledonia
Roman Retreat
Revolt of the Red Witch
Druid's Gold
Trajan's Hunters
The Last Frontier
Hero of Rome
Roman Hawk
Roman Treachery
Roman Wall
Roman Courage

The Wolf Warrior series
(Britain in the late 6th Century)
Saxon Dawn
Saxon Revenge
Saxon England
Saxon Blood
Saxon Slayer
Saxon Slaughter
Saxon Bane
Saxon Fall: Rise of the Warlord
Saxon Throne
Saxon Sword

Medieval History

The Dragon Heart Series
Viking Slave
Viking Warrior
Viking Jarl
Viking Kingdom
Viking Wolf
Viking War
Viking Sword
Viking Wrath
Viking Raid
Viking Legend
Viking Vengeance
Viking Dragon
Viking Treasure
Viking Enemy
Viking Witch
Viking Blood
Viking Weregeld
Viking Storm
Viking Warband
Viking Shadow
Viking Legacy
Viking Clan
Viking Bravery

The Norman Genesis Series
Hrolf the Viking
Horseman
The Battle for a Home
Revenge of the Franks
The Land of the Northmen
Ragnvald Hrolfsson
Brothers in Blood
Lord of Rouen
Drekar in the Seine
Duke of Normandy
The Duke and the King

Danelaw
(England and Denmark in the 11th Century)
Dragon Sword
Oathsword
Bloodsword

New World Series
Blood on the Blade
Across the Seas
The Savage Wilderness
The Bear and the Wolf
Erik The Navigator
Erik's Clan

The Vengeance Trail

The Reconquista Chronicles
Castilian Knight
El Campeador
The Lord of Valencia

The Aelfraed Series
(Britain and Byzantium 1050 A.D. - 1085 A.D.)
Housecarl
Outlaw
Varangian

**The Anarchy Series England
1120-1180**
English Knight
Knight of the Empress
Northern Knight
Baron of the North
Earl
King Henry's Champion
The King is Dead
Warlord of the North
Enemy at the Gate

The Fallen Crown
Warlord's War
Kingmaker
Henry II
Crusader
The Welsh Marches
Irish War
Poisonous Plots
The Princes' Revolt
Earl Marshal
The Perfect Knight

Border Knight
1182-1300
Sword for Hire
Return of the Knight
Baron's War
Magna Carta
Welsh Wars
Henry III
The Bloody Border
Baron's Crusade
Sentinel of the North
War in the West
Debt of Honour
The Blood of the Warlord
The Fettered King

Sir John Hawkwood Series
France and Italy 1339- 1387
Crécy: The Age of the Archer
Man At Arms
The White Company
Leader of Men

Lord Edward's Archer
Lord Edward's Archer
King in Waiting
An Archer's Crusade

The Bloody Border

Targets of Treachery
The Great Cause

Struggle for a Crown
1360- 1485
Blood on the Crown
To Murder a King
The Throne
King Henry IV
The Road to Agincourt
St Crispin's Day
The Battle for France
The Last Knight
Queen's Knight

Tales from the Sword I
(Short stories from the Medieval period)

Tudor Warrior series
England and Scotland in the late 14th and early 15th century
Tudor Warrior
Tudor Spy

Conquistador
England and America in the 16th Century
Conquistador

Modern History

The Napoleonic Horseman Series
Chasseur à Cheval
Napoleon's Guard
British Light Dragoon
Soldier Spy
1808: The Road to Coruña
Talavera
The Lines of Torres Vedras
Bloody Badajoz

The Bloody Border

The Road to France
Waterloo

The Lucky Jack American Civil War series
Rebel Raiders
Confederate Rangers
The Road to Gettysburg

Soldier of the Queen series
Soldier of the Queen

The British Ace Series
1914
1915 Fokker Scourge
1916 Angels over the Somme
1917 Eagles Fall
1918 We will remember them
From Arctic Snow to Desert Sand
Wings over Persia

Combined Operations series
1940-1945
Commando
Raider
Behind Enemy Lines
Dieppe
Toehold in Europe
Sword Beach
Breakout
The Battle for Antwerp
King Tiger
Beyond the Rhine
Korea
Korean Winter

Tales from the Sword II
(Short stories from the Modern period)

Other Books

The Bloody Border

Great Granny's Ghost (Aimed at 9-14-year-old young people)

For more information on all of the books then please visit the author's website at www.griffhosker.com where there is a link to contact him or visit his Facebook page: GriffHosker at Sword Books